NO PLACE
FOR AN ANGEL

Gail Whitiker

Harlequin (UK) Limited's policy is to use papers that are natural, renewable and recyclable products and made from wood grown in sustainable forests. The logging and manufacturing processes conform to the legal environmental regulations of the country of origin.

Printed and bound in Spain
by Blackprint CPI, Barcelona

MILLS
BOON

Published in Great Britain 2014
by Mills & Boon, an imprint of Harlequin (UK) Limited,
Eton House, 18-24 Paradise Road, Richmond, Surrey, TW9 1SR

© 2014 Gail Whitiker

ISBN: 978 0 263 90965 4

Harlequin (UK) policy is to use papers that are natural, renewable and recyclable products and made from wood grown in sustainable forests. The logging and manufacturing processes conform to the legal environmental regulations of the country of origin.

Printed and bound in Spain
by CPI, Barcelona

Valbourg turned and drew her against him, one hand gently grasping her chin and tilting it back.

His fingers were warm against her skin, the scent of him sweet in her nostrils. Catherine tried to pull away but he held her too firmly. Then his mouth closed over hers—and she had no desire to go anywhere.

Desire exploded like a dried-up seed bursting in the welcome rains of a long-awaited storm. The touch of his mouth, the slow, sensual caress of his lips, set her blood pounding and made her heart race, so that in an instant the protective wall she had built around herself shattered, leaving her vulnerable and exposed.

But, oh, how she wanted this. To feel the strength of his arms around her and to experience the mastery of his kiss. It was everything she had imagined it would be and more. Equal parts heaven…and hell.

AUTHOR NOTE

For the final book in my *Gryphon Theatre* trilogy I decided to focus on two characters who made their first appearance in NO OCCUPATION FOR A LADY: the dashing Lord Valbourg, eldest son of the Marquess of Alderbury, and the beautiful Catherine Jones, a gifted actress whose ethereal voice earns her the nickname 'Angel of London'.

Catherine has come a long way from her humble beginnings in remote Wales. Celebrated now as one of London's finest talents, she lives life on her own terms, refusing to take lovers or to be cast in the role of rich man's mistress, as so many actresses are. But her reasons for remaining chaste aren't prompted by a desire to maintain her virginal reputation. Something far more important is at stake. Something Catherine isn't willing to put at risk.

Valbourg, too, has reasons for keeping the beautiful songbird at a distance. As sole guardian of his late sister's child, and heir to his father's title, he knows what entering into a relationship with her would do. But when it comes to love logic seldom enters into it. Sometimes the only way of keeping what you have is giving up what you desire most.

I thoroughly enjoyed exploring the world of Regency theatre, as I did creating the cast of characters who populated it. Then, as now, the theatre is a vibrant world filled with gifted performers, eccentric characters and diverse personalities. I hope the characters whose lives revolved around the Gryphon Theatre engaged and entertained you as much as they did me.

Gail Whitiker was born on the west coast of Wales and moved to Canada at an early age. Though she grew up reading everything from John Wyndham to Victoria Holt, frequent trips back to Wales inspired a fascination with castles and history, so it wasn't surprising that her first published book was set in Regency England. Now an award-winning author of both historical and contemporary novels, Gail lives on Vancouver Island, where she continues to indulge her fascination with the past as well as enjoying travel, music and spectacular scenery. Visit Gail at www.gailwhitiker.com

Previous novels by this author:

A MOST IMPROPER PROPOSAL*
THE GUARDIAN'S DILEMMA*
A SCANDALOUS COURTSHIP
A MOST UNSUITABLE BRIDE
A PROMISE TO RETURN
COURTING MISS VALLOIS
BRUSHED BY SCANDAL
IMPROPER MISS DARLING
NO OCCUPATION FOR A LADY**
NO ROLE FOR A GENTLEMAN**

*part of *The Steepwood Scandal* mini-series
**linked by character

**Did you know that some of these novels
are also available as eBooks?
Visit www.millsandboon.co.uk**

Chapter One

The Gryphon Theatre, London—summer 1828

The single rose arrived precisely on schedule, exactly one half-hour after Catherine Jones took her bows and walked off the stage at the Gryphon Theatre.

The rose, cut at the peak of perfection and tied with a white satin bow, was brought to her dressing room by the same young man who appeared after every performance; an envoy sent to deliver the long-stemmed tribute on behalf of an admirer who preferred to remain…anonymous.

'Curious, don't you think, Lily,' Catherine mused to her dresser, 'that after all this time, the gentleman still refuses to identify himself.'

'Downright queer, if you ask me, miss,' Lily said bluntly. 'The other men who send you gifts all *want* you to know who they are in the hopes you'll offer them the appropriate thanks. Why not this one?'

'I don't know.' Catherine drew the velvety pink petals across her lips. 'Perhaps he is married and does not wish his wife to know he has been showering roses on another woman for the better part of five months. I know I wouldn't.'

'I'm not sure rich men care about that sort of thing, miss,' Lily said. 'And he must be rich, given what he's spent on all those flowers. Lord, what if he's a duke…or one of those handsome Arabian sheiks!'

Amused that the girl would think one as significant as the other, Catherine smiled. 'It can be of no consequence to me *what* he is. A dear friend once told me I can encourage neither prince nor pauper, no matter how rich one or poor the other. And she was right.'

'But why? You're not married or engaged, so why shouldn't you enjoy the company of gentlemen the same as everyone else?'

'Because I have responsibilities and obligations others do not,' Catherine said quietly, preferring not to think about the meeting she was to have in two weeks' time with the man who had taken control of her life five years ago. A man who might have been her father-in-law had a terrible accident not happened to prevent it. 'Never mind that. What's this I hear about you and Mr Hawkins walking out together? Is it true?'

The question, introduced as a way of diverting Lily's attention, launched the girl into a blushing recital of the young man's attributes, allowing Catherine—who wasn't expected to answer— to close her eyes and let the sound of the girl's voice drift around her. She didn't mind that Lily enjoyed the occasional night out. The girl had a good head on her shoulders and knew better than to let any man take advantage of her. Still, it was difficult at times not to feel a little envious of her dresser's amorous adventures.

What wouldn't she have given, Catherine mused, to be able to flirt with a gentleman without fear of reprisal? To have the freedom to spend an evening in his company and not have to worry about who might be watching. To indulge in a few hours of harmless pleasure for a change.

But such choices were no longer hers to make. The errors of her past dictated the path of her future, and the price for straying from that path was too high. She had already sacrificed more than any woman should have to…

'I mended the tear in your rose-coloured silk,' Lily said now. '*And* I added a new piece of lace around the neckline. But I don't know why you would want to wear that gown tonight when your turquoise satin is far more fashionable.'

'Yes, but it is also a great deal more revealing and, given that I shall be performing in front of the Marquess of Alderbury's entire family, I think it best I appear in something a little more conservative,' Catherine said. Plunging necklines and diaphanous gowns were all very well for her performances on stage, but for private concerts like the one she was giving tonight, she preferred a more modest appearance. One never knew who might be watching.

She glanced at her rose again and stroked the petals with a lingering caress. Who was he, this mystery man who bestowed such exquisite flowers yet refused to show his face? Someone who had no desire to reveal his identity—or someone who dared not?

'Are you sure you're up to singing at Lady Mary's reception tonight, miss?' Lily asked. 'You've already been on stage the best part of four hours, and Mr Templeton's scheduled an early rehearsal for the morning. You should be home resting.'

'I will have plenty of time to rest when I get back from my trip,' Catherine said, slipping the rose into the vase with the others. 'Besides, I have only been asked to sing six songs. Hardly an arduous task.'

'I might agree if you hadn't performed twice that many in the last four hours,' Lily said, pinning the last of Catherine's golden curls into place. 'Still, I suppose you know best. Is it to be the pearls or the rubies tonight?'

'The pearls, I think. They look better with the gown.'

'Either work nicely.' Lily unlocked the jewellery box. 'Both make you look like a lady.'

Yes, Catherine reflected, just as jewels and costumes had made her look the part of a siren, a goddess, a street waif and a witch. All roles cast by the charismatic theatre owner, Theodore Templeton, and for which she had achieved a level of fame unimaginable five years ago, when she had left Miss Marsh's house in Cheltenham with few hopes and even less money. Now she had the wherewithal to afford a house in a decent part of town, the staff to maintain it and the clothes necessary to play the part. She might not be as well known as the illustrious Mrs Siddons, but many favourable comparisons had been made in terms of their acting abilities.

But it was her voice that had catapulted Catherine to the forefront of the industry, her incredible four-octave range making her one of the most talked-about performers of the day. She had even been invited to sing before one of the royal dukes on his birthday.

Sometimes it was hard to remember she had been born the only daughter of a governess and a schoolmaster, so far had she risen from those humble beginnings.

'Here's your shawl, miss,' Lily said, draping a lightweight silk wrap around Catherine's shoulders. 'I'll just get my things and we can be off.'

'*We?*' Catherine glanced at her dresser in confusion. 'It isn't your job to accompany me to private engagements, Lily.'

'I know, but you had to send poor Mrs Rankin home early, and I know she doesn't approve of you going out on your own,' Lily said, referring to the widow who had been Catherine's companion since her arrival in London. 'So I thought I would go myself.'

'But you told me you were seeing Mr Hawkins this evening.'

'I was, until Mrs Rankin fell ill. Then I told him I wasn't available.'

'Well, go and find him and tell him you *are* available,' Catherine said, slipping the strap of her fan over her wrist. 'I doubt he will have left the theatre yet. He's likely still helping Mr Templeton take the sets down.'

'But what if that man Stubbs sees you gallivanting around Mayfair without a chaperon?' Lily persisted. 'Mrs Rankin told me he makes notes of everything you do and everyone you see.'

'I will hardly be gallivanting and so I shall tell Mr Stubbs if and when I see him,' Catherine said, surprised the normally tight-lipped Mrs Rankin had been so forthcoming with information. 'Lord Alderbury is sending a private carriage to collect me, and at the end of the evening, I shall take a hackney home. Now go and find your young man.'

Lily did not look convinced. 'I don't think

Mrs Rankin is going to be very pleased about this, miss.'

'Don't worry, Lily, everything will be fine. I shall go to Lord Alderbury's house, sing for his guests and then leave,' Catherine said confidently. 'You'll see. There won't be any trouble at all.'

'Are you going to read me a story tonight, Uncle Val?' the little boy asked. 'I'm really not very sleepy.'

'You never are, even when you don't have a fever,' Valbourg said, stowing the last of his nephew's toys in the large wooden box. 'I would be quite worn out if I did all you do in a day.'

'Is that because you're old?'

'I beg your pardon?' Valbourg straightened. 'Who told you I was old?'

'Aunt Dorothy. Right before she told Grandfather it was time you were married.' Sebastian gazed up at his uncle with wide, trusting eyes. '*Are* you getting married, Uncle Val?'

'I wasn't planning on it, no.'

'It would be all right if you did. I mean, as long as you didn't send me away.'

'Send you away? Why on earth would I do that?' Valbourg asked, sitting down on the edge of Sebastian's bed. 'This is your home now and has been for the past two years.'

'I know, but Aunt Dorothy said the lady you marry might not want me to stay here any more,' the boy whispered, his flushed face evidence of the fever that had only recently broken. 'She said she might prefer to have her own children around her rather than someone else's.'

Anger swelled like a balloon in Valbourg's chest. Damn Dorothy! Why couldn't she mind her own business? She should have known better than to say something so hurtful in front of an impressionable young boy. 'I am not going to send you away, and you mustn't listen to anything Aunt Dorothy says. I shall marry when I am good and ready and not a moment before. So let's have no more talk about you leaving, understood?'

'Understood,' Sebastian said, relief chasing the shadows from his eyes. '*I'm* not getting married either. I think girls are silly,' he proclaimed with all the certainty of a six-year-old. 'Don't you?'

'They certainly can be.'

'Uncle Hugh doesn't think so. He said I'll come to like girls very much when I am his age, because he started liking them very much when he was mine.'

Valbourg sighed, wondering if there was any member of his family he wasn't going to have a word with. 'I think we'll leave that discussion for another time. Your aunt Mary's betrothal ball is this evening and she won't be pleased if I am late.' He tucked Brynley Bear, Sebastian's loyal companion, into the bed next to him. 'Nanny Lamb will be in to read you a story, all right?'

'Yes, all right,' Sebastian said, though Valbourg could tell from the expression on the boy's face that his thoughts were still distracted. 'Don't you want to get married, Uncle Val?'

'I suppose, when the right lady comes along. But for now, it's just going to be you, me and Brynley Bear rattling around in this big old house. And here's Nanny Lamb to read you a story.' Valbourg leaned forward and kissed his nephew on the forehead. 'Sleep well and I'll see you in the morning.'

'Uncle Val?'

'Hmm?'

'I'm glad you don't want me to leave. I do miss Mama and Papa, but I'm happy I came to live here with you rather than with Aunt Dorothy,' Sebastian confided. 'She looks a *lot* older than you and, sometimes, she smells funny.'

Valbourg's mouth twitched. 'Yes, she does, but it isn't polite to tell ladies things like that, so we'd best keep that to ourselves, all right?'

'If you say so. Goodnight, Uncle Val.'

Valbourg ruffled the boy's dark curls and then vacated his seat on the bed. He regretted not being able to stay and read Sebastian a story. Reading to his nephew had become one of the highlights of his day. The childishly innocent stories took him back to his own untroubled youth, and the quiet time he spent with Sebastian was a reminder of what really mattered in life. It was only when he had an important engagement like this evening's that he let Nanny Lamb take over.

It might seem a surprisingly domestic arrangement for the Marquess of Alderbury's eldest son and heir, but Valbourg had no complaints. Having Sebastian living with him was the best thing that could have happened to him—even if it had come about as the result of the most unfortunate circumstances and a promise rashly given to his youngest sister six years ago.

A promise he never thought he'd be called upon to fulfil.

'Ah, good evening, my lord,' Finholm said as Valbourg arrived at the bottom of the stairs. 'Is Master Sebastian feeling better?'

'I believe so, though Dr Tennison said he would stop by again in the morning,' Valbourg said. 'If you need me, just send word to Alderbury House.'

'I'm sure everything will be fine,' the butler said. 'Master Sebastian is a plucky little lad. I doubt there will be any cause for concern.'

'I hope not, Finholm. Goodnight.'

With the butler's reassurances ringing in his ears, Valbourg set off for his sister's engagement celebration, content in the knowledge that he was leaving Sebastian in good hands. It was amazing how completely the responsibility for raising a child changed his priorities. Before his nephew had come to live with him, Valbourg had lived a life as irresponsible as most; gambling too often, drinking too much and amusing himself with a string of beautiful young mistresses. He had given no thought to his future because he'd had no reason to expect it would be any different from his past.

He certainly hadn't expected Fate to walk in and turn his life upside down. Who could have foreseen that his youngest sister and her husband—both only twenty years old—would be struck down by illness, forcing Valbourg into the role of guardian to their four-year-old son? Who could have known that with Sarah's death, the sybaritic lifestyle he'd led would come to an abrupt end? That the room he had used as a study would be converted to a nursery, or that Nanny Lamb would be coaxed out of retirement and that overnight, the heir to a marquessate and one of London's most eligible bachelors would become a sober and responsible family man.

Certainly not him.

But, in fact, that was precisely what had happened, and in the two years since Sebastian's arrival, Valbourg had become a model of sobriety and restraint. A paragon with no vices and few regrets.

Except one—and he would be seeing her tonight. Miss Catherine Jones. The Angel of London. The one temptation he had tried—and so far succeeded in—resisting.

It must be Fate interfering in his life again, Valbourg reflected moodily as he set out on foot for his father's house. Only a perverse deity would bring the Angel into his life at a time when he could do absolutely nothing about it—because only Fate knew how desperately he wanted her. He had, ever since the first time he had seen her on the stage of the Gryphon Theatre in the role of Flora, goddess of spring.

Garbed in a flowing white gown and with her silken hair caught up in a coronet of roses, Catherine Jones had appeared to him like something out of a dream; a golden-haired goddess sent to bewitch and beguile him. Her incredible, bell-like voice had filled the theatre and caused the chattering crowd to raise their lorgnettes and peer with wonder at the glorious creature standing before them.

Unfortunately, it was not only her voice that had captivated Valbourg. When at the end of that first performance, she had stared out into that vast auditorium, raised her sapphire-blue eyes to the first row of boxes, and her gaze had connected with his—and she had smiled. From that moment on, Valbourg had been lost. The thought of holding Catherine in his arms kept him awake at night, while the desire to lose himself in the softness of her body made him ache.

Quite simply, the woman was intoxicating; more seductive than the finest wine, more addictive than the strongest opium. And like an addict, Valbourg kept returning to the Gryphon Theatre night after night, simply for the pleasure of watching her. She never glanced in his direction again, but it didn't matter. The die had been cast. Valbourg became her greatest admirer...and she didn't even know his name.

But she would after tonight, because tonight, she would be singing at his sister's betrothal celebration. Mary had specifically asked him to engage Miss Jones to entertain their guests, and his father had asked him to look after the young lady while she was in his house.

Not an onerous responsibility. Indeed, Valbourg could think of a hundred men who would have jumped at the opportunity. But not him. For him it would be an exercise in frustration. A test of will-power...because the day he had become Sebastian's guardian was the day he had vowed to lead an exemplary life. One that gave no one any room to criticise his behaviour or a reason to take Sebastian away—which a liaison with Catherine Jones would most certainly do. That meant he had no choice but to keep her at arm's length. He would greet her when she arrived at his father's house and introduce her to his sister and her fiancé at the appropriate time. If called upon to do so, he would even talk to her as though she was any other woman and not the bewitching creature who charmed with her music and ensnared with her beauty.

He had a reputation to uphold and a six-year-old boy to take care of. Not even the glorious Catherine Jones could be allowed to jeopardise that!

The Marquess of Alderbury's town house was an imposing Georgian edifice graced with five levels of windows, a row of sculpted Gothic columns and a fringe of grinning gargoyles that glared down on unsuspecting visitors. A house built to impress and intimidate.

Catherine was not intimidated. She might have been when she had first arrived in London five years ago, but so much had changed in her life since then she no longer gazed with open-mouthed wonder at such things. Her employer, Theo Templeton, owned an exceedingly gracious residence just a few streets away, and she had often been invited to attend receptions given by the former actor and his flamboyant wife, also a former stage actress. Together, they had introduced Catherine to an eclectic group of actors, writers, artists and entrepreneurs, few of whom would have been made to feel welcome in the drawing rooms of polite society, but all of whom were accepted and embraced in the Templetons'.

Catherine had been similarly welcomed, because in that gloriously ornate room, no one knew about the scandals in her past. No one knew about Will Hailey, the young man with whom she had fallen in love and committed that one terrible mistake, or about Thomas, the beautiful, golden-haired child who had resulted from it. No one knew about Will's father, the Reverend James Hailey, who had ripped Thomas from her arms when he was but a baby and then told her to leave. A man whose hard-hearted actions had necessitated the dramatic changes in her life.

No one knew any of that because here she was just Catherine Jones, the much-admired singer who had taken London by storm; a woman celebrated for her talent rather than looked down upon for her sins.

A woman who had buried her pain so deep no one even knew it existed.

Catherine glanced down at her gloved hands and sighed. She must be talented indeed to be able to fool all of London into believing she was happy.

The marquess's carriage rolled to a stop at the bottom of the stone steps and one of the liveried footmen jumped down to open the door. He was too well trained to peer inside, but Catherine knew he was waiting for her to disembark... something *she* knew better than to do. Actresses were not deposited at the front door of elegant residences. They were admitted through the servants' entrance and taken up the back stairs, hopefully without being seen by any of the guests.

No doubt, the butler would soon come out and instruct the driver to move on.

But to her dismay, no such direction came. And when a shout rang out from one of the carriages in line behind them, the footman finally poked his head in and said, 'Excuse me, miss, but we have to move on.'

Catherine bit her lip, wondering who was responsible for the mistake. She glanced at the crowds milling beyond the carriage door and knew exactly what they would think if she were to emerge from Lord Alderbury's carriage now. Unmarried women of good birth did not arrive unescorted at evening events and certainly not in the carriages of their hosts. That suggested an association well-bred people chose to ignore. But what choice did she have? She couldn't sit in the carriage all night.

And so she climbed out, trying to appear nonchalant as she stepped into the crowd of richly dressed women and their elegant escorts. A few of the ladies raised well-groomed eyebrows while others just whispered and smiled behind their fans.

Catherine smoothed out the folds in her gown and pretended not to notice. She wanted to tell them she had been specifically invited by the Marquess of Alderbury to perform at this evening's soirée, but if that was the case, why had no one been sent to meet her? Had his lordship forgotten she was coming—?

'Good evening, Miss Jones. Welcome to Alderbury House.'

The voice, polite, reserved and as smooth as warm honey, came from somewhere to her left and, turning around, Catherine saw a gentleman walking towards her. He wasn't old enough to be the marquess, but neither could he be mistaken for a member of the household staff. Tall, dignified and impossibly handsome in exquisitely tailored evening clothes, his self-sufficient air suggested a man who was at home in his surroundings. One who had been born to the role. Another member of the family, perhaps? 'Thank you, Mr...?'

'Valbourg,' he said. 'My father is engaged elsewhere, but asked that I be on hand to greet you. I apologise for having kept you waiting.'

'My apologies, Lord Valbourg,' Catherine said, belatedly aware that she was addressing the marquess's eldest son. 'I hope you will convey my gratitude to your father for having been so kind as to send a carriage to collect me from the theatre.'

'Actually, that was my doing,' Valbourg said. 'Since I asked you to come immediately after your performance, I thought the least I could do was provide comfortable transportation to bring you here. A carriage will also be made available to take you home at the end of the evening.'

'Thank you, but that won't be necessary,' Cath-

erine said, well aware that the infamous Stubbs
would be watching for her arrival and preferring
not to have to pay him extra to forget what he
had seen. 'I am able to make my own way around
London.'

'I'm sure you are, but you will not be required
to do so this evening.' He indicated the stairs.
'Shall we?'

There was nothing in his tone to indicate disapproval of her response, but Catherine felt it none
the less. Obviously Lord Valbourg did not deem it
appropriate for a woman to travel around London
on her own and had no doubt formed an opinion
as to her character and morals as a result. Pity.
She didn't like being judged on appearances, especially when those appearances were misleading.

The truth was, she seldom went anywhere on
her own because Mrs Rankin, the lady who had
been with her since her arrival in London and
who acted as both companion and chaperon,
made sure she did not. It was only as a result of
the lady being so dreadfully ill—and Lily being
otherwise engaged—that Catherine had come on
her own tonight. However, suspecting there was
little she could say that would change his opinion,
she gathered her skirts and started up the stairs
beside him. She would deal with the issue of the
ride home later.

They entered the hall, a magnificent room

sumptuously furnished and sprinkled with price-less artwork and gilt-edged mirrors. Guests were directed up the white marble staircase and to the left, where Catherine assumed the marquess and his family were receiving.

She was taken up the stairs and to the right.

'I thought you would like to see where you will be performing,' Valbourg said politely. 'Refreshments, if desired, will be brought to you there.'

Catherine inclined her head. 'Thank you, my lord.' As kind as Valbourg's offer was, she knew what he was saying. She was the paid entertainment; not an invited guest. Strange how that still had the power to hurt. 'Actually, I never eat before a performance,' she added in a voice as remote as his. 'I find it affects my voice.'

'Then I wonder at you having the stamina to perform so magnificently in *Promises* night after night.'

Her head came round sharply. 'You've seen the play?'

'Indeed. I was curious to know what all of London was talking about.'

'Really.' She resented having to ask, but curiosity got the better of her. 'Did you enjoy it?'

'Very much.' Valbourg glanced briefly in her direction. 'And you were…exceptional.'

His gaze lingered for no more than a moment, but it was long enough for Catherine to form an impression of sculpted cheekbones, dark eyes and a firm, sensuous mouth. Lord Valbourg was an elegant and powerful man; one whose slightest glance would bring women flocking to his side in the hopes of securing his affection.

How fortunate she was not one of those women.

'Thank you,' she said, returning her gaze to the stairs. 'I would not have thought *Promises* the type of play a man like you would enjoy, but I shall certainly pass your comments along to Mr Templeton.' She flicked another glance in his direction. 'I cannot recall having seen you in the audience.'

'Why would you? I am but one of the many thousands who stare at you every night,' Valbourg said. 'In such crowds, all faces blur into one, none of them distinguishable or particularly memorable.'

And yet, yours would be, Catherine found herself thinking. In fact, as she glanced at Valbourg again, she realised there *was* something familiar about his features. The black, wavy hair, the dark slash of eyebrows above expressive eyes and a slender, aristocratic nose. And that mouth, capable, no doubt, of humbling a man with a few carefully chosen words, or of bringing a woman to ecstasy with a lingering kiss—

'I say, Brother, what gem have you brought into the house tonight?' A very different voice cut into her musings. 'Can it be the Angel of London come to grace us with her presence?'

Valbourg stopped and turned around, causing Catherine to do the same.

'Ah, Hugh, I wondered when I would be seeing you. Miss Jones, allow me to introduce my brother, Lord Hugh Nelson. Hugh, Miss Catherine Jones.'

Brother. Yes, Catherine could see the resemblance. Though he looked to be younger than Valbourg, Lord Hugh shared his brother's dark hair, sculpted cheekbones and slender, aristocratic nose. But where Valbourg's eyes were a warm chocolate brown, Lord Hugh's were the cool clear grey of a winter morning. His clothes were more dandified than Valbourg's, and where the latter's build suggested a man who enjoyed outdoor pursuits, Lord Hugh's was already tending towards corpulence.

But it was in their attitudes towards her that Catherine saw the biggest difference. Valbourg's regard was polite but uninterested. Lord Hugh's was engaged and appreciative, leaving her in no doubt as to the nature of his thoughts.

'So, we are to be treated to a performance by the Angel of London,' he murmured, reaching for her hand. 'How honoured we are.'

His words were as flattering as his regard, but Catherine suspected honour had very little to do with them. 'Thank you. I was delighted to be asked and look forward to performing for your father's guests.'

'Not nearly as pleased as we are to have you. I say, Val, why don't you leave Miss Jones in my care until Mary is ready for her to sing?' Lord Hugh said, his hands pressing moist heat into hers. 'I'm sure you have more important things to do.'

'As a matter of fact, I do not,' Valbourg said, pointedly freeing Catherine's hand from his brother's. 'Mary charged me with the responsibility of looking after our guest and that is what I intend to do. Come, Miss Jones, the music room is just ahead. I'm sure you would like a chance to rehearse before the guests start arriving. One of the footmen will keep watch outside.' He levelled a warning glance in his brother's direction. 'I have left instructions that *no one* is to be admitted until you are ready to begin.'

With that, he placed his hand in the middle of Catherine's back and gently propelled her forward.

Catherine was not sorry to walk away. She was familiar with Lord Hugh's type: men who had been indulged since birth and were used to having what—and who—they wanted. He no doubt enjoyed the company of actresses and ballet dancers, many of whom were, for the most part, elegant prostitutes, and while Catherine did not think of herself in that way, she was realistic enough to know that others did.

For that reason, she was surprised when a few minutes later, Valbourg said, 'I apologise for my brother's behaviour, Miss Jones. There is nothing he likes better than to find himself in the company of beautiful women, and while I cannot say he would not have made an improper advance, he would certainly have tried to monopolise your time.'

Catherine slowed, her expression thoughtful. *Valbourg thought her beautiful?* 'Thank you, my lord, but there is no need to apologise. I have encountered your brother's type before and am perfectly able to take care of myself.'

'Are you?' A glint of amusement warmed the brown eyes that suddenly turned to meet hers. 'Have you a bronzed Nubian bodyguard you call upon at such times?'

Catherine allowed herself a small smile. 'No, but I do know a few techniques that can come in useful. Ways in which to deflect a gentleman's unwanted amorous attentions.'

'If force is required to put distance between you and an admirer, he can hardly be called a gentleman.'

'Ah, but he can,' Catherine said. 'A man will always treat a lady with respect, but he is not obliged to show the same consideration when in the company of an actress.'

'He is when in this house,' Valbourg said. 'If you are treated with anything less than the respect you deserve, you are to find me at once and I shall deal with it.'

There was no trace of amusement in his voice now and Catherine was flattered by his concern. For all her fame, actresses were seldom accorded such consideration. It was refreshing to know there were still decent men in the world and that Lord Valbourg was one of them. What a pity their situations in life would prevent her from having a chance to know him better.

'Thank you, my lord, but I doubt any of your father's guests would be so inconsiderate as to misbehave beneath his roof. It would be a poor repayment of his hospitality.'

'It would indeed, Miss Jones,' Valbourg said. 'And for everyone's sake, I hope they remain aware of it.'

After making sure that Miss Jones was safely ensconced in the music room, Valbourg left her alone to practise, insisting she lock the door as soon as he left. The lady might believe herself wise to the ways of the world, but Valbourg knew there was very little she would be able to do against a man who had serious seduction on his mind. For that reason, he waited until he heard the click of the lock falling into place before making his way back to the ballroom.

Not surprisingly, his brother was waiting for him; a drink in his hand and a scowl on his face. 'I say, Val, I didn't care for the way you spoke to me back there. You had no right to be so dismissive in front of Miss Jones.'

'And you had no right to move in on her the way you did. Dear God, Hugh, she is a guest in our father's house,' Valbourg said tersely. 'Could you not have restrained yourself?'

'She is an actress, not a guest,' Hugh informed him. 'One no doubt possessed of the same questionable morals as all the rest. She is only here to sing for her supper, and you can be damn sure she'll be looking for a wealthy man to take her home. For a hefty price, of course.'

'Which just goes to show how little you know about her. Catherine Jones hasn't been any man's mistress since she arrived in London,' Valbourg said. 'Her reputation is spotless. Would that the same could be said of yours.'

'I'll thank you to keep your opinions to yourself,' Hugh said, securing a glass of wine from the tray of a passing waiter. 'Just because *you* choose to live like a bloody monk doesn't mean I have to.'

'No, but something resembling restraint would be nice for a change,' Valbourg drawled. 'Speaking of conduct, watch what you say around Sebastian in future. I'd rather *not* have him thinking your conduct with women is one worth emulating. As for Miss Jones, keep your distance. She is here for our sister's enjoyment. Not for your own personal pleasure.'

His brother's eyes narrowed. 'Why so protective, Valbourg? It's not like you to warn me away from a woman. Can it be you've a mind to bed the wench yourself?'

Valbourg manufactured a smile for the benefit of a passing guest. 'I won't dignify that with a reply, but I trust we understand one another, Hugh.'

'Miss Jones is off limits.'

For a moment, it was as though they were boys again; each determined to emerge the victor in an ongoing battle of wills. Hugh, three years younger and always the more competitive, still felt the need to prove himself, even though it was usually the elder brother who triumphed. Valbourg refused to allow emotion to cloud his judgement and took the time to weigh the pros and cons of a situation before deciding how to act. Logic trumped anger; reason suppressed passion. It was the only way of making intelligent and rational decisions.

Not that reason or intelligence had anything to do with how a man behaved when it came to a woman, Valbourg reflected narrowly. 'I want your word on this, Hugh. Miss Jones is a guest in this house. Whatever her occupation or background, she is to be treated with respect while she is here. I will not allow you to harass or embarrass her.'

It was a hollow threat and they both knew it. Catherine Jones was an actress and as such, fair game for any man who wanted her. Indeed, for many actresses, becoming an aristocrat's mistress was the far more desirable career. By ordering Hugh to behave like a gentleman, Valbourg had all but thrown down the gauntlet—and his brother had never been slow to pick it up.

Surprisingly, however, Hugh only shrugged his shoulders and said, 'Very well, I won't try to take advantage of Miss Jones. While it galls me to have to play the part of the gentleman, neither do I have any desire to be raked over the coals by you, or by Father after you trumpet your knowledge of my conduct to him. But mind you watch all the others, Brother,' Hugh said, lowering his voice. 'You can't protect her from every red-blooded male who walks through that door, nor from the thousands who go to see her at the theatre every night. Catherine Jones is a beautiful and desirable woman. And you and I both know there's nothing a man wants more than a woman someone tells him he can't have.'

Chapter Two

∼⦻∼

Valbourg mulled over the significance of his brother's words as he stood listening to Catherine Jones perform a few hours later. The guests had all assembled in the music room, and when Catherine appeared, elegant in a gown of rose-coloured silk and with pearls glowing at her ears and throat, they had burst into applause, aware that a special treat was in store for them. She had positioned herself beside the piano, waiting for her lady accompanist to begin the opening strains of her first song.

A hush had fallen over the room as Catherine began to sing. In contrast to her petite body, her magnificent voice had swelled to fill every corner of the room, each note crystal clear and perfectly struck. It was as though the music lived within her, the glorious sound bursting forth every time she opened her mouth.

Even her physical appearance changed as she

sang. Caught up in the music, her body began to sway, her arms and hands floating gracefully in time. Indeed, there was something decidedly sensual in the way she moved and, judging from the expressions on the faces of most of the men in the room, Valbourg wasn't the only one who was aware of it.

'Oh, Val, isn't she wonderful,' his sister Mary whispered in his ear. 'I cannot thank you enough for arranging to have her sing for us.'

'The pleasure was all mine, dearest. After all, what kind of brother would I be if I did not see to your every wish, especially on a night like this?'

'You would be like Hugh, who neither sees nor cares about anyone's desires but his own.'

'Now, Mary, Hugh is a product of his upbringing,' Valbourg felt compelled to point out. 'Third in birth order and second in line to the title, he has always felt the need to compete with me for our parents' affection and respect.'

'And never succeeded. At least not with Papa,' Mary said in a wry tone. 'Mama spoiled him outrageously, but you were always Papa's favourite.'

'Actually, I believe Sarah held that honour,' Valbourg said softly. 'Father never spent as much time with any of us as he did with her.'

'Perhaps because he sensed he wouldn't *have* as much time with her as he would with the rest of us.' Mary sighed. 'Thank goodness we still have Sebastian. Every time I look at him, I see a little reminder of Sarah in his face. Is he feeling better today? Papa told me you had to have the doctor round to see him.'

'I did, but thankfully his fever broke last night,' Valbourg said. 'He will likely be weak for a few more days, but Tennison said he should make a full recovery.'

'Thank goodness. I know how worried you were about him.' Mary hesitated a moment before adding, 'Still no regrets about having him come to live with you?'

'Not a one.'

'Then you don't mind living the life of a monk? Sorry, dearest. Hugh's words, not mine,' Mary said with a smile. 'But I don't suppose they're all that far off the mark. Everyone knows how much you've changed your life to accommodate Sebastian's arrival and I really couldn't blame you for feeling a little put out. I understand your evening entertainment is now restricted to tame forms of cards and the company of safely married couples.'

'Dear God, have I truly become so boring?'

'I'm afraid so. And we all know you've Dorothy to thank for that.'

Yes, because when his eldest sister Dorothy had heard that Valbourg was assuming responsibility for Sebastian's upbringing, she had bluntly called it the most idiotic idea she had ever heard. It didn't matter that Sarah had asked *him*, rather than Dorothy or, God forbid, Hugh, to care for Sebastian in the event something should happen to her and her husband. Dorothy maintained it was ridiculous that a man who was only concerned with drinking and whoring should be responsible for the well-being of a child. Even their father had suggested it might be in everyone's best interests if Sebastian went to live with Dorothy and her husband, given that they already had a son and a daughter in the nursery.

But Valbourg had stood firm. He informed them he had given Sarah his word that he would honour her request and honour it he would. For the most part, he just ignored Dorothy hovering in the background like a dark foreboding cloud.

And then, as though summoned by the mention of her name, Dorothy appeared, drab in a fawn-coloured gown that did nothing for her complexion or her figure.

Not, Valbourg reflected, that his eldest sister had been particularly blessed in either regard. 'Good evening, Dorothy.'

'Valbourg,' she said, adding with a brisk nod, 'Mary.'

'Hello, Dorothy. I was beginning to wonder whether or not you were coming.'

'I was delayed by a crisis below stairs,' Dorothy said. 'Some scandal involving one of the maids. Mrs Plinkin came to see me about it just as I was leaving. I told her I had neither the time nor the patience to deal with it and that she should just get rid of the girl.'

'Compassionate, as always,' Valbourg murmured.

'Don't take that tone with me, Brother,' Dorothy snapped. 'I don't want my children exposed to behaviour like that under my own roof. Speaking of servants, I really must talk to Papa about his new valet. The man is rude and condescending and needs to be taught his place. But I suppose that is what you invite when you hire an Irishman.'

'I don't know why you would say that,' Mary objected. 'I find Tully very pleasant to deal with.'

'Of course, because you find *everyone* pleasant. It is the reason you will fail so miserably as a wife,' Dorothy stated. 'Servants need to be taught their place. You do that by maintaining a firm hand. I don't care if my servants like me. All I require is their obedience and their willingness to work hard.'

'Which I am sure they do,' Valbourg remarked. 'But if Mary's servants work hard it will be because they like and respect her, not because they are afraid of her. As for her new role, I have no doubt she will make Tyne an excellent wife.'

'Of course I will,' Mary said, stung by her sister's criticism. 'I love him and he loves me.'

'Love,' Dorothy said with a sneer. 'A highly overrated emotion that serves as no useful foundation for marriage whatsoever. You would have been better off accepting Lord Troon's proposal.'

'Troon? The man is sixty if he's a day,' Mary said, incredulous. 'And he is not at all handsome.'

'Handsome? Of what value are looks when in twenty years' time they will have vanished, leaving you shackled to a man with whom you likely have nothing in common and with no financial recompense to salve your wounds for being so silly as to accept his proposal in the first place. At least Troon is a worthy catch. He is heir to a dukedom.'

Mary blinked at the harshness of her sister's reply, but Valbourg simply smiled. 'I shouldn't worry about it, Mary. Tyne may not be as wealthy as Troon, but I suspect his looks will last far longer so that even in thirty years' time, you will have no reason to regret your decision to marry him.'

'Oh, yes, be sarcastic if you like, but people would do a lot better if they made decisions based on logic rather than emotion,' Dorothy said. 'Speaking of which, when do *you* intend to do your duty and settle down, Brother? You are past thirty now and responsible for the welfare of a young boy. No doubt you would both benefit from the influence of a sensible woman in your lives.'

'Is that a criticism of the way I am raising Sebastian?' Valbourg enquired, unwilling to let the remark pass.

'Not at all. Much to my surprise, you have cast off your dissolute ways and emerged a surprisingly respectable man,' Dorothy said. 'But it is past time you gave some serious thought to settling down. You are Papa's heir, after all.'

Valbourg's sarcastic rejoinder was lost in the burst of applause that greeted Catherine as she finished her song. He looked up in time to see her execute a graceful curtsy, and though her face was lightly flushed and her blue eyes still sparkled, he could see how weary she was. And why not? It was nearly three in the morning and she had already performed her required six songs as well as three encores. It was time to pay the girl and send her home.

'Come, Mary,' Valbourg said. 'If you wish to meet Miss Jones, now would be the time.'

'Meet her?' Dorothy's pencil-thin eyebrows rose. 'Why on earth would you wish to meet her?'

'Because she was kind enough to come here and sing for our guests,' Mary said.

'Are you not paying Miss Jones for her time, Valbourg?'

'Of course.'

'Then let that be an end of it. One must be careful around women like that, Mary,' Dorothy warned. 'Flattery goes to their heads. Gives them airs. Worse, Miss Jones may think Valbourg is interested in her and he certainly doesn't need that kind of complication in his life. No, tell Harrison to give the girl her money and send her on her way. Now, if you will excuse me, I shall go and have a word with Papa. See if I can talk some sense into him before the Irishman robs him blind.'

With a curt nod, Dorothy left, taupe-coloured feathers bending in the breeze.

Mary leaned over and whispered in Valbourg's ear, 'Is it truly awful to admit that one doesn't care much for one's sister?'

'Not as awful as it is honest.'

'It doesn't seem very charitable.'

'Honesty seldom is,' Valbourg said in a wry tone. 'Come, let us speak to Miss Jones while the Dragon is otherwise engaged.'

They lined up to speak to her. Knights and their ladies, barons and their baronesses, even a viscount and his viscountess—all took a moment to express their admiration of her voice. Only one crusty old earl and his equally crusty countess left without acknowledging her, but Catherine took the snub in her stride. The majority of guests had been kind enough to speak with her, rendering unimportant the few who were not.

The gentlemen, of course, suffered no such inhibitions. Anxious to convey their compliments, they all rushed forward, asking if they might fetch a plate of refreshments or assist her to a chair. Catherine accepted Mr Brinkley's offer of a glass of wine and Lord Styles's insistence on a small plate of food, but the other offers she kindly but firmly refused. All she wanted to do now was go home. She had enjoyed performing for Lady Mary, but the euphoria was wearing off and it was only a matter of time before weariness rushed in to take its place. She wanted to be home in her own bed before that happened. She had to be up again in a few hours.

Suddenly, a path opened and Lord Valbourg, Lady Mary Nelson and her fiancé, Lord Tyne, approached. Valbourg and his sister made a striking pair, Catherine noted. Both so beautiful and blessed with all the good things life had to offer. Oblivious to the darker, more insidious side of human nature—

'Miss Jones, I cannot thank you enough for coming to sing for us tonight,' Lady Mary said, taking both of Catherine's hands in hers. 'I see why they call you the Angel of London, for truly God's own choir could not contain a more divine voice.'

'Thank you, my lady,' Catherine said, genuinely touched by the woman's charity. 'It was a pleasure to sing for you and Lord Tyne, and I am so glad you enjoyed it.'

'We did. My brother, too,' Lady Mary said, reaching for Valbourg's arm. '"The True Lover's Farewell" is one of our family's favourites.

Mama used to sing it to my sister and I before we went to bed.'

'I'm so pleased. Is your sister here?' Catherine asked, glancing around the room for a younger version of Lady Mary. 'I don't believe we have been introduced.'

She turned back in time to catch the look that passed between brother and sister and wondered if she had said something wrong. Seconds later, she realised she had when Valbourg said, 'Sadly, my sister is no longer with us. She passed away two years ago.'

Catherine's eyes widened in dismay. So, all was not blissful in the house of Alderbury. Tragedy had touched this golden family, stealing one of their own and leaving an empty place in their hearts. 'I am so sorry,' she whispered. 'I would not have performed the song, had I known.'

'But you did not and therefore owe us no apology,' Valbourg said. 'I doubt there is a song in the world that doesn't evoke poignant memories for someone.'

That might be true, but it did not take away from the fact that *she* had been the one to bring those painful memories back, Catherine thought regretfully. She might not know Valbourg well, but she sensed he was a man who betrayed little of his feelings, yet felt them keenly, especially when it came to his family.

'Will you take some refreshment, Miss Jones?'

Lady Mary asked, forcing a cheery note into her voice. 'Valbourg told me you came here straight from your performance at the Gryphon.'

'Thank you, but I'm really not hungry,' Catherine replied. 'Lord Styles has gone to fetch a plate, but at the risk of sounding rude, I would rather go home. It is late and I have an early rehearsal in the morning.'

'Of course. How selfish of us to keep you here talking. Val, have arrangements been made for Miss Jones's transportation?'

'Indeed. I shall go and see to the carriage now.'

'Oh, please don't bother,' Catherine said quickly. 'As I said before, I am quite capable of travelling around London on my own.'

'And as I said earlier, that will not be necessary. It is late and you have been kind enough to perform at my sister's betrothal celebration,' Valbourg said. 'I suspect Theo Templeton would have something to say if I did not take the very best care of you.'

Catherine lowered her eyes, as much to hide her confusion as to acknowledge the unexpected kindness. What was wrong with her? It had been years since a gentleman's words had brought colour rushing to her cheeks, but Valbourg had done it several times this evening, and with no effort at all.

She would have to be careful. While he might not approve of her, he nevertheless aroused feelings Catherine thought gone for ever; feelings that had lain dormant since Will's death. It was unsettling to discover they had simply been... misplaced.

Especially now when she was so close to achieving her goal of regaining custody of her son. To forfeit that now through a careless or unguarded action would be the height of folly and something for which she would *never* forgive herself.

'Well, I suppose we should be returning to our guests,' Lady Mary said to her fiancé.

'And I shall go and see to the carriage,' Valbourg said. 'If you would be good enough to wait here, Miss Jones, I shall make the arrangements and then come back for you. In the interim, please do enjoy some of what Lord Styles brings you. My father really does have one of the finest chefs in London.'

He left with his sister and her fiancé, and moments later, Mr Brinkley returned with the promised glass of wine and Lord Styles with a *small* plate of food. Catherine was quite sure there was enough on it to feed Mrs Rankin and herself for three days, but smiling her thanks, she took the glass and the plate and sat down at a small table as the room continued to empty and the majority of guests returned to the ballroom. Unfortunately, several of the gentlemen lingered.

'A delightful performance, Miss Jones,' Lord

Tantemon said. 'The music is as beautiful as its mistress.'

'Thank you, my lord,' Catherine said, avoiding his gaze. Tantemon was one of her more persistent admirers. He had never strayed beyond the bounds of polite behaviour, but neither was he reluctant to make his feelings known.

'I heard Valbourg say he was going to arrange for a carriage, but mine is already waiting close by,' he said now. 'Perhaps you would allow me the pleasure of taking you home.'

'I say, steady on, Tantemon,' Lord Styles objected. 'I brought Miss Jones supper, so I claim the right to take her home.'

'Don't be ridiculous, Styles. This is not a supper dance. Doing one does not entitle you to the other.'

'I am grateful to both of you for your offers,' Catherine intervened, 'but since Lord Valbourg has already gone to the trouble of arranging a carriage, I do not intend to offend him by leaving with someone else.'

'You are gracious, dear lady, but Valbourg won't care,' the ever-dapper Mr Brinkley said. 'He is only seeing to your welfare because his sister asked him to. I, on the other hand, would welcome the opportunity of spending time alone with you.' He leaned down and whispered in her ear, 'My offer still stands. You have but to say the word.'

'Thank you, Mr Brinkley, but so does the answer I gave when first you made it.'

Catherine heard a guffaw from one of the other gentlemen. 'I told you you were wasting your time, Brinkley. The lady has better taste than that.'

'Obviously,' the barrister snapped. 'She refused you!'

'Now, gentlemen, you are unkind to pester Miss Jones in this manner,' Lord Hugh Nelson said, strolling across the room to join them. 'Can you not see that the poor girl is trying to eat? I suggest you all go away and leave her alone.'

'What, so that you can proposition her with no one around to listen?'

'You malign me, sir,' the gentleman said, affecting a look of injury. 'My intentions towards Miss Jones are strictly honourable.'

'Fustian, you've never had an honourable thought in your life,' Styles said. 'And standing so close to the Angel, I doubt you're having one now!'

Ribald laughter followed the inappropriate comment, and knowing it would only get worse, Catherine put down her glass and stood up. 'Well, gentlemen, if you will excuse me—'

'Oh, no, sweet angel, you cannot leave yet,' Lord Tantemon objected. 'We so seldom have the opportunity of enjoying the pleasure of your company in such a private setting. Surely you would not be so cruel as to deprive us of it now?'

'I'm afraid she would,' Valbourg said coldly from the doorway. 'Miss Jones, are you ready to leave?'

It wasn't really a question and, grateful for the timeliness of Valbourg's return, Catherine stood up. 'I am, my lord.' She wanted nothing more than to turn her back on every one of the powerful men gathered around her, but aware that she was still performing and that it would not be in her best interests to alienate any of them, she added with forced affability, 'Though the company is very pleasant, I am exceedingly weary.'

A number of polite objections and expressions of sympathy greeted her remark, but Valbourg merely stepped forward and offered his arm. For a moment, their eyes met…and Catherine's widened in surprise. *He knows. Despite his chilly demeanour, he knows how uncomfortable I am and he is offering me a dignified escape.*

Humbly, she placed her hand on his arm, gratitude warring with pride as she lifted her chin and walked out of the room with him. She had no wish to feel indebted to him. Valbourg had made his feelings about her quite clear, both by his attitude and his remarks. But at the moment, his position and authority offered her the protection she needed and for that, Catherine was grateful.

At the top of the staircase, she swept up her

skirts and, with one hand on his arm, gracefully began to descend. Heads turned in their direction. Some guests even called out to them, but Valbourg did not stop. He just kept on walking, leading her towards the front door and freedom.

It seemed, however, that her departure was to be delayed further.

'My apologies, Miss Jones. I thought the carriage would have been here by now,' Valbourg said after a glance outside assured him that such was not the case. He hesitated, then led her into a small chamber that opened off the hall. 'If you would be good enough to wait here, I will go and see what is keeping it.'

Catherine nodded, suddenly too weary to do much more. Lily was right. Two performances in one night were exhausting, especially given the emotional overtones of the latter part of the evening. She wasn't used to dealing with men like Valbourg and having to pretend a lack of interest drew heavily on her emotional reserves. How fortunate that after tonight, she would have no reason to see him again.

The room in which she waited was beautifully decorated. Silk wallpaper festooned with exotic flowers and birds covered the walls, while more birds were painted on the domed ceiling. Catherine walked around, stopping to admire an exquisite tapestry hanging on the far wall when an all-too-familiar voice said, 'Well, well, what's this? A beautiful bird trapped in a gilded cage. How…appropriate.'

Catherine turned around, not at all pleased to see one of her more troublesome admirers leaning against the now-closed door. 'Good evening, Lord Lassiter.'

His eyes widened. 'You remember me?'

'How could I not? You made quite an impression when you appeared at my dressing-room door with a diamond the size of Gibraltar dangling from your fingers.'

'Sadly, it did nothing to tempt you into my bed.'

'It would have taken a great deal more than a diamond to do that, even if I had been interested,' Catherine said. 'Which I was not.'

'Feisty Miss Jones,' Lassiter said, pushing away from the door. 'Still playing hard to get. But I rather like that in a woman. It makes the eventual capitulation all the more exciting, don't you think?'

'I couldn't say.' Catherine's smile was cool. 'I don't play hard to get because I am not interested in being caught. By you or anyone else.'

'Really. So you prefer to live alone, scraping by on the pittance you earn on stage rather than being able to enjoy the many pleasures life has to offer.'

'I enjoy life well enough,' Catherine said. 'As I told you at the time, I've no need of help from you.' She wasn't afraid of Lassiter, but neither did she wish to cause a scene in Lord Alderbury's house. Pity she hadn't seen him come in. She could have made a dash for the door—beyond which the sounds of the reception were now decidedly muted. As, no doubt, would be any sounds that might emanate from this room.

'I fail to see why you persist in playing this ridiculous game, my love,' Lassiter said, beginning to circle her like a hungry wolf stalking its prey. 'I am a wealthy man and a generous one. You could have anything you wanted. Jewels, gowns, a carriage at your disposal day or night. All yours simply for the asking.'

'*If* I agree to become your mistress.'

'Of course. One must be prepared to give in order to receive,' Lassiter said, narrowing the distance between them. 'And surely giving yourself to me would not be such a hardship. I am not unattractive, nor nearly so old as Crosby, whom I understand you also sent away.'

'Yes, with the same answer I gave you,' Catherine said, backing up until she felt the edge of the credenza against her lower back. 'At least he was gentleman enough to accept my decision.'

'Only because he found another mistress.' Lassiter leered at her in a way that made him look even more like a wolf. 'I, however, have not and I am willing to overlook your earlier error in judgement. So, what do you say? Is it to be your bed tonight…or mine?'

He was so close Catherine could see the network of veins on his nose and smell the staleness of his breath as he opened his mouth, his tongue flicking suggestively, obscenely, over yellowed teeth. 'Come, sweet angel,' he murmured, 'give me but a taste of those honeyed lips.'

He placed his palms against the wall on either side of her head, his body angled in such a way that if Catherine brought her knee up and connected in just the right place, he would drop like a felled tree, giving her the time she needed to bolt for the door. It wouldn't have been the first time she had employed such methods, but she had learned that success was all in the timing. If she didn't get it right, she would find herself in an even worse predicament.

She closed her eyes and counted it down in her head. Three…two…one…

Suddenly, there was a muffled curse, a screech, and the weight of Lassiter was gone—but not because of anything Catherine had done. She opened her eyes to see the viscount sprawled on the floor on the other side of the room, while a few feet away, with his legs firmly planted and his arms crossed over his chest, stood Valbourg.

'What the hell do you think you're doing?' Lassiter demanded. 'I wasn't accosting the wench.'

'Mind your language, Lassiter. There is a lady present.'

'Lady? She's no—'

'Miss Jones, are you unharmed?' Valbourg interrupted, all the while keeping his eyes on the fallen peer.

Catherine swallowed. The question, like the threat, had been quietly spoken, but there was no mistaking the rage simmering just below the surface. 'I am. No harm done.'

'How fortunate for you, my lord,' Valbourg murmured. 'Otherwise you would have found yourself in a very unpleasant situation. Now remove yourself from my father's house before I forget I am a gentleman and give you the thrashing you so richly deserve.'

Lassiter blanched. The threat, all the more dangerous for the silken tone in which it had been uttered, left no room for discussion. He clambered to his feet and bolted, leaving the door open behind him.

Valbourg walked over and closed it. 'Are you sure you're all right?'

His back was towards her, giving Catherine a moment to regain her composure. She *was* shaken—because she hadn't expected to be attacked in a house like this by a man whose upbringing should have prevented it. 'I am, my lord, though I don't think I was in any real danger. I was about to give Lord Lassiter his come-uppance.'

'You were?' He turned around. 'You will understand if I say it didn't look that way from where I was standing.'

'No, I suppose not. But in truth, I was just waiting for...the right moment.'

'The right moment,' Valbourg repeated with a smile. 'So despite the fact he had you pinned against the wall so tightly the outline of his fob is likely imprinted on your skin, you still felt there was going to be...a right moment.'

'Yes.' Catherine raised her chin. 'I can explain how if you like. I can even show you—'

'That won't be necessary,' he said, holding up a hand to forestall the demonstration. 'It's time we got you home. Your carriage awaits, my lady.'

My lady. Valbourg's words brought the blood rushing to Catherine's cheeks far more than Tantemon's innuendos or Lassiter's advances. If his intention was to humiliate her, he had more than succeeded. She was not a lady and never would be. She was an unwed mother and actress. And tonight she had been on stage, just as when she was performing at the Gryphon. She had appeared in costume and walked into Valbourg's world as though she belonged there—but she did not. The fairy tale had come to an end. It was time to go home, where there were no costumes to hide behind or masks to disguise who and what she really was.

She walked out to the carriage in silence, a few steps ahead of Valbourg. It wasn't the magnificent barouche in which she had arrived, but a smaller, more intimate carriage drawn by two gleaming black horses and with a single driver up top. A carriage that was still very much the property of a gentleman.

'Thank you, my lord,' she said, turning to face him. 'I had...a most enjoyable evening.'

'I doubt that, but it is kind of you to say so.' Valbourg handed her an envelope. 'I hope this makes up for what you suffered tonight.'

Catherine took the envelope, but did not open it. She had no reason to suspect the marquess of short-changing her. Instead, she climbed into the carriage and immediately became aware of the lingering scent of lavender, making her wonder who had been in the carriage last. Lady Mary, perhaps, or another equally elegant lady of commendable family and high birth? The sort of lady Valbourg would be expected to marry.

Chiding herself for allowing her thoughts to drift in that direction, Catherine turned to bid him goodnight—only to gasp when she realised he was climbing into the carriage after her. 'My lord?'

'Don't worry, Miss Jones, you are perfectly safe with me,' Valbourg said, settling on to the seat opposite and pulling the door closed. 'But if you think I intend to let you drive through the streets of London alone at this time of night, you are mistaken.'

'But I am perfectly safe in a closed carriage!'

'That was what I thought when I left you in the music room and then again in the Chinese Salon,' he said drily. 'I will see you safely home if for no other reason than to assure myself a good night's sleep.'

They travelled without speaking for a time, Valbourg keeping his attention on the street, his expression remote, his eyes as dark as the night that surrounded them. Catherine took advantage of his distraction to study him. When she had first seen him walking towards her on the steps of Alderbury House, she had thought him older. But now, having spent time in his company, she realised he couldn't have been more than thirty, despite the fine lines that fanned out from the corners of his eyes—

'Why haven't you taken a lover?'

The question made her jump. 'I *beg* your pardon?'

'A lover. Forgive me if you find the word offensive, but I doubt the topic is one with which you've not had some experience.'

Catherine bristled. 'If by experience you mean I have been *approached* about such things, you're right. If, however, you refer to my having *accepted* such offers—'

'I do not…because I know you *have* not. But let there be honesty between us, Miss Jones,' Valbourg said. 'You admit the subject has been raised in the past, in which case I hardly expect you to suffer a fit of maidenly outrage when I bring it up.'

No, she wasn't likely to do that, Catherine acknowledged. But the fact he felt free to talk to her about the subject told her exactly what he thought of her…and that *did* bother her.

'I fail to understand why you would ask such a question, my lord. What possible interest can it be of yours?'

'I should think what happened to you this evening would be a more than sufficient explanation.'

'I don't follow.'

'If you were under someone's protection, you would not have been taken advantage of the way you were earlier.'

'Oh, yes, of course,' Catherine retorted. 'Being someone's mistress would entitle me to a greater degree of respect than what I currently enjoy.'

'Come, Miss Jones, we both know being a gentleman's mistress earns you no more respect than being an actress does,' Valbourg said. 'But it does come with certain advantages. For one, you would be better taken care of.'

'Indeed. I would be given food and lodging in

exchange for pleasures owed to my keeper whenever and wherever he chose to exact them,' Catherine was stung into replying. 'Forgive me if I do not find that preferable to the situation in which I currently find myself. Now, if you don't mind, I would rather not continue this conversation. As surprising as it may seem, I find it…degrading.'

Valbourg shook his head. 'I do not find that surprising at all. And it was not my intention to offend you, Catherine. I know you haven't taken a lover, and while I do not know what your circumstances were before you arrived in London, I doubt they were all that much different from what they are now.'

Catherine raised an eyebrow at the casual use of her first name. Did he think to disarm her with familiarity? 'Why would you say that?'

'Because the opportunities you have in London would be far superior to any you might have been offered in the country. If you were willing to become some shop-owner's mistress, you would not hesitate to become the mistress of a much wealthier man here.'

The implication stung. 'You flatter me, Lord Valbourg. Obviously, your opinion of me is very high.'

'Actually, it is,' he said quietly, 'which is why it pains me to have to ask you the question.'

It was surely one of the strangest conversations Catherine had ever had. A gentleman, asking her why she hadn't become some other man's mistress…but not because he seemed to have any interest in making her his. 'For what it's worth, I choose not to be a mistress,' she said. 'Singing is my passion and I am grateful to Mr Templeton for having given me the opportunity to do what I love night after night in his beautiful theatre. *And* to pay me for the privilege.'

'Granted, but what of your future? There will come a time when the public tires of you. Or when the work becomes too demanding. What will you do then? Retire? Move away? Marry?'

'I will never marry,' Catherine said. 'I have a career. One I love and that I intend to pursue. If I were to marry, all of that would change. A husband would not allow me to appear in public.'

'He would if he were a fellow performer.'

'It has been my experience that actors make poor husbands.'

'Personal experience?'

'No. Experience gained from watching those around me.'

'So you're not hiding an abandoned husband in some remote country village,' Valbourg said with a small smile.

Catherine did not return it. 'I assure you, I am not.'

Thankfully, the carriage began to slow. Catherine turned her gaze towards the window, aware that they had arrived in a part of town she knew well, but that was still a few streets from where she lived…which was exactly what she had intended when she had given the false address. It would have been bad enough for Stubbs to see her arriving home in a nobleman's carriage. It would have been disastrous had he seen the owner of the carriage sitting in the carriage *with* her.

'I take it you're not going to tell me why you refuse to take a lover?' Valbourg said, the question dragging her back into the moment.

Catherine sighed. Why couldn't he just leave it alone? She didn't want to lie to him, but she could not…*would not*…tell him the truth. 'Lord Valbourg, it would be impossible for you to understand what my life has been to this point. Or for me to predict how it will be in the future. I can tell you that events in my past dictate how my future will be lived and it doesn't matter whether I like it or not. The past is the past. It cannot be changed.'

'So you're telling me you did something you regret and your life is now ruled by that event.'

'Something like that. Now I really must go,' Catherine said. 'It has been a long day and I am exhausted.'

He didn't say a word. He simply looked at her in silence. But when she went to reach for the door handle, he leaned forward and held out his hand.

Confused, Catherine sat back. What was he doing? His expression, while serious, was in no way threatening, leading her to believe he wasn't about to try to ravish her. So what *did* he want?

Her gaze rested on his a moment longer and then, with a sigh, she cautiously placed her hand into his.

Valbourg's fingers closed around hers, warm and reassuring. 'Thank you for agreeing to perform for my family and guests this evening, Miss Jones. While I regret the unfortunate incident that took place, I do not regret the time we were able to spend together. You are a beautiful and talented woman and I know you will do well in the future. But if you *ever* have need of my help, you have only to ask and it will be given.'

With that, he raised her hand to his lips and kissed it.

Catherine stared back at him, her thoughts a confusing tangle of emotions. What was she to make of all this? Did he dislike her—or desire her? Was he inviting her in or warning her to stay away? She had no idea. But too tired to figure any of it out, she gathered up her skirts and climbed out of the carriage.

By the time she looked up, it was already pulling away, leaving her standing alone in the middle of the darkened street. A few minutes later, it began to rain.

Fortunately, or perhaps miraculously, a hackney came trotting around the corner and Catherine hailed it, relieved she wouldn't have to travel the rest of the way on foot.

She was unlocking her front door when a dark figure separated itself from the shadows. 'Good evening, Miss Jones.'

Catherine gasped, a combination of fear and exhaustion prompting the unguarded response. But when she realised who it was, she closed her eyes and said tersely, 'Dash it all, Stubbs! You frightened the life out of me!'

'My apologies, but you're coming in later than usual and without the ever-watchful Mrs Rankin by your side.'

'Mrs Rankin is ill. I sent her home and went alone to Lord Alderbury's house.'

'The *Marquess* of Alderbury?' Stubbs repeated. 'Well, well, and what would someone like you be doing at a fine house like that until this time in the morning?'

'Performing.'

'Oh, aye.' He smiled and winked suggestively. 'For a gentleman?'

'No. For Lord Alderbury and about a hundred of his guests, at a ball to celebrate his daughter's engagement,' Catherine said with as much patience as she could muster. 'I was invited to sing.'

'Well, ain't that nice,' the man said. 'Expect me to believe that, do you?'

'I expect you to believe it because it's the truth,'

Catherine said. Had the circumstances been different, she would have told Stubbs to mind his own business, or at the very least to go away and leave her alone. But it would have been foolhardy to do one and she knew better than to expect the other. 'You can verify it easily enough, Stubbs. No doubt details of the reception will appear in the society columns tomorrow.'

'No doubt they will,' Stubbs agreed, his gold tooth briefly catching the light from the overhead lamp. 'Enjoy moving with the toffs, do you, Miss Jones?'

'I don't move with them, Stubbs. I sing *for* them. There's a difference.'

'But they pay you well for your trouble.'

'Of course. I wouldn't do it otherwise.'

'I wonder you do it at all, a famous actress like you,' Stubbs said, his cracked leathery face reminding Catherine of one of the gargoyles crouched atop the marquess's house. 'Would have thought you already had everything you need. Except your boy, of course. And believe me, money's no guarantee of ever getting him back.'

Despite the warmth of the evening, Catherine shivered. 'What do you know about Thomas?'

'I know the vicar believes he's watching out for the boy's soul. And that it would suffer if he were to come to live with a fallen woman like you,' Stubbs said, leaning against the wall. 'If Hailey were to hear you'd done something foolish with one of your toffs—'

'He won't hear that because I haven't *done* anything foolish,' Catherine said. 'You know what kind of life I lead, Stubbs. Where I go and who I see. I've maintained the same lifestyle for the past five years. Why would I be so foolish as to do something to jeopardise it now?'

'Who knows? Stronger women than you have given in to temptation. Women who do everything they can, but still can't make ends meet.'

'Well, I *can* and Reverend Hailey knows it. And when the Gryphon shuts down in a week's time, I intend to go and collect Thomas.'

'Do you now? Well, let me give you a word of advice. The vicar ain't your only worry when it comes to the boy. His wife's taken a real fancy to him and all. Takes him with her wherever she goes. Treats him like her own son.'

'But he's not her son. He's *mine*!'

'Damn it, woman, keep your voice down!' Stubbs said, casting a nervous glance over his shoulder. 'You'll have the whole bloody street awake. And there's no point blowing up at me. I've got nothing to do with it.'

No, he didn't, and belatedly, Catherine realised she would gain nothing by lashing out at him. Stubbs was only a pawn. Her real fight was with the man—and now, by all accounts, the woman—

for whom Stubbs worked. 'So, are you going to report my evening's activities to your master?'

'Depends. How much is it worth to you that I *not* say anything?'

Catherine clenched her teeth and pulled out the marquess's envelope. This was always how the game was played and it was the reason she continued to give private concerts. Stubbs threatened to send a false report back to Hailey and she paid him not to do so. In short, blackmail. It didn't matter that she had nothing to hide. Stubbs was in the position of power and he didn't hesitate to use it. 'I trust this will help convince you that nothing worth reporting happened tonight.' She handed him his usual stipend. 'Do we have an accord?'

Stubbs made a pretence of counting the money before stuffing it into a small leather pouch he carried for the purpose. 'A pleasure doing business with you, Miss Jones.' He doffed his battered beaver and scurried away like a rat into the night.

Catherine unlocked the front door and went inside. It had been an unpleasant end to the evening, but in truth, she had been lucky to escape as lightly as she had. If Stubbs had seen her getting out of Valbourg's carriage—with Valbourg still inside—it would have taken a *lot* more than five pounds to guarantee his silence. Worse, it could have been Moody, the other man Hailey employed to keep an eye on her, in which case she would have been forced to hand over a great deal more of her night's earnings. Moody was a nasty piece of work; a man who had been in and out of prison and who seemed to have no conscience whatsoever.

Sell his own kid for a bob, Stubbs had once told her. And with someone like that hanging around, Catherine knew she couldn't risk stepping out of line. Any association, no matter how innocent, between herself and a man of wealth or title would be turned into something sordid and dirty. Between Moody and Stubbs, she had more than enough reasons for avoiding *any* kind of involvement. With Lord Valbourg or anyone else.

Chapter Three

The following afternoon brought a bit of welcome news in the form of a letter from Miss Gwendolyn Marsh, the spinster with whom Catherine had lived for her pregnancy and the first few months of Thomas's life and with whom she still maintained a friendship.

Gwen wrote in an elegant, flowing hand.

My dearest Catherine,
How I look forward to seeing you again. It feels as though it has been much longer than six months between visits this time. I have followed your success, of course. I understand Promises *is still the rage in London, and I am smiling to myself, remembering the nervous young girl who came to stay with me all those years ago, with nary a thought of performing on stage, let alone becoming one of its brightest stars!*

But I digress. I am glad to hear you will
be travelling to Grafton to collect Thomas.
I am so happy for you, my dear. You have
worked very hard for this, forgoing the plea-
sures enjoyed by most young women your
age, and you deserve now to reap the re-
wards...

Catherine let the letter fall to her lap, her
mind casting back over the events of the past
five years. Yes, she had worked hard, but what
choice had she had? Making a success of her life
was the *only* hope she'd had of regaining custody
of Thomas.

She remembered as though it were yesterday
the day she had arrived on Gwendolyn Marsh's
doorstep, pregnant with Will Hailey's child. Will,
the only son of the Reverend James Hailey and
his first wife, Ruth, had been Catherine's first
love; an attachment formed when Will had started
coming to her house to take lessons with her father. A thoughtful, quietly spoken lad, Will had
actually been eight months younger than Catherine, but his gentle manners and studious air
had made him seem older, and it was, perhaps,
inevitable that a friendship would spring up between them.

They saw a great deal of each other over the
next few months, the friendship deepening into
an attraction and eventually into love. Unfortu-

nately, Will didn't tell his parents about his feelings for Catherine. Nor did he know, on the day he was thrown from his horse and killed, that she was carrying his child. For that reason, Reverend Hailey had refused to believe Catherine when she told him of their involvement. As far as Hailey was concerned, Catherine was just the schoolmaster's daughter. He had been horrified to learn she was carrying his dead son's child and had refused to have anything to do with her.

Nor had her own father been much better, Catherine reflected. Having recently lost his wife and struggling to come to terms with his own grief, Peter Jones had been unable to help her, his sadness prompting him to say things Catherine would never forget. So she had written to Miss Gwendolyn Marsh, a spinster and close friend of her late mother. Miss Marsh lived in Cheltenham, and it was to her Catherine had poured out her heart, going so far as to ask Miss Marsh if she might come and live with her until her baby was born.

Thankfully, Miss Marsh had said yes, and it was there in the comfort of her home that Catherine had spent the long, unhappy months of her pregnancy, blissfully unaware of the storm brewing on the horizon. A storm the effects of which she was still feeling today.

She picked up Gwen's letter and continued reading.

You are welcome to stay with me for as long as you like, both before and after you collect Thomas. Cheltenham is empty of company at the moment and I should so enjoy having you around again. And of course I am anxious to see Thomas, since all I remember of him is a tiny baby.

Mrs Brown has been busy baking, and Flo and Daisy are quite silly in the way they go on. They will no doubt giggle and blush upon first seeing you. You are quite the star now, my dear, and I could not be happier for you...

Catherine finished the letter and then folded it up and put it on the table next to her chair. Unbidden, the memory of her first trip back to Grafton after Thomas's birth came to mind; an occasion that stood out as one of the worst of her life. She had taken Thomas, then only a month old, to see Reverend Hailey and his new wife, Eliza, whom he had married shortly after Catherine left Grafton.

Pretty and spoiled, Eliza possessed neither the compassion nor the gentleness of Hailey's first wife, and Catherine had disliked her on the spot. She'd had difficulty understanding why Hailey had married such a woman, though she suspected it had much to do with the fact Eliza *was* so pretty and that she played the part of the helpless female so well. Reverend Hailey wasn't a bad man, just a weak one. And weak men, whether they be men of God or tillers of the soil, were easily manipulated. Catherine had recognised that the moment she had walked into the manse. She had been greeted at the door by the new housekeeper, a brusque north-country woman who had arrived with the new Mrs Hailey, and rather than being shown into the drawing room, where family and guests were usually entertained, Catherine had been ushered into the vicar's private study, where Reverend Hailey and Eliza stood glaring at her from behind his desk. There, she had drawn back the blanket and shown them their grandson.

Hailey's reaction was not at all what Catherine had been expecting. Asking if he might hold the child, Catherine had willingly passed Thomas over, hopeful his birth might help break down the barriers that existed between them. But only moments after taking Thomas, Reverend Hailey had handed him to his wife, as though reluctant to hold the child any longer than was absolutely necessary.

He'd said that, under the circumstances, he felt it best that the child remain with them. Given Catherine's position as an unwed mother, with no employment and few prospects, she was the last person who should be taking care of a baby. He had gone on to say it was in Thomas's best interests that he be raised in a Christian household, untainted by his mother's immoral and sinful ways.

Stunned by the unexpected turn of events, Catherine had immediately asked Reverend Hailey to hand Thomas back to her, but the man had coldly and adamantly refused. He had quoted biblical text, saying his son's death was a punishment from God, and that Catherine would burn in hell for her sins of lust and fornication. Eliza hadn't said a word, but her expression had warned Catherine against trying to plead her case. At that point, she had returned to Miss Marsh's house, where, devastated by the very real possibility of never seeing her son again, she had broken down and burst into tears.

A kind though practical woman, Miss Marsh had let Catherine cry, and when at last the tears came to an end, she had sat Catherine down and talked about what must be done. She told Catherine she truly was in no position to look after Thomas because until she was able to earn a living that provided a reasonable level of income, she would not be able to adequately provide for her son. Then she had said the words that had set Catherine on the road to her new life.

'You have two gifts, my dear. A beautiful face and a remarkable voice. You must use both to make a career for yourself.'

'A career?' Catherine had said, confused. 'Doing what?'

'Why, performing, of course,' Miss Marsh said. 'Good actresses can command very high salaries.'

An actress? Miss Marsh wanted her to go on stage and *perform*? Catherine had been appalled. Everyone knew actresses were fallen women who allowed themselves to be kept by wealthy men who paid for their lodgings and gowns in exchange for the kinds of pleasures otherwise found in brothels. Surely Miss Marsh did not wish to see Catherine end up that way.

Thankfully, Miss Marsh—being a great deal more familiar with the ways of the world—had agreed that, yes, while many actresses were possessed of questionable morals, some had genuine talent and managed to make enviable careers for themselves.

'It is the morality of the woman that dictates how she will be viewed by others,' Miss Marsh said. 'If you are skilled at your profession and keep yourself free of scandal, you will be acknowledged and celebrated for your talent. Furthermore, if you are able to capitalise on that talent and prove your financial competence to Reverend Hailey, he might reconsider and give Thomas back to you.'

It was all the encouragement Catherine needed—and while it had seemed the flimsiest of hopes, it was one to which she had clung with desperate ferocity.

Then Miss Marsh had performed her greatest act of charity. She had taken it upon herself to pay a visit to Reverend Hailey, during which she had set out the facts surrounding Catherine's past and future plans. She had then asked Reverend Hailey if he would consider revisiting the issue of Thomas's custody on the occasion of his fifth birthday.

Catherine hadn't held out any hopes of Reverend Hailey agreeing to the suggestion. To her astonishment, however, Miss Marsh had returned with the news that if Catherine was able to prove herself a responsible woman of good moral character and was able to earn an income that would allow her to support herself and Thomas, Reverend Hailey would agree to review the situation when Thomas turned five.

At the time, five years had seemed an eternity, but that date was now upon them, and knowing she had met all of Reverend Hailey's demands, Catherine had written to advise him that she would be coming to Grafton to talk about regaining custody of Thomas.

She had fulfilled her part of the bargain. Now it was time for the clergyman to live up to his.

The following Tuesday saw the final performance of *Promises* and, knowing it was their last show, the cast delivered what Mr Templeton said afterwards was their finest performance of the season. A standing ovation greeted Catherine as she took her bows, and she was showered with bouquets of flowers and expensive gifts when she returned to her dressing room later on.

As always, the diamond brooches and sapphire earrings with accompanying messages and thinly veiled invitations were politely sent back, while the posies of red roses, exotic lilies, pink carnations and sweet-smelling freesia were redistributed amongst the younger cast members; girls who seldom received such tributes.

Only one pink rose, adorned with a white satin bow, was kept.

'Your unseen admirer will have a bit of a rest now,' Lily said as she hung Catherine's costume in the wardrobe. 'Whatever will he do, I wonder?'

'Perhaps he will find someone else to admire,' Catherine said as she removed her necklace of paste emeralds. 'An actress in one of the other theatres.'

'He won't find anyone as talented as you,' Lily said. 'I peeked into the audience when you were singing tonight and I swear there wasn't a dry eye in the house.' She closed the wardrobe door and glanced around the dressing room. 'I'll make sure everything is packed, and I've asked Mr Hawkins to give us a hand with the trunk. Are you and Mrs Rankin still leaving in two days' time?'

'Yes,' Catherine said, turning around so that Lily could fasten the pins at the back of her gown.

'Mrs Rankin is looking into arrangements for the coach.'

'I'm glad I don't have to go.' Lily wrinkled her nose. 'I don't like travelling on public coaches.'

'Neither do I, but at least we will be riding inside.' Catherine stood up and smoothed back an errant curl. 'There, I think I'm ready. I shall meet you outside the theatre in half an hour.'

Catherine heard the sound of voices and laughter long before she walked into the crowded lobby, but as soon as she did, people turned and began to cheer her arrival. It still humbled her, these overwhelming tributes to her performances. Never in her wildest dreams had she imagined that one day, she would achieve this kind of fame. Indeed, when Miss Marsh had first put forward the idea of singing on the stage, Catherine had been convinced that *no one* would pay good money to hear her sing, let alone provide her with enough to establish herself as an independent woman. But they *had* paid to see her, filling the seats and the boxes of the Gryphon Theatre night after night and giving her back far more than she could possibly have given them.

'Catherine!'

She looked up to see Theo Templeton shouldering his way through the crowd, dapper as always in formal evening attire, his trademark black cape swirling around him. Theo didn't study the dictates of fashion. He set them; dressing as he pleased because he was rich enough to do so. Even his hair, once as black as midnight but now liberally sprinkled with grey, was worn longer than fashion decreed, but it looked dashing on him and he had the confidence to carry it off.

He reached her side and embraced her in a fatherly hug. 'A marvellous night, my dear, and you were wonderful. Come and meet your adoring public and celebrate your success!'

He stayed by her side for the next twenty minutes, acting as both buffer and host as Catherine moved through the crowd, acknowledging the accolades and compliments. The gentlemen were all there, of course: the green lads begging for kisses or calling out invitations for supper, the older men like Lords Styles and Tantemon lounging by the stage door, watching her with barely veiled desire. Others, like Lord Hugh Nelson and Mr Stanton, merely smiled and winked.

Caught up in the giddy whirl of the evening, Catherine smiled back, knowing Theo would intervene if any of them came too close. But when she heard *his* voice rising above the others, she stopped and immediately turned around. 'Lord Valbourg,' she said, extending her hand. 'You came.'

'Did you think I would miss your final performance?' He raised her hand to his lips and brushed a kiss against her fingers. 'Which, I must say, was one of your finest.'

Catherine blushed like a schoolgirl, as though she had never been offered a compliment before. 'Thank you. Last performances are always special,' she said, wondering if she would ever develop an immunity to this man's charm. 'We strive to send the audience home with good memories.'

'Judging from what I saw tonight, you succeeded admirably. So, what now?' he asked, drawing her to one side as Theo moved away to speak to Lady Pearcy. 'A well-deserved holiday, perhaps?'

'You could say that. I leave for Cheltenham the day after tomorrow.'

'Cheltenham! What a coincidence. So do I.'

Catherine's stomach tightened. 'Really?'

'Lord and Lady Brocklehume are hosting a gathering at their country estate,' Valbourg said, nodding at an acquaintance before turning a thoughtful gaze back on her. 'Would you care to travel with me?'

Catherine hesitated, but only for a moment. 'Thank you, but I have already made my arrangements.'

'And they are?'

'To take the coach into Gloucester and rendezvous with the lady with whom I shall be staying. She has written to say she will meet me in the square.'

'She still can, but since we are both bound for

the same destination, why not journey together?' Valbourg said. 'Time always goes faster when one has company.'

'But I will have company. My companion, Mrs Rankin, will be travelling with me,' Catherine said, aware even as she said it that it was a flimsy excuse. A lady of quality never travelled without a maid or a companion, but the thought of spending two days in a carriage with Valbourg and having to make conversation with him was disquieting to say the least. 'There won't be room for all of us in your carriage.'

'There will be if I take the barouche.'

'But surely your father will need it while you are gone?'

'Not for the brief time it takes to drive there and back, no.'

Catherine bit her lip. For every objection she put forward, he countered with a solution. If only there weren't the risks... 'Lord Valbourg, I am most grateful for your offer, but I'm really not sure it would be wise.'

'And you, Miss Jones, must stop throwing up roadblocks in my path. If it is your reputation you are worried about, don't be,' Valbourg said. 'You will be travelling with a respectable companion and I can hardly ravish you with her looking on, now can I?'

Shocked, Catherine burst out laughing, only to regret it a moment later when she realised that amusement would *not* have been the reaction of a well-brought-up young lady. 'No, I am quite sure you can't. And were I a respectable young lady, the presence of a companion would likely be enough to quiet wagging tongues. But I am an actress and therefore anyone travelling with me might be equally suspect.'

'Even though Mrs Rankin is a widow?'

'Perhaps more so because of it.'

'Very well. Then I shall make one further suggestion. You and your companion can travel in the carriage and set off first thing in the morning while I shall set out on horseback a few hours later,' Valbourg said. 'I will no doubt catch up with you at some point along the road, but for all intents and purposes, we would be leaving London separately, thereby giving the gossips nothing to talk about. Does that meet with your approval?'

Catherine wanted to find fault with his suggestion, but found she was unable to do so without sounding ungracious. Yes, there was a possibility she would be seen riding in the Marquess of Alderbury's carriage, but what harm could come of it if neither the marquess nor Valbourg were with her? Especially since Mrs Rankin would be at her side the entire time. 'Very well, Lord Valbourg, I accept your offer and thank you for it.'

'Splendid. Because I have a favour to ask in return. Would you consider singing for Lady Brocklchume and her guests one evening?' he asked. 'For a fee, of course.'

Catherine looked at him in surprise. 'You have taken it upon yourself to arrange your hosts' entertainments?'

'Only when it comes to you. The countess enjoys your performances, and I am hopeful if she is very pleased with the arrangements, she will put in a good word for me with her husband. I have been trying to persuade him to sell me one of his prize stallions for some months now.'

It was such a male justification that Catherine couldn't help but smile. 'Fine. If that is all that is required by way of repayment, I am happy to comply.'

'Ah, but I did not say that was *all* that was required,' he said, his voice dropping. 'Have you given any more thought to what we talked about the other night?'

In a heartbeat, Catherine's mood of joyous optimism faded. She knew what he was referring to and wished with all her heart he would let the matter drop. 'I have given it no further thought whatsoever. I told you how I felt about the subject at the time.'

'Yes, but I am not willing to let the matter rest. However, this is neither the time nor the place to discuss it,' Valbourg said as a cluster of giggling girls made their way across the lobby towards them. 'Hopefully, we will have an opportunity to converse during the journey to Cheltenham. Or while you are at Swansdowne. I will, of course, arrange for a carriage to collect you from wherever you are staying and return you there after your performance. Unless you wish to spend the night at the manor?'

Catherine's head whipped round, her gaze locking with his. What was he suggesting? That she might like to stay at Swansdowne for the night...or that he *wanted* her to? Was he rethinking his decision about the role he wished her to play in his life? She supposed it was possible, but if he thought to initiate an affair at Swansdowne, the chances of it being discovered were exceedingly high. Bedroom hopping was a commonplace event at country-house gatherings, and though a blind eye was often turned to those who were discreet, Catherine suspected an affair between Valbourg and an actress would not be so casually overlooked.

Besides, she would have Thomas with her by then. She had no desire to leave him alone at Gwendolyn's house after having so recently been reunited with him. 'Thank you, my lord, but I think it best I return home at the conclusion of the performance. I would not wish to offend my friend by spending a night away so soon after my arrival.'

'If your friend is aware of how popular a performer you are, I dare say she would understand. However, the decision is yours.'

Catherine nodded, the complexity of her thoughts threatening to bring on a headache. 'I must be leaving. My maid is waiting for me in the carriage.'

Valbourg bowed. 'Then I shall escort you to it.'

Catherine was tempted to argue, but the lobby was still crowded with admirers, and none of the gentlemen she wished to avoid had left. No doubt some were waiting to see what she did, perhaps hoping to catch her alone. As such, walking to her carriage on her own might not be the wisest course of action. Theo had moved away and she was reluctant to call him back, though she had a feeling Valbourg would prove a far more effective barrier.

'What is your address in Cheltenham?' Valbourg enquired as they walked out to the carriage together.

'High Street, near the park, but I think it best I make my own way to Swansdowne and back,' Catherine told him. She saw Lily, who had been waiting by the carriage, bob a curtsy and quickly climb inside. 'It would be more prudent.'

'But not nearly as entertaining. However, I bow to your wishes. I shall arrange for the carriage to pick you up from Green Street at eight o'clock Thursday morning.'

Halfway into the carriage, Catherine stopped

and turned around. 'What makes you think I live on Green Street?'

'Because while you may be a very talented actress, you are an extremely poor liar.' He helped her the rest of the way into the carriage and then closed the door. 'Good evening, Miss Jones.'

He nodded at the coachman, and the carriage sprang forward, leaving Catherine with no opportunity to reply. She stared at Lily in bewilderment. 'How did he know where I lived?'

'Don't look at me, miss. I certainly didn't tell him,' Lily said. 'But I doubt it would be all that difficult for a man like that to find out. Is there a reason you don't want him knowing where you live?'

'Not really. It's just that...' Catherine stopped, thinking about the night she had instructed his coachman to drop her off a few streets over from where she lived. Had Valbourg known even then that she was lying? 'Never mind. I don't suppose it matters.'

'Did I hear him say he would be seeing you in Cheltenham, miss?'

'Hmm? Oh, yes. Apparently Lord and Lady Brocklehume are holding a gathering in the area, and when I told Lord Valbourg I was also travelling to Cheltenham, he asked if I would be willing to sing for them. I said I would, at which point he kindly offered me the use of his father's carriage.'

'And very nice, too!' Lily said, her expression

of curiosity changing to one of satisfaction. 'I suspect that's because he's sweet on you.'

'He is not sweet on me!' Catherine said, cheeks burning. 'A man like that would never be interested in someone like me.'

'But a man like that doesn't do things for people like you unless he wants to...and he clearly likes doing things for you,' Lily pointed out. 'So you can interpret it how you like. I still say he's sweet on you.'

Catherine didn't bother to reply. What was the point? Lily was a hopeless romantic who was forever devouring penny novels with the belief that dark, handsome heroes existed to sweep beautiful young women off their feet. It didn't matter how often she was told that fiction seldom resembled real life or that the heroines of most stories didn't live happily ever after. Lily preferred her own way of looking at the world.

Still, Catherine couldn't deny that whether by chance or design, she *was* seeing rather a lot of Valbourg, nor could she deny that she was flattered by his regard. He was handsome, charming and considerate; more so than any man she had ever met. Unfortunately, he was also a marquess's son and the type of man for whom a woman happily and willingly did foolish things.

Catherine could not afford to be foolish. Valbourg was just passing through her life. The best she could hope for with him was the kind of tawdry relationship she had been offered and turned down so many times before.

Besides, how would he feel about her when he learned about Thomas? Would he turn away in disgust? Ask why she was keeping herself chaste when her son's existence proved she was anything but?

Best not go down that road, Catherine warned herself. She had endured enough heartache over the past five years. She had no desire to live through any more in the future.

The night after the Gryphon closed, Theo and Tandy Templeton threw one of their lavish dinner parties. The entire company was invited, and Catherine was persuaded, as were several other members of the cast, to stage an informal entertainment after dinner. Victor Trumphani would recite a passage from a Shakespearean play, Tommy Silver, one of the newcomers to the troupe, would perform wondrous tricks of magic and illusion, and Catherine would sing a selection of songs.

Anthea Templeton, or Tandy as she liked to be called, always invited an eclectic mixture of guests to her dinner parties; everyone from a viscount and his lady to a doctor and his unmarried sister. Catherine was introduced to a barrister and his beautiful French fiancée, several extremely wealthy gentlemen whose conversations led her to believe they spent more time out of the country than in it and a delightful Italian count whose broken English was colourful if not always correct.

'He can be quite outrageous,' Tandy confided. 'But he is such an interesting man, no one really minds. Just don't take anything he says to heart. Italians can be such notorious flirts. I should know. I almost married one!'

As always, the guests mingled together well, no doubt due to the relaxed atmosphere Theo and Tandy took such care to foster. Catherine spotted the viscountess laughing with the barrister's wife, saw the doctor chatting with Victor Trumphani and heard Theo speaking quite respectable French to the barrister's fiancée. The Italian count flirted with every lady he could, but Catherine soon discovered that Tandy was right. He was harmless as long as you didn't let his blandishments go to your head.

Then, to Catherine's dismay, *he* walked in. Valbourg, with Lord and Lady Castingrote and their eldest daughter, Lady Susan Wimsley, at his side. She had no idea if he was with Lady Susan or if they had simply arrived at the same time, but the sight of him laughing so easily with an earl's daughter caused a painful and entirely unexpected constriction in her chest.

'They're not together,' Tandy whispered as she sailed past. 'But I do not think Lady Susan's mother would be unhappy to see them end up that way.'

She was gone before Catherine had a chance to say she barely knew Valbourg and didn't *care* if he was there with someone, even though she knew in some twisted corner of her heart that she did. Nor did it help that he made a point of walking across the room to speak to her.

'Good evening, Miss Jones. We seem destined to keep bumping into one another.'

'We do indeed, my lord,' Catherine replied, drawing on her skills as an actress to make it sound as though such meetings were of no great importance. 'Though I am surprised to find you mingling at a gathering like this.'

'Why? Because not all of the guests are wealthy blue bloods?'

'Your words, not mine.'

'You are unjust, Miss Jones,' Valbourg retorted. 'I often attend gatherings where I am the only titled gentleman present and suffer no feelings of guilt or superiority whatsoever.'

She struggled not to smile. 'I stand corrected. I had no idea you were so liberal.'

'How could you? We have not spent enough time in each other's company for you to have formed an opinion about my character.'

And yet, she had, Catherine reflected, and she suspected it wasn't all that far off the mark. He was a man committed to doing what was right for those he loved, and even for those he did not. How could one not admire such a man?

'I'm glad you do not set yourself so high as to feel you must avoid gatherings like these,' Catherine said, the smile on her lips there for the benefit of those around them. 'They can be a lot of fun.'

'Truth be told, I enjoy these occasions far more than the stuffy soirées where one is forced to partake of meagre refreshments while not being able to move without bumping into a duke or a marquess.' He glanced across the room to where Count D'Abrezzi and Victor Trumphani were engaged in a spirited conversation in Italian. 'Tandy can always be counted upon to invite the most interesting people to her dinners.'

'You have attended gatherings here before?' Catherine asked in surprise.

'Indeed. I've known Theo and Tandy for years. He and I did business together in the past, and though I was in America for several years, we kept in touch. He is an exceedingly amiable and generous man.'

'Yes, he is and I owe him everything,' Catherine said softly. 'He was very kind to me the first time we met.'

'And where was that, exactly?'

She hesitated, fearful of giving away too much about her past. And yet in truth, where was the harm? It wasn't as though Valbourg was interested in her. 'Newport.'

'Ah. That explains the Welsh lilt. Were you born there?'

'No. I was born in a small village east of Monmouth. I was performing at a theatre in Newport the first time Mr Templeton saw me.'

'Is that also where you took your formal training?'

Surprise bubbled up. 'How did you know I was formally trained?'

'The manner in which you sing. Most young ladies are able to perform quite adequately in the confines of a small drawing room, but to develop a voice like yours and be able to project it in a theatre the size of the Gryphon suggests the influence of a teacher trained in operatic performance.'

In spite of herself, Catherine was impressed. Most men were more interested in her appearance than in her talent. *This* man complimented her voice.

Of course, *this* man had also suggested she take a lover. If that didn't tell her where she stood in his estimation, nothing would.

'A friend I was staying with at the time arranged for me to have lessons,' Catherine said. 'She told me that while I had a good voice, it could be improved with training. And as she happened to be friends with a German lady who had performed on stage, she arranged for me to take lessons with her.'

'She obviously recognised your potential. Still, Newport's a long way from London,' Valbourg commented. 'How did you end up here?'

'You ask a great many questions, my lord.'

'I suffer from a terminal case of curiosity for which no known cure exists. My sister despairs of me for that reason.'

In spite of her wariness, Catherine laughed. 'I fear your condition is wasted on me. I lead a very simple life, unlike many in this room who are far more interesting and about whom you *should* be curious.'

'Yet, I am not.' He gazed down at her, his eyes lingering on the creamy expanse of neck and shoulders left bare by the daring décolletage of the crimson gown. 'As unwise as it may be, I have a burning desire to know a great deal more about you.'

Catherine snapped open her fan and waved it in front of her face. Madness! Engaging in a flirtation with Valbourg was inviting trouble. If she were smart, she would ask him to leave or simply turn and walk away.

And yet she stayed; drawn like a lemming to the precipice over which it must plunge.

'Mr Templeton happened to be in Newport when I was performing at the local theatre,' she said finally. 'At the end of the evening, he came backstage to speak with me and said if I ever wanted to come to London, he would put me up in lodgings and guarantee me a place in his company.'

'So you did and quickly became his shining star.'

'Not at all,' Catherine said, recalling the trials of her early days in London; the strangeness of living in a huge city and the feeling of being completely on her own, not to mention the professional jealousies she had encountered from those who suspected her of being Templeton's mistress. It wasn't until Theo had made her get up on stage and perform a difficult duet with Victor Trumphani without the benefit of a prior rehearsal that she had been accepted and welcomed by the rest of the troupe.

'I had to prove my worth,' Catherine said, 'but I've no complaints about the way it all turned out. Mr Templeton demands a lot of his performers, but no more than we ask of ourselves.'

'And you earn enough money to provide an adequate living for yourself?'

Catherine stiffened. Was this a subtle return to their previous conversation? An attempt, perhaps, to point out how much better off she would be if she placed herself under the protection of a wealthy man? 'I earn enough to look after myself. And the private concerts I give augment my income.'

'And that is enough for you?'

'Why would it not be?'

'Do you not desire the company of a gentleman? Perhaps occasionally wish to be taken out to dinner or an elegant soirée?'

'Not at all. Men are complicated,' Catherine said. 'My life is not. And I intend to keep it that way.'

Once again, the conversation had strayed beyond the level of comfort; veering off in a direction Catherine had no intention of going. Thankfully, dinner was announced shortly thereafter, and the order of precedence, which even Tandy paid some mind to, did not put Catherine in close proximity to Valbourg at the table. She was glad to be spared the difficulty of trading barbs or witticisms with him. Sparring with Valbourg was like dancing with a tiger.

One never knew when the beast was going to strike.

Chapter Four

At length, the remnants of a most excellent meal were cleared away and the ladies rose and retired to the drawing room for coffee and conversation. Valbourg, whose culinary standards were exceedingly high, expressed himself well satisfied with the meal, as he was with the exceptionally fine port and cigars his host handed around afterwards. Conversation was stimulating, mainly because the gentlemen came from a wide variety of backgrounds and were able to discuss an assortment of subjects with very little considered off limits.

It served as a refreshing change from the guarded discussions that usually took place in the dining rooms of the aristocracy, and Valbourg was slightly disappointed when Theo said it was time to rejoin the ladies for the evening's entertainments—until he remembered that Catherine would be one of the performers. Somehow that cast the rest of the evening in an entirely different light.

Not surprisingly, she was the first person he looked for upon entering the drawing room and he knew he was not alone in his admiration of her. Catherine drew men's eyes like air drew flame, and in the crimson gown that wrapped so lovingly around every curve, she glowed like a column of fire. Rubies flashed at her ears and throat, dazzling red against the creaminess of her skin. If they were paste, they were truly exceptional.

Of course, they might well be genuine, Valbourg reminded himself. He knew of several gentlemen who routinely sent her jewellery, along with offers of various other kinds, and though the offers were summarily rejected, he had no idea if the gifts were likewise sent back.

Wisely, however, he did not make his way to her side. People had been watching them during their conversation before dinner, and, guessing at the nature of their thoughts, Valbourg decided to keep his distance. It would not be to his benefit to let anyone know how he really felt about her... especially since the more time he spent with her, the harder it was becoming to remain steadfast in his intent not to get involved.

The more he learned about Catherine, the more powerful her effect on him. He found her unusual combination of innocence and sensuality intensely intriguing, and more than once, he had to stop himself from smiling in her direction. Too many people were watching, eyes alert for the first sign of scandal. And the Marquess of Alderbury's heir taking up with an actress would definitely qualify as scandal.

At length, the post-dinner entertainments began. Young Tommy the Conjurer led off, dazzling his audience with inexplicable feats of magic. The boy made silver balls vanish and bunches of flowers appear out of thin air, pulled rabbits from hats and amazed them all with displays of sleight of hand and card wizardry. The lad clearly had a promising future ahead of him.

Next came Victor Trumphani, taking the makeshift stage for a moving recital of one of Shakespeare's most famous soliloquies. Trumphani was a consummate performer, his finely cultivated baritone rising and falling with emotion, his expression alternately joyous or mournful as called for by the part. Valbourg noticed Lady Susan wipe a tear from her eye and applaud most enthusiastically at the end of the performance.

Finally, Catherine got up and walked towards the piano while the barrister's fiancée sat down at the harp. To Valbourg's surprise, they both began to play their respective instruments while Catherine sang along, resulting in a most enchanting duet.

'I had no idea Miss Jones could play the piano,'

Lady Castingrote commented. She was seated to his right on the chesterfield. 'I have only ever heard her sing before.'

'Which she does sublimely,' Lady Susan said, leaning in front of her mother to add, 'Do you not think so, Lord Valbourg?'

'Indeed, the lady has many talents.'

'And Valbourg would know,' Tantemon murmured, collapsing into the vacant chair to Valbourg's right. 'From what I hear, he doesn't miss many of her performances.'

'I enjoy going to the theatre,' Valbourg remarked, 'whether it be the Gryphon, the Theatre Royal or any other.'

'True, but you have shown a marked preference for the Gryphon,' Tantemon said. 'If one didn't know better, one might think you were contemplating giving the Angel a slip on her quite heavenly shoulder.'

Valbourg shot the peer a withering glance. He'd never cared much for Tantemon, and after having seen him form part of the pack that had circled Catherine like hyenas, he liked him even less. 'I don't partake of the pretty muslin company, Tantemon. I thought you knew that.'

'A man has to spend his nights somewhere.'

'I prefer to spend mine at home. The hells and brothels hold no attraction for me any more.'

'Of course not, because you are a respectable family man,' Tantemon drawled. 'Still, I couldn't help but notice how protective you were of Miss Jones at your sister's engagement ball. Or the cosy way the two of you were chatting before dinner this evening. Such conduct would lead one to believe you were...interested in her.'

'Then one would be mistaken,' Valbourg said, returning his attention to the two ladies at the front of the room. 'Miss Jones has a rare talent and I enjoy listening to her sing. Nothing more.'

'Probably just as well. Now that you have your nephew living with you, you can't afford to put your reputation at risk,' Tantemon said. 'Wouldn't do for the lad to venture into your room and see a naked woman lying in your bed. Or a fully clothed one dashing out of it in the morning. Difficult to explain, wouldn't you agree?'

'You tell me.' Valbourg pinned the other man with a steely gaze. 'I understand you often invited Miss Moyen to stay at your house when your wife and children were at home. Is that why she is no longer in your employ?'

Tantemon offered up a thin smile. 'Miss Moyen was cataloguing my library, which turned out to be a lengthy and time-consuming affair. She found it easier to be...close at hand. Now that the cataloguing is done, her services are no longer required.'

'Of course.' Valbourg flicked a piece of dust from his cuff. It was amusing the lies some men told themselves.

'After she left, I briefly toyed with the idea of making Miss Jones my mistress,' Tantemon went on, 'but in the end I decided against it. It's not an angel a man wants in his bed, but a woman who makes his blood boil. I seriously doubt that a lady some have dubbed the Ice Queen would be capable of doing that. Still, the next few weeks should be interesting. Have you seen the latest wager on the book at White's?'

Valbourg didn't bother looking over. 'No. Should I?'

'You might find it amusing. Lord Hornston has wagered Mr Tattingbone one hundred pounds that the Angel won't be quite so angelic by Christmas, if you take my meaning.'

Somewhere close by, a chair creaked. Across the room, a gentleman coughed, and next to Valbourg, Lady Castingrote laughed, the shrill sound echoing in his ears. All he heard, however, was the underlying message in Tantemon's words. 'And is Hornston intending to…clip the angel's wings?' he asked coldly.

'I suspect he will be one of those making the attempt,' Tantemon said, adding with an unpleasant smile, 'Miss Jones may find herself wishing she had accepted one of the offers put to her. At least then she would have had the choice of going to the gentleman's bed on *her* terms.'

With that parting remark, Tantemon left, claiming he needed a drink.

Valbourg needed one, too, but for an entirely different reason. So, his concerns about Catherine were not misplaced. The wager on the betting book indicated that someone was planning to seduce her, and if no one was around to prevent it, she might well find herself in a very unpleasant situation. It wouldn't matter that she had a rare talent, or that taking her by force might break her spirit. Men like that saw only a beautiful and desirable woman who was unencumbered by good birth or doting parents. She would be taken against her will, after which she would be cast aside or settled in a house, kept a virtual prisoner by a man whose only interest was in controlling and subduing her.

Valbourg couldn't let that happen. He'd never forgive himself if he found out Catherine had been so abused, and he'd likely throttle the man who'd done it. The only solution was to convince Catherine to take a lover. It didn't matter that he wanted her for himself or that he would have already made her an offer if Sebastian hadn't been in his life. Sebastian *was* in his life and nothing could come before that. But neither could he sit back and knowingly allow harm to come to her.

There had to be a way of protecting Catherine without jeopardising his own reputation. And for everyone's sake, he had to come up with one fast.

* * *

When, at last, the evening's entertainment came to an end, Catherine took her bows along with the rest of the performers and rejoined the guests. She was glad Lord Tantemon had left, surprised he had been invited in the first place, and was determined to avoid Valbourg for the rest of the evening. As such, she sat down with Tandy and Miss Bilodeau, the barrister's fiancée, only to find out too late that the young lady was talking about the very man she wished to avoid.

'Lord Valbourg is so dashing, is 'e not?' the girl said in her delightful French accent. 'And 'e seems to be a great admirer of yours, Mees Jones. I noticed 'im watching you during your performance.'

'You mistake enjoyment for interest, Miss Bilodeau,' Catherine said, again calling on her skills as an actress to feign indifference. 'Lord Valbourg is a patron of the arts. He appreciates good music, and his enjoyment of my performance was simply that.'

'Ah, *non*, mademoiselle. I am French. I recognise zat look in a man's eyes!'

The telltale rush of heat to Catherine's cheeks was extremely unwelcome, especially given the way Tandy was looking at her. 'I can assure you, Miss Bilodeau, that Lord Valbourg is not in the least interested in me,' Catherine said. 'I am an actress. He is a marquess's son and a thoroughly respectable man.'

'But 'e is still a man and will always be'ave like one. *Alors*, 'ere he is,' Miss Bilodeau said, green eyes bright with interest as Valbourg strolled towards them. '*Mon Dieu*, 'e is 'andsome, is 'e not?'

He was, Catherine thought, but aware that he was close enough to hear anything she said, she merely tilted her head and smiled. 'Still here, my lord?'

'Yes, but I will be leaving shortly. I wonder, Miss Jones, if you would allow me the pleasure of seeing you home?'

'Thank you, but I prefer to make my own way.'

'But why would you wish to?' Miss Bilodeau asked. 'I am sure Lord Valbourg 'as a very nice carriage. And surely it is safer to travel with 'im than on your own.'

'Actually—'

'Miss Bilodeau is right, Catherine,' Tandy said. 'It's late and I would prefer to see someone escort you. I could ask Theo—'

'No! I wouldn't dream of taking him away from his guests,' Catherine objected. 'Nor is it necessary. I am perfectly capable of hiring a hackney.'

'But why do zat when Lord Valbourg 'as made such a kind offer?' Miss Bilodeau persisted with a wide-eyed innocence Catherine knew better than to believe.

'Because it is not proper for a single man to offer a single lady a ride in his carriage,' she said. 'At least, not in England.'

'Then perhaps you would allow me to walk you home,' Valbourg said. 'I can have my carriage follow at a discreet distance, close enough that my coachman is able to see us at all times. Because there is something very important I must speak to you about.'

'*Bien!* Now you *must* say yes, mademoiselle,' Miss Bilodeau said, a satisfied smile on her prettily rouged lips.

It seemed pointless to argue and, aware that it would now be ungracious to do so, Catherine reluctantly agreed, though she was in no way looking forward to the outing. She had a sneaking suspicion Valbourg intended to continue their conversation about her taking a lover, even though she had said all she intended to the last time.

What did he think he could say *this* time that would possibly make the slightest bit of difference?

Yet another carriage waited in the street; this one a smart little equipage drawn by a single black horse.

'Have you an endless supply of these at your disposal, my lord?' Catherine enquired as they walked towards it.

'A gentleman requires a variety of carriages to accommodate the needs of the evening, Miss Jones. This is but one of them.'

'I see.' Catherine glanced at the young boy holding the carriage, quite sure he wasn't old enough to drive, and asked, 'Where is your coachman?'

'At home with a toothache.'

She stopped dead. 'There is no one to act as chaperon?'

'No, but that needn't be a problem. You and I have ridden in a carriage before.'

'Yes, with a coachman in the box and a valet on the back! You lied to me, Valbourg, and I do not like being lied to,' Catherine said tersely. 'I shall find a hackney and make my own way home.'

'Wait. I'm sorry I had to deceive you, Catherine, but it is of vital importance that you listen to what I have to say. And I doubt you will wish anyone else to hear it.'

Torn between curiosity and annoyance, Catherine glanced back at the house. She had been ready to walk away...until that last remark. 'Very well, my lord, but I'm warning you. If you intend to bring up what we talked about the other night—'

'I said I had something important to say.' Valbourg cut across her objections. 'Can we leave it at that for the moment?'

Aware she had little choice in the matter, Catherine sighed and allowed him to help her up into the carriage. He climbed in beside her and set the horse to a trot, its high-stepping hooves clattering on the cobbles. She could feel the warmth of Valbourg's leg pressing against hers, but was unable to move away in the close confines of the carriage.

'You surprised me this evening, Catherine,' Valbourg began in a conversational tone. 'I had no idea you could play the piano. You are, indeed, a woman of many talents. And, of course, your beauty made you the belle of the ball.'

'Thank you, but I could never be the belle of any ball at which Miss Bilodeau was present,' Catherine said, refusing to be charmed. 'She is an exceptionally lovely young lady, though I hope her forthright manner does not prevent her from being embraced by English society.'

'I suspect her fiancé will take steps to instil a proper sense of decorum in her.' Valbourg sent her a sideways glance. 'Does that matter to you? The opinion of others?'

'A strange question, given my career,' Catherine mused. 'But, yes, I suppose it does. I like to think people judge me for who I am rather than what I do, but I realise many don't and that there's nothing I can do about it. The people I care about know who I am. The others I just try to avoid.'

'I can't imagine there would be all that many.'

'You would be surprised,' Catherine murmured. 'But now we have engaged in polite chit-chat long enough. I wish to know what was so important that you felt you had to trick me into coming with you.'

'I did not trick you,' Valbourg said, skilfully navigating a sharp corner. 'I simply manipulated the truth a little. However, you remember that when we were last together, I asked you a question?'

'As I recall, you asked several.'

'None of which you answered.'

'The reasons for which I made clear.'

'Not really. You said the course of your future was dictated by the mistakes of your past.'

'That's right.'

'Then…and I promise this is my last question, if you could change what happened in your past, would you?'

Catherine turned her head away. Such a simple question. One to which a glib *yes* would likely prevent further questioning and send Valbourg on his way. Unfortunately, it wasn't that simple. Did she regret having been foolish enough to fall in love with Will Hailey and to have given in to the desires that overtook them both? Of course she did. But could she honestly say she regretted the outcome of her mistake…Thomas…enough to make her wish it had never happened?

She turned back and met his gaze. 'No, I would not.'

There. She had told him what he wanted to

know. What was he thinking now? What would *she* have made of such an answer had she been the one to ask the question? 'Have you nothing to say?'

'I'm not sure what the right response is,' Valbourg said, pulling the horse to a halt and securing the reins. 'To be honest, I was expecting a different answer. However, it does lead me to my next question.'

'No. You promised only one more and you have asked it.'

'Agreed. But I don't intend to *ask* this question,' he murmured. 'At least, not in words.'

Giving her no more warning than that, Valbourg turned and drew her against him, one hand gently grasping her chin and tilting it back. His fingers were warm against her skin, the scent of him sweet in her nostrils. Catherine tried to pull away, but he held her firmly. Then his mouth closed over hers—and she had no desire to go anywhere.

Desire exploded like a dried-up seed bursting in the welcome rains of a long-awaited storm. The touch of his mouth, the slow, sensual caress of his lips, set her blood pounding so that in an instant, the protective wall she had built around herself shattered, leaving her vulnerable and exposed.

But, oh, how she wanted this. To feel the strength of his arms around her and to experience the mastery of his kiss. It was everything she had imagined it would be, and more. Equal parts heaven…and hell.

When he finally drew back, he sat for a moment gazing down into her eyes. Catherine wanted to look away, but he held her fast, his thumb caressing the smoothness of her cheek.

'Find someone to take care of you, Catherine,' Valbourg said, his voice a whisper in the darkness. 'You are a creature of passion. What just happened between us proves that. You need a man to protect you.'

'I do not. I *cannot*!' Catherine closed her eyes, desperate to shut out the sight of his face. 'You don't understand. You don't know—'

'I know all I need to,' he said softly, his lips brushing hers again. 'There is a wager on the book at White's. An insidious wager in which your virtue is the prize.'

'*Me?* But why—?'

'Because you have become a challenge to them, my dear. A game they are determined to win and they will not let you go. For that reason, you *must* choose a champion. A woman on her own, a woman like you, cannot hope to survive.'

'I have survived until now.'

'Circumstances change. And as much as I might wish otherwise, I cannot be there to protect you from the Lassiters and the Tantemons of the world,' Valbourg said, his expression darkening. 'You need to put yourself under someone's protection and to do so as quickly as possible. I will help you in any way I can. I have friends. Men whose values I respect and who would treat you with kindness—'

'Stop it!' Catherine jerked her face away. 'I will *not* become some man's mistress simply because you think I should or because some other man feels entitled to put me down as the prize in his disgusting wager!'

'Then you invite trouble, Catherine, and trust me, it will find you,' Valbourg said. 'I *urge* you to give this matter the consideration it deserves. And I beg you to do it soon.'

He might have said more, but Catherine was already clambering out of the carriage. She didn't wait for him to help. She ran blindly for her door, tears of anger and shame rolling down her face.

How could this have happened to her? How could she suddenly have become the object of some twisted man's lust? She had never spoken badly of anyone. Had never caused any of these men embarrassment or pain, yet still they pursued her and now with money as the means to spur them on.

You have become a challenge to them... A game they are determined to win and they will not let you go.

It was hard to believe that fine, upstanding members of society would stoop to such a vile and cowardly act! And yet, had she not seen evidence of such cruelty before? Had she not seen the coldness with which men cast aside their mistresses when the women no longer pleased them? Had she not heard stories about husbands who betrayed their wives after vowing before God and witnesses to be faithful?

Had a man of God not taken her child and denied her the right to see him?

How could she doubt that *any* man would stoop to such conduct when she had more than enough proof to the contrary?

Valbourg did not doubt it. Otherwise he would not have told her of the wager. She had to be grateful to him for that.

As to the matter of her recent behaviour, Catherine could find no words to excuse what she had just done. For five years, she had kept herself apart; maintaining a distance from the men who pursued her, knowing it was the only way of avoiding this kind of involvement. Yet tonight, the first time Valbourg had touched her, she had melted into his arms. She had let him kiss her until her lips softened and her body trembled, and now she was truly undone. She had allowed herself to be seduced by his kindness and reassured by his air of nobility—only to find herself faced with a most painful truth.

The game was already lost. She had chosen her champion…knowing full well she would never be the lady for whose honour he fought.

* * *

Catherine saw no sign of Stubbs or Moody as she let herself into the house and locked the door, and for that she was grateful. There was no way on earth she would have been able to deliver as convincing a performance as the one she had given the other night. Not with the memory of Valbourg's kiss still sweet on her lips.

Thank God she was leaving London. She had to get away from here and to put herself beyond Valbourg's reach. He was a threat to everything she had built for herself. Everything that mattered.

'Find someone to take care of you... You are a creature of passion.'

The implication behind the words stung, yet it was their lack of truth that made Catherine want to cry. She was *not* a creature of passion. The roles she enacted on stage might call for her to engage in emotional and sometimes passionate scenes, but she was *not* that way inclined herself. Until Valbourg, she had not even felt the desire to *be* with a man. She had shut herself off from those feelings; convinced they didn't matter. No man since Will Hailey had aroused even the slightest stirrings of her heart.

And yet, she had experienced every one of those feelings with Valbourg tonight. Why? What was it about him that made him so different from everyone else? Wealthy men appeared at her dressing-room door every night. Many with promises of jewels and gowns, others with offers of carriages and homes, yet she had turned them all down. No man had touched her...until tonight, when Valbourg had kissed her and turned her world upside down.

And what had she done to discourage him? Had she shouted or screamed for help? Slapped his face and demanded that he let her go? No. She had offered no resistance whatsoever. She hadn't even asked for an apology.

Well, it was time for a change, Catherine decided as she closed her bedroom door and began to get ready for bed. Circumstances might force her into associating with Valbourg on the journey tomorrow and at Lord and Lady Brocklehume's soirée the following evening, but after that she intended to have nothing more to do with him. She was too vulnerable where he was concerned. Her reaction to his kiss had prompted him to call her a creature of passion and to *insist* she take a lover. He had even gone so far as to offer to introduce her to a few of his friends. But not once had he offered to give her the protection of *his* own name. Even though he knew what was at stake, he had not given her that option.

How much clearer could he make it that he had absolutely no interest in her?

The marquess's carriage arrived at precisely eight o'clock Thursday morning, and by half past,

Catherine was on her way, her luggage securely stowed on the racks overhead and Mrs Rankin— who was still feeling the effects of her illness— dozing in the seat across from her.

Catherine didn't mind. Mrs Rankin's lethargy left her free to think about Thomas. It was hard to believe they were soon to be reunited as mother and child. The visits she had made to Grafton over the past five years had been sweet torture; long anticipated, but too soon over. And she was never allowed more than two visits per year. For that reason, Catherine spent every moment of those visits with her son, even if it meant sitting in his bedroom, watching his dear little face as he slept.

Her last visit had been particularly memorable because at four and a half, Thomas had been more aware of what was going on around him and of the people he met. He actually remembered Catherine and greeted her at the door with his bright, beautiful smile.

Eliza, who insisted on remaining with Thomas at all times during Catherine's visits, hadn't looked pleased, but Catherine hadn't cared. All that mattered was Thomas and the fact she was with him.

'You're smiling,' she heard Mrs Rankin say in a weak voice. 'You must be thinking about Thomas.'

'I was.' Catherine looked up and smiled. 'Are you feeling any better, Margaret?'

'A little. I'm so sorry to have been such a bother, Catherine. It seems you've spent more time looking after me than the other way around.'

'Don't be silly. You've done so much for me these past five years, I can't begin to thank you. In fact, I don't know how I would have managed without you,' Catherine said with a smile. 'Those early days in London were very difficult for me, but you were always there with words of wisdom and support. You encouraged me when I was uncertain and let me lean on you when I was down. I'll never forget that.'

'Nor will I ever forget you,' Mrs Rankin said. 'The weeks following my husband's death were very hard. I suddenly found myself with too many empty hours on my hands and not enough activities to fill them. But when Gwendolyn wrote to me and told me about you, I thought it might be the perfect opportunity to pick myself up and brush myself off...and it was. Being a part of your life these last five years and watching you grow from a nervous young girl into the successful actress you are today has been marvellous. And I am, of course, delighted that you and Thomas are finally to be reunited. It has been a long time coming, but now happiness is within your grasp. Ohh...' She leaned back and closed her eyes. 'Will this dreadful nausea never end?'

'You should have stayed home,' Catherine said, concerned about her friend's welfare. 'A long carriage ride was the last thing you needed today.'

'Never mind. I wasn't about to see you travel halfway across the country without a chaperon. I feel bad enough you had to go to Lord Alderbury's reception on your own,' Mrs Rankin said. 'Had I known Lily wasn't going with you—'

'It's not Lily's fault. She had already made other plans.'

'With a fellow, no doubt.'

Catherine smiled. 'Yes, with Mr Hawkins's son. And knowing how Lily feels about him, I wasn't going to spoil her plans by insisting she come with me.'

'But how did you explain things to Mr Stubbs? He must have been surprised to see you out on your own.'

Remembering the conversation, Catherine sighed. 'He was. But everything turned out fine in the end.'

'Hmm.' Mrs Rankin looked far from convinced. 'How much did you give him this time?'

'Five pounds.'

'Five pounds! Oh, Catherine, that was far too much,' Mrs Rankin said. 'You know he'll only demand more the next time.'

'There isn't going to *be* a next time,' Catherine assured her. 'When we leave Grafton this time, Thomas will be coming with us. Then there will be no more Stubbs, no more reports and no more being spied upon.'

'I do hope so,' Mrs Rankin said. 'I would like nothing better than to see you and your dear little boy together again. But to be honest, I haven't a great deal of faith in Reverend Hailey's promises, for all his being a man of God. What man separates a mother from her child so heartlessly?'

'I know, but I like to think Reverend Hailey did what he felt best for Thomas,' Catherine said, repeating the words as though they might hold more truth now than they had in the past. 'I had no way of taking care of Thomas at the time.'

'He could have made allowances for that. You would have found employment. You wouldn't have let that little boy starve.'

'Of course not, but I don't think Reverend Hailey believed I was capable of finding a job.'

'Nonsense! You're an intelligent young woman. You could have worked in a shop or taken a position as a governess,' Mrs Rankin said. 'But to be honest, I don't think Reverend Hailey is the one who wanted the boy to stay. I've thought all along it was his wife. She's the one who doesn't want to give Thomas up.'

Her words had a disturbingly familiar ring, and Catherine was about to tell her what Stubbs had said when the carriage suddenly drew to a halt. Fearing an accident, Catherine glanced through the window, only to breathe a sigh of relief when she saw Valbourg approaching on a magnificent black horse that pranced and tossed its head as it drew level with the carriage.

'Good day, Miss Jones, Mrs Rankin,' Valbourg called through the open window. 'I trust you've had a good journey thus far.'

'A very pleasant one, my lord, thank you,' Catherine replied for the benefit of the marquess's servants riding atop the carriage. 'We seem to be making good time.'

'I suspect we will reach Newbury in time for dinner. We can put up at the George and Pelican. The rooms are comfortable and they serve an excellent roast beef.'

Unsure of how she felt about the prospect of sharing a meal with Valbourg, Catherine nevertheless nodded her agreement and returned her attention to her book as the carriage set off again.

'A charming man, Lord Valbourg,' Mrs Rankin said casually. 'What a coincidence he should be travelling to Gloucester the same day as us. And that he should catch up with us on the road.'

'Yes, isn't it,' Catherine said, keeping her eyes on the page.

'Of course, we are riding in his father's carriage, so perhaps he feels obligated to check on our progress. And to make arrangements for our dinner and accommodation.'

'I suspect he does.' Catherine turned the page. 'He travels these roads more often than we do and so knows better than most where to stop for such things.'

'Yes, I'm sure that's all it is.'

Catherine heard the note of amusement in the other woman's voice, but by the time she looked up, Mrs Rankin's eyes were already closed.

She breathed a sigh of frustration and returned her attention to her book. Clearly, Lily wasn't the only one prone to imagining romantic fantasies where none existed.

At midday, they stopped for a meal at a small country inn perched on the brow of a hill. Mrs Rankin went inside straight away, but, grateful for the opportunity to stretch her legs, Catherine walked to the edge of the property and stood gazing across the rolling countryside. She had almost forgotten how sweet the country air was, blissfully unpolluted by coal dust or the stench of sewage. And it was quiet. No clatter of carts and carriages, no chattering voices, just the sound of birdsong and the rustle of the afternoon breeze through the trees.

'You should travel to the country more often,' Valbourg remarked. 'That is by far the most contented smile I have ever seen on your face.'

Catherine kept her eyes on the view, determined to maintain an emotional distance between herself and Valbourg. 'I had forgotten how refreshing it is to be able to take a deep breath of fresh air and not feel it catch in your throat.'

'Agreed, but it's not just that,' he replied. 'You seem more at ease here than you did in London. I always had the feeling you were looking over your shoulder.'

'I was. You said yourself, a single woman has to be aware of what is going on around her. Especially when there are men willing to wager on her virtue.'

'You were guarded before I told you about the wager,' Valbourg said. 'Have you some other reason for being fearful?'

'Not fearful. Just…cautious.'

His expression tightened. 'Has this something to do with your past?'

'To a degree.' Catherine stared into the distance, tired of pretending that everything was all right. 'There are people who are interested in what I do and with whom I spend my time.'

'How do you know that?'

'I've seen them.'

'Why haven't you told me about this before?' Valbourg asked.

'Because it has nothing to do with you.'

'Are we not friends?'

Catherine turned to look at him. 'I hadn't thought of us in that way, no. You are who and what you are and I am who and what I am.'

'That doesn't mean I cannot be concerned

about you. If someone is watching you, I'll take steps to put an end to it.'

'That won't be necessary,' Catherine informed him. 'It will be coming to an end soon.'

'Really.' His tone was patently disbelieving. 'How do you know that?'

'Because I know *why* they are watching me. And, no, I do not intend to tell you what those reasons are.'

'But if this should turn dangerous—'

'It won't. This is a private matter, Valbourg, and a personal one,' Catherine assured him. 'My safety is not at risk.' *Only her future happiness.* 'And now, I suggest we return to the inn and have something to eat. I am anxious to continue on, as I'm sure you are.'

She knew from the expression on his face that he wasn't pleased with her answer, but this time, she didn't care. She had no intention of enlightening Valbourg further as to the identity of Stubbs and Moody, or to explain her reasons for coming to the country. There was no simple way of telling a man like him that she was going to collect the son she had given up at birth and hopefully to start her life over with him.

She doubted any man would be able to understand something like that.

The rest of the trip was uneventful. Valbourg secured two rooms at the George and Pelican, as well as a private dining room where he and Catherine partook of a most satisfactory meal. Mrs Rankin, as feared, had not benefited from the journey and had gone to bed early, preferring to take supper on a tray in her room.

Guiltily, Catherine didn't miss the woman's presence, given that Valbourg went out of his way to be a charming dinner companion. He seemed determined to distract her and made no mention of the past, the men who were watching her or her reasons for travelling to the country. Instead, he entertained her with stories about his childhood, regaling her with anecdotes about his brother and older sister, with whom he was not close, and his younger sister Mary, with whom he was. But it was Sarah, the sister who had died, of whom he had the fondest memories.

'Sarah wasn't anything like Mary or Dorothy,' Valbourg said when the remnants of their meal had been cleared away. 'She was determined to do things her own way, but never in a manner that made it seem as though she was doing it to flaunt our parents' wishes. She simply knew her own mind and refused to be pushed in any direction she had no desire to go.'

'That doesn't sound like typical behaviour for the youngest daughter in a family like yours,' Catherine said. 'Most girls are far more biddable.'

'Were you?'

'I like to think I was. I loved my parents dearly,

but I suppose I did have a bit of a wayward streak. Otherwise I wouldn't have ended up in London singing for my supper.'

Or bearing a child at the age of seventeen.

'With a voice like yours, it would have been a crime had you *not* sung for your supper,' Valbourg said. 'When did you start singing?'

'To be honest, I can't remember a time when I did not. Mama and I used to sing duets when I was little, and I sang in the church choir from the time I was eight.'

'And no one ever remarked about how amazing your voice was?'

'I'm not sure anyone heard me,' Catherine said. 'I never sang solos. I was far too shy.'

'Yet now you get up on stage and sing in front of thousands of people. How were you able to overcome your shyness enough to allow you to do that?'

'Theo helped me. He made me see that when I was on stage, I actually became someone else,' Catherine explained. 'He said it wasn't me singing any more, but the character I was playing. Somehow, that allowed me to feel more at ease and to concentrate on my performance.'

'I'm glad he was able to do so.' Valbourg smiled, the creases at the corners of his eyes becoming more pronounced—and making him look even more attractive. 'Otherwise, you would have deprived London of a most formidable talent.'

'To say nothing of the fact that you and I would never have—' Catherine broke off, too late realising what she had almost said and how it might be interpreted. 'Forgive me. I didn't mean to suggest—'

'What? That I, too, recognise how fortunate it is that we met? Or that getting to know you better hasn't brought me a great deal of pleasure?' Valbourg said. 'Because it has.'

The air around Catherine thinned and it suddenly became difficult to breathe. 'You don't have to say that. You don't even like me all that much.'

'Why would you say that?'

'Because you keep insisting I find another man to be my lover.'

'Only because I cannot. You need a man who is able to take care of you, Catherine,' Valbourg said. 'One who has no restrictions on what he does in his life. I can't be that man. But that doesn't mean I don't care about you…because I do. And a great deal more than I should.'

He uttered the last quietly, but Catherine heard every word. She also heard the regret he was unable to conceal. He *liked* her, even though his conduct led her to believe otherwise.

She wasn't surprised when he stood up and said, 'I think it's time we turned in.'

Catherine nodded, the pounding of her heart deafening in her ears. 'Thank you for dinner, Lord Valbourg.'

'My pleasure.' He didn't touch her. He simply bowed and said, 'Sleep well. We leave at half past seven.'

'I shall be ready.'

And she would, Catherine promised herself. Because the earlier they left, the sooner they would reach Gloucester and the sooner this enforced intimacy with Valbourg would come to an end.

Chapter Five

They arrived on the outskirts of Gloucester the following day, having stopped only once to change horses. Valbourg rode the entire way, sometimes within sight of the carriage, sometimes disappearing into the distance ahead. He did not try to engage Catherine in conversation again, and when they parted, it was only to remind her that he was looking forward to seeing her at Swansdowne the following evening.

Catherine said she would be there around nine and then sat back against the velvet cushions and closed her eyes. She had no desire to enter into a conversation with Mrs Rankin. The woman was far too intuitive when it came to other people's emotions. She was able to detect by the slightest shift in tonal inflection, or changes in facial expression, how other people were feeling—and she was very seldom wrong. That meant trouble when it came to Valbourg because Catherine was finding it harder and harder to pretend he wasn't having an effect on her.

The truth was, time spent with Valbourg was both exhilarating and exhausting. Exhausting because she was constantly aware of having to watch what she said, but exhilarating because every moment she spent in his company made her feel alive. Last night, he had made her laugh, he had made her think and he had made her *feel* things. Things she didn't want to feel. Things she had no right to feel...and that was why she had to bring it to an end. Despite what he had said to her over dinner, there was no point imagining his feelings for her might lead to anything permanent between them. Not given his family's expectations and her own plans when it came to Thomas. Her son would need her every day and every day she intended to be there for him; devoting her life to fulfilling the role she had set out upon five long years ago.

That wasn't to say there weren't inherent problems with that situation as well, Catherine reminded herself. Thomas had no idea she *was* his mother. The Haileys had insisted that she refer to herself as a friend of the family's during her twice-annual visits, explaining that anything else would only confuse Thomas and make him very unhappy. At no time was she to intimate that she knew who Thomas's father was or that she had been in any way acquainted with him.

Yet now she was coming back into the boy's life as his mother. How was she to approach that conversation? Thomas would be shocked when he learned the truth, but would his overriding emotion be one of happiness or despair? He had spent the first five years of his life with the Haileys. He had seen Catherine less than ten times over that same period. And it was only during the last four visits that he seemed to remember who she was.

Now she was coming to take him away; effectively removing him from the only home and family he had ever known. How would any normal five-year-old child react to such an upheaval in his life?

Catherine arrived in the market square in Gloucester to find Gwendolyn Marsh waiting for her in a stylish new carriage that, much to Catherine's surprise, the lady drove herself.

'I've always wanted to learn how to tool the ribbons,' Gwen said, setting off as soon as the three of them were comfortably settled. 'So I approached a gentleman who was selling his carriage and asked him how much he wanted for it. He said he would give it to me if I allowed him to show me how to drive. I decided that was a fair request and agreed. It has worked out very well for both of us.'

'I tend to think you got the better of the deal,' Catherine said, holding on to her bonnet as they clipped along. 'The gentleman is without a carriage and with nothing in his pocket to show for it.'

'True, but given that he proposed to me two weeks later, I suppose he considered it a worthwhile investment.'

'Proposed!' Catherine glanced at her friend in delight. 'Did you accept?'

'Heavens, no, though I suspect he will ask again.' Gwen winked at her. 'He is a most persistent gentleman.'

Catherine laughed and suddenly felt lighter in spirit than she had in weeks. Being with Gwendolyn was as refreshing as breathing the clean country air. Both filled her with optimism, and cheered her, as did their eventual arrival at Hollyhock Cottage, Gwen's charming country home. Over two hundred years old, the stone cottage had been lovingly restored and made into a warm, inviting home that welcomed family and guests alike.

Catherine climbed the stairs to her old room and smiled when she opened the door to find that nothing had changed. The desk and the chest of drawers were in the same place, the cheval glass stood next to the four-poster bed, and the same blue-and-white curtains hung at the window. Only the bedspread of white lace and blue edging was new.

* * *

Half an hour later, having changed out of her travelling clothes and into more appropriate attire, Catherine closed her bedroom door and walked down the hall to Mrs Rankin's room.

'Are you all right, Margaret?' she asked through the closed door.

A moment later it opened. 'I'm fine,' Mrs Rankin said, though there wasn't a trace of colour in her face. 'I'm just going to rest up for a bit. I think the journey must have tired me out.'

'I'm sure it did,' Catherine said. 'I'll have a dinner tray sent up, shall I? That way, you won't have to get dressed and go downstairs.'

'Oh, that would be nice. Mrs Searling invited me to join her for dinner, but I said it might be better if we waited until tomorrow. I'm sure I'll be right as rain by then.'

'I'm sure you will. I'll see you in the morning.'

Catherine closed the door and then went downstairs to find Gwendolyn waiting for her in the drawing room with two glasses of sherry and a tray of cheese pastries. 'Sorry to have kept you waiting, Gwen.'

'My dearest girl, you don't owe me any apologies. I'm just delighted you're finally here. And I can't believe how little you've changed,' she said as Catherine sat down across from her. 'Except to grow more beautiful. If I didn't know better, I'd swear you were in love.'

'Which, I can assure you, I am not,' Catherine said, quickly thrusting images of Valbourg's face from her mind. 'You were right to say I can encourage neither prince nor pauper. If I had, I wouldn't be here today in the hopes of regaining custody of Thomas tomorrow.'

'But have princes or paupers been knocking at your door?'

'Constantly. And they have all been sent away with the same response,' Catherine said, determined to keep the moment light.

'Still, they did come, as I warned you they would,' Gwen said. 'You are too beautiful to be left alone, Catherine, and when you sing, men see the passion in your eyes and wish to possess it. It has always been the way. But once you have Thomas, you will be free to entertain their advances. Or perhaps you already have. I couldn't help but notice that you arrived in a very stylish barouche bearing a very fine coat of arms.'

'Compliments of the Marquess of Alderbury,' Catherine admitted. 'Or rather, his son.'

Gwen's eyes widened. 'Valbourg?'

'Yes. Do you know him?'

'We met several years ago in London. Sadly, his sister had just died and the family was in mourning, but I remember thinking what a handsome man he was even then. Did he ever marry?'

'No, though his name has been connected of

late with that of Lady Susan Wimsley,' Catherine said in an offhand manner.

'She would be fortunate to secure his affection,' Gwen said. 'Valbourg has long been one of London's most eligible bachelors, and I suspect his father is anxious that he marry, given that Valbourg is the legal guardian of his late sister's child, Sebastian.'

Catherine stared at her friend in astonishment. 'He is?'

'You didn't know?'

'No one had any reason to tell me.'

'It was the talk of the town when it happened,' Gwen said. 'Shortly after Lady Sarah died, her four-year-old son went to live with Valbourg and, as far as I know, is still there.'

'But is it not unusual for a single man to be given the charge of such a young boy?' Catherine said. 'Surely someone else in the family would have been better equipped to look after him.'

'I'm not sure anyone was given the chance. As I recall, it was Lady Sarah's wish that Valbourg look after the boy.'

'And Valbourg agreed?' Catherine asked in surprise.

'Yes, though I am sure it turned his life upside down,' Gwen said with a chuckle. 'He had been quite the rake to that point. Gambling, drinking, carousing. The usual vices of a young man in his position. But he gave it all up and settled down to the life of a responsible family man. All he was missing was a wife.'

It was as though a veil had been lifted, allowing Catherine to see clearly for the first time. No wonder Valbourg hadn't asked her to be his mistress. Any return to his former lifestyle would have put the guardianship of his nephew at risk. And if that was the case, he had done exactly what she had; attempted to live a life free of sin for the well-being of a child.

Her respect for him increased tenfold.

'Speaking of families, you must be thrilled at the prospect of finally being reunited with Thomas,' Gwen said.

'I haven't been able to sleep,' Catherine admitted. 'But as excited as I am, I am fearful, too. I have no idea how Thomas will react to my coming into his life. He has no idea I *am* his mother, yet I will be taking him away from the two people who have fulfilled that role since he was a baby.'

'Surely Reverend Hailey hasn't encouraged the boy to think of him and Eliza as his parents?'

'I don't know what they have led him to believe, though to be honest, I would not be surprised,' Catherine murmured. 'I shall never forget the way Eliza looked at Thomas the first time she saw him. There was…a hunger in her eyes. A yearning I found highly disturbing.'

'There may be a reason for that,' Gwen said. 'She and Reverend Hailey have been married seven years, but she hasn't given him any children. We know Hailey can father a child, so the problem may well lie with Eliza. And if she suspects as much, she may not be willing to let Thomas go.'

'She *has* to let him go,' Catherine said. 'I have done *everything* Hailey asked of me. He cannot renege on his promise now.'

'I'm not saying he will,' Gwen said quickly, 'but if Eliza is the one trying to keep Thomas, it won't matter that you have abided by her husband's rules. She will find some other excuse for not giving him back. And, as much as I hate to say it, they are operating from a stronger position than you, my dear. They've had Thomas since he was a baby. You left Grafton six years ago and have only been back to see him on a handful of occasions—'

'Because I was only allowed to see him on a handful of occasions!' Catherine said in frustration. 'Twice a year, and even then, I was warned against telling Thomas who I really was.'

'I know, and the Haileys certainly haven't let anyone believe you have a connection to him. But you must prepare yourself for the possibility that they want to keep Thomas and that it may be very difficult for you to stop them from doing so.'

'Then I shall consult a lawyer. Let him put forward my case.'

'And who do you expect to take your side,

Catherine? An unwed actress petitioning against a clergyman and his wife, who are in truth the child's grandparents, for the right to keep a little boy no one but a handful of people know is not rightfully theirs?' Gwen said. 'How do you think that will look in the eyes of the law?'

'I don't care how it *looks*,' Catherine retorted. 'Thomas is my son and Hailey has no right to keep him. The only reason I gave in five years ago was because I was unmarried and unemployed. If you hadn't taken me in, I don't know what I would have done. I do know that no court in the land would have recommended that I look after Thomas rather than a respected minister of the church and his wife,' Catherine said. 'But everything is different now. I'm not that naïve seventeen-year-old girl. I am older and wiser and have more than enough money to take care of us both. That is what I intend to make clear to Reverend Hailey when I see him tomorrow.'

There was nothing more to be said, and, not wanting her concerns over Thomas to weigh the evening down, Catherine spent the rest of it enjoying Gwen's lively and amiable company. The morning would come soon enough and with it, her fate. She was within hours of having what her heart desired most and starting the next chapter of her life.

She could not…*would* not…allow herself to consider the alternative.

* * *

The manse was a large brick house set well back from the road and surrounded on all sides by a high stone wall. Wild flowers bloomed in the garden and in boxes beneath the windows. A neatly tended vegetable patch was situated to the left of the house and to the right stood a shed, a chicken coop and, beyond that, a paddock where two horses and a cow chewed contentedly on the lush green grass.

Catherine took a deep breath and went to open the wrought-iron gate, only to pause with her hand resting on the latch.

'Are you all right?' Mrs Rankin enquired.

'I'm fine. It's just that I have waited so long for this moment, now that it is finally here, I am terrified of something going wrong,' Catherine said softly. 'What if Hailey changes his mind?'

'He is *not* going to change his mind,' Mrs Rankin said with far more confidence than Catherine was feeling. 'It won't be long before the three of us are heading back to London and you will be asking yourself what all the worrying was for.'

Wishing she shared the woman's conviction, Catherine nodded and pushed open the gate. She walked up the path and, after a moment's hesitation, knocked on the door.

It was opened by the same hard-faced housekeeper who appeared every time Catherine called. 'Oh, it's you again, is it?'

'Good afternoon, Mrs Comstock,' Catherine said, determined to be pleasant. 'Reverend Hailey is expecting me.'

Mrs Comstock didn't move, and Catherine, fearing they were to be turned away without even seeing the vicar, made ready to do battle when, at last, the woman grunted and stepped back. 'This way,' she said before turning and leading the way down the long corridor and into Reverend Hailey's office. 'Wait here. I'll tell the master you've arrived.'

The door closed with a bang. Standing slightly behind Catherine, Mrs Rankin sniffed. 'The years certainly don't sweeten her disposition.'

'No, but I expect she knows why I am here and doesn't think very highly of me.'

'It is not up to her to think one way or the other about you. She works for the vicar, nothing more.'

Suspecting the housekeeper's position in the house was more pivotal than that, Catherine waited in silence for Reverend Hailey to appear. She practised the calming breathing techniques Theo had taught her and took several long, deep breaths to steady herself. It always worked for her on the stage and in some ways the upcoming meeting was no different. She and Hailey were the two lead actors in a dramatic scene. The only problem was that Catherine had no idea what her lines were—or what his might turn out to be.

After what seemed like an eternity, the door

opened and Reverend Hailey walked in. He had been a pleasant-looking man in his youth, but over the years, his round face had thinned out, his black eyebrows had grown bushy and the hair on his head had thinned. He spared a brief glance for Catherine as he walked past, frowned at the presence of Mrs Rankin and then sat down at his desk. 'So, you've come back.'

'I have, as you knew I would. Thomas's fifth birthday is a week away and I am anxious to have him back,' Catherine said, determined not to be put off by Hailey's lack of enthusiasm. 'How is he? I am so looking forward to seeing him again.'

'The boy is fine. However, as to your seeing him, I'm afraid that won't be possible.'

'I beg your pardon?' Catherine risked a quick glance at Mrs Rankin and saw the expression of concern on her face. One, no doubt, that was reflected on her own. 'We agreed that Thomas was to be returned to me when he turned five. I wrote and told you I was coming.'

'And I received your letter. But your memory is faulty when it comes to the terms of our agreement, Miss Jones. I agreed to *review* the situation when the boy turned five and to make my decision based on the information I had at hand. That is what I have done. And based on information that has recently come into my possession, I cannot allow you to take Thomas away.'

'But I don't understand.' A hard knot formed

in the pit of Catherine's stomach. 'What kind of information did you receive?'

'Information regarding your conduct with the Marquess of Alderbury's heir,' Eliza Hailey said, walking into the room. 'Disgraceful conduct that neither myself nor my husband were pleased to hear about.'

Catherine looked over as Eliza Hailey took her place beside her husband. Unlike Hailey, Eliza had flourished in the intervening years. Her figure was still slim and attractively curved, her hair was the same shade of light golden blonde and her clothes, while suitable for a clergyman's wife, were of finer material than one might expect. 'It seems you have not been leading the life of a good Christian woman, Miss Jones,' she said, 'as much as you might like us to believe otherwise.'

'If you heard anything that would cause you to be disappointed, you have been misinformed,' Catherine said. 'I have done nothing for which I have reason to be ashamed.'

'Perhaps not in your eyes, but what is acceptable conduct in the eyes of an actress would be vastly different from what is acceptable to my husband and myself,' Eliza said.

'But that's not fair—!' Mrs Rankin exclaimed.

'Mrs Rankin, perhaps it would be best if you waited outside,' Catherine said quickly. 'I would like to speak to Reverend Hailey alone.'

Mrs Rankin frowned and, after casting a dark

glance in Eliza's direction, left the room. Catherine waited until the door closed before turning to face the vicar. 'Perhaps you would be good enough to tell me what this is all about.'

'I don't think we need go into it—' Eliza began.

'I would prefer to hear it from your husband, Mrs Hailey,' Catherine said, not about to be dismissed by the vicar's wife. 'Reverend Hailey?'

The vicar was clearly uncomfortable relaying the details of his case. 'Yes, well, as my wife said, we have received reports of…conduct unbecoming—'

'What manner of unbecoming conduct?'

'We have heard that you…well, that you have been seen in the company of men.'

'I am often in the company of men, Reverend Hailey, just as I am often in the company of women,' Catherine said. 'I am an actress. It is the nature of my business to be seen in the company of the theatre-going public.'

'I understand that, but I have been informed that you have spent rather more time than is appropriate with *one* particular gentleman—'

'Lord Valbourg,' Eliza was quick to add.

'And that you have been seen getting in and out of his carriage on several occasions,' Reverend Hailey continued.

'I do not deny it,' Catherine said. 'We were at a reception together and he made his carriage available to take me home.'

'Why? A man like that would hardly bother with a person like you unless there was a good reason for it.'

Anger flared, but knowing it would not help her, Catherine fought it back. 'I am well aware that you have been keeping watch on me these past five years, Reverend Hailey, and that you have received regular reports with regard to my conduct. As such, you will know that I have led an exemplary life.'

'You are an actress,' Eliza said cynically. 'Pray tell us how that entitles you to make such a ridiculous claim.'

'I am not saying I have led as normal a life as most,' Catherine allowed, 'but neither have I done anything for which I need feel ashamed. I was born with an ability to sing and I have used that ability to make a career for myself. One that has allowed me to earn enough money to provide for myself and my son.'

'But your misconduct with Lord Valbourg—'

'There has been no misconduct,' Catherine said. 'On the night of his sister's engagement celebration, Lord Valbourg sent a carriage to fetch me from the theatre and to take me home afterwards—'

'We are not talking simply about the use of his carriage,' Eliza interrupted. 'We are talking about something far more…intimate.'

'We refer, Miss Jones, to a kiss,' Reverend Hailey said, his cheeks darkening. 'A passionate kiss between you and Lord Valbourg that took place in his carriage the night after your final performance. One that left no one in any doubt as to the licentious nature of the relationship that exists between you.'

Catherine stared at the man as a sickening awareness of what he was referring to sank in. So, her emotional embrace with Valbourg had not gone unnoticed. Stubbs must have been lurking in the neighbourhood, keeping watch on her activities. Then, having witnessed the exchange, he had decided to make Hailey aware of her transgression rather than demand a hefty bribe to ensure his silence. 'It was not what you think—'

'It was *exactly* what we think,' Eliza said. 'A kiss between an unmarried aristocrat and his mistress.'

Catherine gasped. 'I am *not* Lord Valbourg's mistress!'

'There is no point in trying to deny it, Miss Jones,' Reverend Hailey said. 'You were observed in his arms. Clearly, an understanding exists between the two of you, and as such, my wife and I are not prepared to give Thomas into your care.'

'But this is a mistake!' Catherine cried. 'If Lord Valbourg were here, he would tell you so!'

'I can only judge the situation by what I hear, and what I hear does not permit me to let you have Thomas,' Reverend Hailey said. 'Clearly, you lack the Christian morals necessary for raising a child in an appropriate manner and it would be wrong of me to consign the boy to your care. I cannot allow you to corrupt him with your behaviour!'

'He is my son!'

'And he is *my* grandson! The only link I have to William, God rest his soul.'

'You've changed your tone, Reverend Hailey,' Catherine was stung into replying. 'You told me Will's death was a punishment from God for the sin he committed with me.'

'My son is no concern of yours. If anything, he is dead *because* of you!'

Catherine blanched. 'How dare you say such a cruel and hateful thing. I loved your son. I had nothing to do with his death.'

'You had *everything* to do with it. You led him astray!' Reverend Hailey cried, rising in agitation. 'You tempted him with your body and he died because of it. I refuse to let you near Thomas. I will do everything I can to protect that poor boy's soul. You can give him nothing—'

'I can give him a mother's love. And I can provide for him.'

'As Lord Valbourg provides for you?' Eliza said waspishly.

'How *dare* you!' Catherine said, finally losing her temper. 'No man has *ever* provided for me. I have made my own way in the world, without help from anyone.'

'You exist on the proceeds of a lewd and vile occupation,' Reverend Hailey said. 'A way of life that would corrupt Thomas as surely as it has corrupted you. That is why I sent him away. I could not afford to run the risk of you poisoning him with your—'

'Sent him away?' Catherine interrupted. 'Where? Where have you sent him?'

'That is of no concern of yours. I have done what I know to be best for the boy. Now I would ask you to leave. I find your presence here extremely distasteful.'

Catherine stared at the man in disbelief. 'Why did you agree to this meeting if you had no intention of giving Thomas back to me?'

'My husband does not have to answer to you,' Eliza said.

'Oh, yes, he does,' Catherine said, rounding on her. 'I asked him a question and I expect an answer.' She turned back to glare at the minister. 'Or have you no voice of your own?'

It was not, perhaps, the most tactful thing to say, but Catherine was beyond caring. Hailey had no right to keep Thomas and certainly not as a result of a kiss that had been bestowed without thought or sentiment.

'I have a voice and I will use it to tell you that I *was* of a mind to give Thomas into your care until this past week, when the letter arrived informing me of your conduct,' Reverend Hailey said. 'And, yes, Miss Jones, I *was* disappointed. What I had heard of your behaviour to that point led me to believe you were leading a life free of sin. Now I see it was all a carefully constructed lie. Mrs Comstock?'

The housekeeper appeared instantly, as if she'd been waiting outside the door. 'Yes, Reverend Hailey?'

'Show Miss Jones out.'

There was nothing more to say. Catherine looked into the faces of the vicar and his wife and saw no kindness or charity there. They were united in their stand against her. She would not be leaving Grafton with her son. Not today or at any time in the foreseeable future.

Catherine was silent on the ride back to Cheltenham, lost in a morass of grief and despair. Mrs Rankin tried to take an optimistic view of the situation, saying she was sure Reverend Hailey would change his mind once he'd had a chance to think things over, but Catherine knew better. She had stood in front of Hailey and his wife and listened to them tear her down and knew there was no hope of them changing their minds. Her hopes lay in ashes, her dream of having Thomas restored to her shattered.

Reverend Hailey still believed her a fallen woman; the evidence a damning letter from Stubbs…and it must have been Stubbs, Catherine reflected bitterly. For once, he hadn't waited in the alley close to her house, but had ventured further afield, hoping to catch her at an inopportune moment—and he had. For the first time since her arrival in London, she had done something she should not—and it had been her downfall.

Gwendolyn, of course, wanted to hear about everything that had taken place, but saying only that matters had gone terribly wrong and that she would explain later, Catherine went up to her room and sat for some time at her dressing table, sadness pressing like a crushing weight on her chest. For the first time, she realised exactly how much she had been looking forward to this day...and how desperately she wanted Thomas back. He was *all* that mattered to her. He had been the justification for the endless hours she had spent working on her voice. The one thing that had made worthwhile all the late nights and early mornings. Now he was gone. A few thoughtless kindnesses, a meaningless kiss, and she had lost everything.

What in God's name was she to do now?

Swansdowne Manor truly was the quintessential country house, Valbourg decided as he stood in front of the mirror dressing for dinner. Lord and Lady Brocklehume provided everything a man might need in the way of recreation and relaxation, and their cook served some of the finest meals to be had this side of London. It was one of the reasons he never hesitated when it came to accepting their invitations.

But for all the amiability of the guests and the excellence of the accommodation, it was Catherine's arrival that Valbourg was most looking forward to. He had informed his host and hostess of her willingness to sing for them and, not surprisingly, they had been thrilled. Valbourg was quite sure it was the reason he had been allotted the finest guest room in the house.

Now, as he headed downstairs and waited for her to arrive, he realised how much time he had devoted to thinking about her and about how important she had become in his life. Not only did he enjoy hearing her sing, but he also genuinely relished spending time with her. She was a rarity: a woman who felt no need to indulge in idle chit-chat and who did not blush or giggle when a gentleman approached. On the few occasions they had engaged in conversation, Catherine had offered intelligent and thoughtful commentary on whatever topic Valbourg had raised. In fact, she had surprised him more than once with the extent of her knowledge about subjects he would not have expected her to be familiar with.

'Ah, there you are, Lord Valbourg,' Letitia, Viscountess Douglas, said. 'I was hoping we would have an opportunity to spend some time together this weekend.'

'Good evening, Letty.' Valbourg's smile was polite but discouraging. 'I see you have put off your blacks. Is it a year already?'

'Close enough.' Her green eyes flashed up at him. 'One grows weary of playing the grieving widow when one doesn't feel the part. But I am done with it now and delighted to be back in society. So when it came time to dress for the occasion, I thought of you.'

'Oh?'

'I recall you once saying you were partial to a particular shade of pink.' She did a graceful pirouette. 'This shade, if I am not mistaken.'

Valbourg inclined his head, thinking the maidenly colour a touch inappropriate for a twice-married woman. But not about to admit that his partiality for the colour drew its inspiration from someone else entirely, he said instead, 'I can hardly admit to liking such a feminine colour, Letty, though I am the first to say how flattering the shade is on you.'

'If I have secured your admiration, I have achieved my purpose,' Letty said, her gaze lingering on his mouth. 'I hope it might encourage the possibility of our spending a little time together this weekend.'

Valbourg knew exactly what kind of time Letty was hopeful of spending with him. They had been lovers in the days before Sebastian's arrival and she had not been pleased at having to let the association go. She had sought him out at various social gatherings since and suggested they could meet at places other than his home.

At first, her invitations had been difficult to refuse. Letty was a beautiful woman and a tigress in bed, and, given that she was married to a man who paid more attention to his books than his wife, there was little chance of their affair being discovered. But as time passed and Valbourg began to re-evaluate what was important in his life, Letty had been one of the easier habits to let go. Now she fell well short—and he knew the reason why. 'Thank you, Letty, but you know I don't indulge in that kind of activity any more.'

'Not even when you are away from home and in the company of trusted friends?'

'I'm not sure anyone can be trusted when it comes to the kind of behaviour you are suggesting.'

'I don't know why you would say that. Many of the guests will be indulging in exactly that same kind of behaviour.'

'True, but while others may do as they please, I must be guided by my principles,' Valbourg said, 'and I know you would not ask me to compromise those when you know what is at stake.'

She was clearly disappointed, but mature enough not to alienate him by trying to change his mind. 'What a waste.' Then, catching sight of someone in the crowd, she added, 'Gracious, is that who I think it is?'

Valbourg turned—along with every other man in the room—as Catherine walked in and stood for a moment in the doorway, resplendent in a gown of pure-white silk overlaid with silver net. Her glorious golden hair was swept up in a Grecian knot, long white gloves covered her arms to her elbows and a strand of diamonds encircled her slender white throat.

She was breathtaking. An angel in white and silver. But something was missing. Her complexion was unusually pale and, in contrast to her normal sparkling vivacity, her smile looked forced and unnatural.

'If you refer to Miss Jones, I venture to say it is,' Valbourg said, wondering what had stolen the roses from her cheeks.

'But what is she doing here? I thought she was still performing in *Promises*.'

'I believe the Gryphon is temporarily closed for repairs. Excuse me, Letty.'

Ignoring the widow's pout, Valbourg made his way across the room. By the time he reached Catherine's side, several other gentlemen had, too, but when she looked up and saw him, it was as though they were the only two people in the room.

'Ah, Valbourg, there you are,' Lady Brocklehume said, pushing aside two younger gentlemen who were standing in his way. 'I cannot thank you enough for persuading Miss Jones to sing for us. I hope he didn't badger you too much, my dear.'

'Not at all.' Catherine managed a smile, but Valbourg saw how her lips trembled. 'I was delighted to be asked.'

'Glad to hear it. I am so happy to welcome you to Swansdowne,' the countess said. 'I have long been one of your greatest admirers.'

Catherine's smile flashed again, but it was a reflex action that disappeared as soon as the countess turned away, making Valbourg wonder what could have happened since her arrival in the country to effect such a change.

Unfortunately, an explanation would have to wait. A footman arrived and whispered something in Catherine's ear. She nodded and then followed him out of the room. A few minutes later, the countess clapped her hands and announced that Miss Catherine Jones would sing for them, after which she asked everyone to follow her into the gold drawing room, where the performance was to take place.

Valbourg followed the rest of the guests into a room sumptuously decorated in crimson and gold and took a seat that gave him a good view of Catherine. She stood by the piano, head down as though to avoid eye contact with anyone. He could almost feel the unhappiness pouring from her, the joy leaching out as though someone had taken a knife and cut a hole in her heart. Something was definitely wrong. At the first opportunity, he intended to take her aside and find out what it was.

Then the pianist began to play and Catherine slowly raised her head. Her eyes were closed, her face turned to one side as though listening to the music. She began to sing, the first note impossibly high yet exquisitely struck, as clear as a silver hammer hitting a bell. She sang in a way he had never heard her sing before, emotion pouring from her very soul—and Valbourg realised he was fighting a losing battle.

He wanted her. Not for an hour or a night. He wanted her for the rest of his life, in every part of his life—and he had absolutely no idea how to make that happen. The kind of relationship he longed for with her was impossible. He was heir to a marquessate, his father a peer of the realm. Their lineage was old and respected, and his ancestors had fought to defend King and country. They had done what was necessary to preserve their way of life. They had married well and produced children who had married well. And if they had loved out of their class, they had kept such things in the appropriate place. What he was considering with Catherine was definitely not appropriate, but neither could he stop thinking about it. Because he knew that with her, one night would never be enough.

At the end of the song, there was a moment's

silence; the kind that could only follow such a brilliant performance. Then applause rang out as people sprang to their feet, calling her name and shouting accolades. It was the kind of recognition every performer must dream of, yet Catherine did not smile. She looked around the room at the cheering crowd and then executed a deep and graceful curtsy.

'Miss Jones, may I say on behalf of everyone here that you are truly a gift to those of us who appreciate fine music,' Lady Brocklehume said, wiping her eyes. 'I am not frequently moved to tears, but I must say, even I was unable to remain dry-eyed throughout that performance.'

A faint dusting of pink chased the pallor from Catherine's cheeks, but her voice was still reserved when she said, 'Thank you, Lady Brocklehume. I am glad you enjoyed it.'

'I did, and I hope we will be able to persuade you to sing a few more songs before you leave us, but for now, stay and enjoy yourself. I am sure many of our guests would be delighted to have this opportunity to speak with you.'

Lady Brocklehume left, humming the song Catherine had performed. Knowing he would have to act quickly, Valbourg inserted himself into the space where his hostess had been. 'Miss Jones, I wonder if you would care to take a walk with me? There is a lovely view of the lake and the surrounding countryside from the terrace.'

She looked up at him and the naked pain in those sapphire-blue eyes stopped him dead. What in God's name had happened to bring about such desolation and anguish?

Thankfully, dancing had resumed in the ballroom and most of the guests were moving in that direction, leaving the terrace deserted. Valbourg walked silently at Catherine's side, aware of her unnatural stillness. 'Are you going to tell me what's wrong?' he asked in a soft voice.

'What makes you think anything is wrong?'

'Because I have seen you perform before, and while there was nothing lacking in your presentation tonight, that indefatigable sense of joy was definitely missing.'

Her gaze remained fixed on the lake shimmering in the distance, her smooth brow unaccountably furrowed. 'I'm sorry my performance did not live up to your expectations, Lord Valbourg.'

'It did. *You* simply didn't sparkle. Why?'

'I don't know.' Her gaze fell. 'I'm sorry. I can't talk to you right now—'

'Don't apologise. Just tell me what's wrong.'

'I can't. There's nothing you can do.'

'How do you know? If I can help in some way—'

'You cannot.' To his dismay, two tears broke free and rolled like liquid stars down her cheeks. 'No one can.'

She groaned softly and started to walk away,

but Valbourg reached for her wrist. '*Tell* me what's wrong, Catherine. Open that locked door and let me in. Because I can't help feeling that the pain and unhappiness you're experiencing now has something to do with what happened in your past.'

She gazed up at him with a look Valbourg could only call fear, but when she closed her eyes and shook her head, he made a decision. 'Stay here. I shall return in a moment.'

He walked back into the drawing room and sought out his hostess.

'Is something wrong, Valbourg?' Lady Brocklehume asked.

'I fear Miss Jones is not well. Is there somewhere she might be able to rest for a moment?'

'Of course, poor dear. I thought she wasn't looking quite the thing when she arrived. Take her upstairs to my private sitting room. She can stay there for as long as she likes. Shall I send up my maid?'

'No, that's fine. I'll stay with her for a while,' Valbourg said. Then, thanking his hostess, he went back out to the terrace to find Catherine where he'd left her, hands resting on the stone balustrade, her gaze still fixed on the distant view.

'I have secured the use of Lady Brocklehume's private sitting room,' he told her. 'And I will stay with you as long as you need.'

'I don't want to stay here,' Catherine whispered, the sadness in her voice tearing at his heart. 'I just want to go home.'

'I know, but I'm not going to let you do that until you've told me what's wrong. You don't have to go through this alone, Catherine. Trust me with your secrets. *Tell* me why these men are watching you and who has this hold on you,' he urged. 'I've already said I will do everything I can to help, but I can't do anything if you won't let me in.'

Catherine took a long, deep breath—but the stiffness in her body remained. 'Very well, but there really is no point.' She turned to face him, and it was not pain Valbourg saw in her eyes, but resignation. 'Because when I tell you the truth, I doubt very much you will *want* to help me.'

Chapter Six

In the privacy of Lady Brocklehume's sitting room, Catherine took a moment to gather her thoughts. She was relieved to be away from the chattering crowds and grateful to Valbourg for having arranged it, but even so, the weight pressing on her chest was suffocating.

'Do you remember…in the carriage,' she began, 'when I said that the path of my future was dictated by the mistakes of my past?'

'Yes. You also said you did not regret those mistakes.'

'I don't. Because they brought me something… someone…I love more than anything or anyone else in the world.'

Valbourg's eyebrows rose, but there was no re-crimination in his voice when he said, 'Tell me.'

'His name is Thomas and he is five years old,' Catherine said. 'He is the reason I came to London five years ago. The reason I go up on stage every night. He is the reason I never took a lover and the reason I am here now.' She turned to look at Valbourg, needing to see the impact her words were having. 'He is my son. And I came here to get him and to take him back to London to live with me.'

Stark silence greeted her words and, in a heartbeat, Catherine knew she had made a mistake. Valbourg wasn't looking at her. He was staring at the floor. But she could tell from the rigidness of his shoulders and the tension in his hands that everything had changed.

'Am I to assume from your present unhappiness that something has happened to prevent you from taking…your son back to London?'

His hesitation confirmed what she suspected, but it was too late to turn back or to try to undo the damage her confession had done. 'His grandfather has refused to give him up.'

'Grandfather?' Valbourg's head snapped up. 'The boy *lives* with his grandparents?'

'Yes.'

'Your parents?'

'No. His paternal grandfather and his second wife.'

'And your husband is…?'

'Dead.' Catherine felt the heat rising in her face. 'And he never was…my husband.'

'I see.'

The two words spoke volumes. Clearly Valbourg had filled in the parts of the story she had left out and put his own interpretation on the rest of it. 'He did love me,' Catherine said, wanting to make that clear. 'Thomas's father. And I loved him.'

'But he didn't marry you.'

'He was killed before we had the chance,' Catherine said. 'But he told me he wanted to marry me and I believed him. It was the only reason I... the only reason that we—'

'I understand,' Valbourg said, sparing her the necessity of having to explain. He turned and walked towards the window. 'Did you willingly give the child into his grandfather's care?'

'No. Reverend Hailey took Thomas from me.'

'*Reverend* Hailey?' Valbourg turned around. 'His grandfather is a clergyman?'

'Yes. I had gone home to show Thomas to them, hoping it might make relations between us better. Thomas's father was Reverend Hailey's only son and I wanted him to know that we loved each other and that Thomas was a child of that love. But it didn't work out that way,' Catherine said, hearing the echo of defeat in her voice. 'Reverend Hailey took Thomas from me, saying it was in my son's best interests that he be raised by someone else.'

'What were your circumstances at the time?'

'I was seventeen and unmarried. When my father found out, he all but said I was a disgrace,

so I left Grafton and went to stay with a friend
of my late mother's in Cheltenham. Thomas was
born there. When he was a month old, I made the
decision to go back to Grafton and show him to
his grandfather. I thought it was…the right thing
to do.'

'But he took the child and told you to get out.'

Catherine winced at the remoteness of his
voice. 'Yes.'

'What did you do then?'

'I didn't know what *to* do. Hailey was the local
minister. I was an unwed mother. What power did
I have against a man like that?'

'It counted for nothing that Thomas was his
dead son's child?'

'Reverend Hailey said that as much as he
grieved for his son, it was God's plan that Will
be punished for his sins, as I was now being punished for mine.'

'A man overflowing with God's charity and
forgiveness,' Valbourg drawled. 'What did his
wife say? It was her grandson, too.'

'Actually, it wasn't. The present Mrs Hailey
is the minister's second wife. Will's mother died
not long after he did, but I know matters would
have been very different had she lived,' Catherine
said. 'She was a compassionate woman. Someone
who cared deeply about her family.'

Valbourg said nothing and Catherine felt the
incredible awkwardness of the moment. But this

was what he had asked for. He was the one who had forced this revelation. 'So, now you know why I didn't *sparkle* tonight,' she said.

'I understand that you have suffered a grave disappointment. And that you are struggling to come to terms with it. The question is…what are you going to do now?'

'I honestly don't know. I was so sure I would be leaving with Thomas I didn't give any thought to the alternative,' Catherine said, feeling a tidal wave of desolation. 'But now I must because they have refused to give him up.'

'What made you think they would?'

'Reverend Hailey said he would be willing to revisit the situation when Thomas turned five if I did as he asked and led an exemplary life.'

'But you were an actress. Surely he couldn't have approved of that.'

'I wasn't an actress at the time,' Catherine said. 'It was Miss Marsh who suggested I had a gift for music and that I use that gift to make a new life for myself. She paid for me to have singing lessons and arranged for me to have a companion when I arrived in London so that I never had to go out alone.'

'But how would Hailey know if you complied with his request?'

'He hired spies to keep watch on my movements.'

'*He's* the one who's been spying on you?' Valbourg said, incredulous.

'He needed reports as to what I was doing. There are usually two men employed at any one time.'

'You know this for a fact?'

'I speak to one of them regularly,' Catherine said. 'He usually waits in an alley close by my house so he can see when I go out and at what time I come back.'

'And he has been sending reports back to Hailey for five years?'

'Yes. Unfortunately, the last report changed Reverend Hailey's mind about giving Thomas back to me.'

'Why? What did it say?'

Catherine almost told him until she remembered that by doing so she would be involving him in something he would have no wish to be a part of. 'It doesn't matter. It wasn't true, but Hailey believed it to be so.'

'Did you tell him the report was in error?'

'Of course, but he didn't believe me. Why would he? I was the one who led his son astray.'

'Forgive me, Catherine, but a man *lets* himself be led. It was not all your fault.'

'Regardless, I am the one who must now bear the shame and accept the punishment,' Catherine said, dangerously close to tears. 'I feel as though my heart has been cut out.'

'Are you sure there is nothing more to be done? No avenue you may have overlooked?'

'If there is, I don't know what it is. Not only have the Haileys forbidden me to see my son, they have sent him away and are refusing to tell me where. But I intend to find out. And when I do, I will get him and take him back to London with me. I don't care how long it takes. I *will* find Thomas.'

'And what then? Hailey isn't going to let you keep the boy without a fight.'

'I'll cross that bridge when I come to it,' Catherine said. 'Right now, I intend to go back to Gwen's house and talk it over with her. Then I shall make my decision.' Knowing there was nothing more to be said, she stood up. 'Thank you, Lord Valbourg. I appreciate everything you have done and the patience you have shown in listening to my sorry tale. But you and I both know this changes everything. I am not an angel; only a fallen woman forced to turn to the stage to earn a living. You will not counsel any of your friends to make me their mistress now. And since there was never any chance of my becoming yours, I will say goodnight. And goodbye.'

Valbourg did not enjoy the rest of the evening. His emotions were too raw, his shock at having found out the truth about Catherine's past too great to allow him to enjoy the company of others. And while he did not speak to her again, he knew at what time she left. He saw her hesitate in the doorway and turn to look at him, but when he made no move to go to her, she quickly walked out.

Lady Brocklehume found him a few minutes later. She assured him that while Miss Jones was feeling better, she still looked dreadfully pale, and that she had refused payment for the evening's work.

Valbourg nodded, drained the contents of his glass and then went to join several other gentlemen for billiards.

At midnight, realising that neither his heart nor his head was in the game, Valbourg bid his host goodnight and went up to his room, making sure to lock his door before he turned in. He had no desire to find Letty slipping into his bed in the middle of the night and he wasn't convinced she wouldn't try. But he had no patience for such things tonight. His thoughts were focused entirely on someone else; a lady who, as it turned out, was something quite different from what she had portrayed.

Catherine Jones; a seemingly virtuous woman who went to church every Sunday and who was seldom seen without her companion at her side. A woman who kept to herself, refusing all offers, respectable and otherwise, and who had appeared to him a lady in every sense of the word.

A woman who was, in fact, an unwed mother with a child; a son presently being kept by her dead lover's father, a clergyman who, because of what Catherine had done, refused to give the child up.

'Thank you, Terence,' Valbourg said, slipping into the silk robe his valet held out for him. 'I won't be needing you any more tonight.'

'Very good, my lord. What time will you be riding in the morning?'

'Seven, but I'll dress myself. I'll see you when I return for breakfast.'

The valet bowed and withdrew. Valbourg crossed to the table where his hostess had set out a bottle of cognac and two glasses and poured himself a generous measure. Swirling the golden liquid in the bowl, he raised the glass to his lips and downed the contents in one go. Then, pouring another, he took the glass and a book and climbed into the elegant four-poster bed.

An hour later, Valbourg's glass was empty and the book still lay closed upon the coverlet. Something didn't add up. Not the part about Catherine's past. She wasn't the first woman who had found herself pregnant and shunned, nor would she be the last. But she had come to Grafton expecting to leave with her son, yet upon arrival, had been told that a report had come from one of the clergyman's spies and the contents of that report had made him change his mind.

Why? What manner of damning information had it contained? Valbourg had heard nothing of a derogatory nature about Catherine's activities in the past two weeks, nor indeed at any time before that. Prior to this evening, he had never seen her look anything but happy and light-hearted. Yet at *some* point since writing her letter to Reverend Hailey, something had happened to change his mind. Something serious enough that he had felt the need to send Catherine's son away and not tell her where.

Had *his* involvement in her life somehow become the topic of that last report? Valbourg wondered. Had the spies hired to watch Catherine seen her coming and going in one of his carriages? Might they even have witnessed him kissing her—?

'Damn!' Valbourg swore. Of *course* that was what had happened. *He* was the reason for the vicar's sudden change of heart. Had he not sent his father's barouche to collect Catherine at the theatre and then ridden home with her afterwards? Worse, had he not driven her home after the dinner party and kissed her passionately in the middle of the street?

Clearly someone had seen them, and because the clergyman *expected* Catherine to misbehave, he had likely assumed that she had sinned in *every* sense of the word. Hailey no doubt believed a fallen woman would always *be* a fallen woman and that the mistakes Catherine had made in the past would be repeated in the future—and that she had repeated them with *him*!

'Damn!' Valbourg swore again. He threw back the covers and rang for his servant.

Terence arrived, shrugging on his robe and looking bleary-eyed. 'My lord?'

'Sorry to rouse you so late, but I need you to find out where this man lives.' He wrote Reverend Hailey's name on a piece of paper and handed it over. 'Tomorrow morning will be fine. And you're not to say anything to anyone, do you understand?'

'Of course, my lord.'

After his valet left, Valbourg began to pace. All right, so Catherine was not the innocent young woman she had led everyone to believe she was. That was the result of a mistake *she* had made and one that by her own admission she did not regret. But if *his* involvement in her life was the cause of her being denied access to her son, that was *his* mistake and a problem that needed to be resolved.

He might not have been the reason she had lost her son in the first place, but Valbourg was damned if he was going to be the cause of her losing him a second time!

* * *

The Reverend Hailey was not at home when Valbourg paid a call the following afternoon. The housekeeper, a stern-faced woman with a north-country accent, informed him that the vicar was likely to be found at the church. She gave him a series of vague directions, then shut the door in his face. Tempted to call her back and inform her that she wouldn't have lasted long in *his* household, Valbourg headed instead for the old stone church.

As it turned out, Reverend Hailey wasn't there, but his daughter, Miss Megan Hailey, was. 'Papa should be back soon,' she informed him as she efficiently sorted the contents of three white porcelain vases. She was a pretty girl with a sweet nature and dimples. 'He went to visit one of his parishioners. Mrs Tupper had a baby last week and hasn't been able to get out.'

Valbourg nodded, wondering how a village parson could be so charitable to some and so cruel to others. 'So, have you other brothers and sisters at home?' he enquired, wondering about Thomas.

'Just one. Thomas will be five next week.'

'And you are…?'

'I shall be sixteen in October,' Megan said, blushing.

'Quite a few years, then, between you and your brother.'

'Actually, Thomas isn't my brother.'

Valbourg feigned surprise. 'He isn't?'

'I had an older brother, but he died. Thomas is my stepmother's nephew.'

'Really? How did he come to be living with you?'

'I don't know,' Megan admitted. 'Papa said it wasn't important that I know. Only that I look after Thomas and be kind to him.' She looked up at Valbourg, eyes bright with curiosity. 'Have you come all the way from London to see Papa?'

'No. I'm staying with Lord and Lady Brocklehume.'

'At Swansdowne?'

'Yes.'

'Oh, how lucky you are! It is such a beautiful house, is it not?' Megan said breathlessly. 'Papa calls there occasionally, but he never takes me with him. I wish he would. I should love to see inside.'

'I'm sure a visit could be arranged,' Valbourg said. 'I shall speak to Lady Brocklehume when I return there this afternoon.'

'You would do that for me?' Megan said, sounding, if possible, even more breathless.

Valbourg smiled. 'I would be happy to.' He picked up a hymnbook and idly flipped through the pages. 'So you don't know who Thomas's real mother is.'

'No. Stepmama brought Thomas here when he was only a month old. Papa said I was to open my heart and love him as though he were my brother, and I do,' Megan said. 'But sometimes I would like to know—'

'Megan! What are you doing here, child?'

Valbourg turned to see a man striding down the aisle towards them. Judging from the collar and gown, it was Reverend Hailey, an assumption confirmed by Megan's greeting. 'Hello, Papa. I came down to change the flowers, but as you can see they are still quite fresh. This is Lord Valbourg. He is staying with Lord and Lady Brocklehume at Swansdowne.'

'Your servant, my lord,' the vicar said, his expression of welcome changing to one of caution. 'Run along now, Megan. Your stepmother is looking for you.'

'All right. Goodbye, Lord Valbourg. It was very nice meeting you.'

'And you, Miss Hailey. I will be sure to mention your wishes to Lady Brocklehume.'

Megan blushed prettily, dropped a charming curtsy and all but skipped out of the church. Her father, clearly not as delighted by Valbourg's presence, said, 'So, my lord, what brings you here?'

'I expect you know the answer to that.' Valbourg crossed his arms over his chest and leaned against one of the pews. 'I believe you had a conversation with Miss Catherine Jones yesterday.'

'I did.' The clergyman's face took on a decidedly closed aspect. 'I suppose I've no need to ask how you know we spoke.'

'I saw her when she came to perform at Swansdowne last evening,' Valbourg said, resenting the man's insinuation. 'Miss Jones was good enough to sing for Lord Brocklehume's guests.'

'Yes, well, that is what actresses do, isn't it,' Hailey said. 'Sing for their suppers.'

'Except on this occasion, she sang as a favour to the countess. No money was exchanged.'

'I commend her generosity. Now I must ask you to let me get on with my work—'

'Not just yet.' Valbourg straightened and uncrossed his arms. 'I'd like to talk to you about the conversation you had with Miss Jones, given that there seems to be some confusion as to the nature of the relationship that exists between us.'

'There is no confusion, Lord Valbourg,' Hailey said stiffly. 'I know what she is and how she makes her living. What *you* do with her is certainly no business of mine.'

'You would do well to mind your words, Reverend Hailey,' Valbourg said quietly. 'I am not doing anything with Miss Jones, and you do us both a disservice by implying that she is my mistress.'

'If she is not your mistress, why are you here?'

'Because she was very upset when she arrived at Swansdowne last night and, eventually, I persuaded her to tell me why.'

'And what did she tell you?'

'That she came to Grafton to collect her son, only to be turned away because you had changed your mind as a result of her perceived association with me.'

'Miss Jones is not morally capable of looking after a child—'

'Miss Jones is *more* than capable of looking after a child,' Valbourg interrupted. 'Gossip travels very quickly in London, Reverend Hailey. I'm sure even a country parson like you must know that. So if Miss Jones did something to bring herself to the attention of scandalmongers, it would be all over London before sunrise the next day. But the drawing rooms of society do not whisper her name and I have no hesitation in saying that the lady is as moral as any I've ever met. Indeed, I consider her a friend, as does the rest of my family.'

'Yet she was seen riding in your carriage and you were observed kissing her in a darkened street. Perhaps in your world that does make her a *friend*, my lord, but God would put a very different name to it.'

'Really? And what would that be?'

'I prefer not to speak of such things in His house, but I'm sure we understand one another,' Hailey said. 'And while I do not know what your true reasons for defending Miss Jones are, I can assure you, they do not matter to me.'

'They should because it is your biased perception of her that has stopped you from restoring custody of her son to her,' Valbourg was stung into replying.

'It is not *my* perception that has caused her to lose her son, but her own immorality.'

'How many more times must I say it?' Valbourg said, feeling his patience wearing thin. 'Miss Jones is *not* my mistress.'

'Lord Valbourg, I may not move in the elevated circles to which birth has entitled you, but I am wise enough to know that the distinction between classes cannot be breached. There is no reason for a man in your position to associate with a woman in Miss Jones's, other than for the one of which I speak. You do not move in the same circles, you have nothing in common beyond an enjoyment of theatrical works, so the only reason for your being in her life is, for the lack of a better word, to be her protector.'

Valbourg slowly set the hymnbook he was holding on the closest pew. 'Are you calling me a liar, Reverend Hailey?'

The vicar blanched. 'Certainly not.'

'Then you will do me the courtesy of not questioning my integrity when I tell you that Miss Jones is *not* my mistress. The only reason I am here is because I wish to see justice served and a boy returned to his mother. Something you were prepared to do until a misleading report found its way to you. Speaking of which,' Valbourg added coldly, 'I find your hiring of men to spy on Miss Jones reprehensible. Not in the least worthy of the conduct of a clergyman.'

'I do not need to justify my conduct to you, Lord Valbourg,' Reverend Hailey said. 'I report to a far higher authority. One who is in a position to judge us all. And when it comes to the well-being of Thomas's soul, I must do as I see— Megan, what are you doing here again? I thought I told you to go home.'

'I did go home,' Megan said quietly from the doorway. 'But Mama asked me to find out whether or not you would be home in time for lunch.'

'Yes, yes, I shall be there directly. Now run along. There's a good girl.'

Valbourg saw Megan cast an embarrassed glance in his direction before turning and walking back out into the sunshine. He wondered how much of the conversation she had heard.

'Lord Valbourg, there really isn't anything more to say,' Hailey said. 'I have made my position clear to Miss Jones, as I have now to you. My wife and I are not willing to relinquish Thomas into her care. Good day.'

It was tantamount to a dismissal. Never having been treated so shabbily by anyone, let alone a country cleric, Valbourg didn't budge. 'Your living here is provided by Lord Brocklehume, is it not, Reverend Hailey?'

'It is.'

'And such livings can be withdrawn, can they not?'

Hailey's eyes narrowed. 'If the bishop or Lord Brocklehume believe I have been negligent in my duties then, yes, it can be withdrawn. But the welfare of my parishioners is of the utmost importance to me and I have done nothing to compromise that obligation.'

'I do not question your dedication, Hailey,' Valbourg said. 'Merely your methods. I wonder what the bishop would say about a clergyman who hires men to spy on a young woman who, under different circumstances, might well have been his daughter-in-law.'

Valbourg didn't wait for the man's reply. Frankly, he didn't care. *Smug, self-righteous prig!* What gave Hailey the right to criticise Catherine's conduct when his was no better? So much for the nobility of the church! Valbourg walked out of the stone building—and came to an abrupt halt.

Catherine Jones was standing at the top of the path. And she did not look happy.

Catherine most definitely was not happy. The last person she had expected to see emerging from the church on this fine sunny morning was Valbourg. 'What are you doing here?' She glanced past him. 'Is Reverend Hailey inside?'

'He is.'

'Please tell me you haven't been talking to him about me.'

'As a matter of fact, I have. And I fear you will gain nothing by going in there and talking to him now.'

'Why? What did you say?'

'Not nearly as much as I would have liked,' Valbourg said, taking her by the arm and leading her away. 'The man is an arrogant—'

'Please tell me you didn't insult him to his face.'

'Not in so many words, but I suspect he got the gist.'

Catherine groaned. If she'd had *any* idea Valbourg was going to come here today and speak to Hailey, she would have done everything she could to dissuade him from it last night. 'How could you, Valbourg? Have you any idea what you've done?'

'I know what I *came* to do,' Valbourg muttered. 'But the man isn't willing to listen to the truth.'

'Of course not, because he believes his own.'

'He needed to know you were not my mistress.'

Catherine gasped. 'Is that what you told him?'

'What else should I have said?'

'You shouldn't have said anything! You had no right to interfere.'

'I had *every* right. It may have escaped your notice, Catherine, but yours is not the only reputation at stake here. Hailey believes we are having an affair. I made it clear we are not.'

'But he didn't believe you.'

'No, and trust me, if you go in there now it will only make matters worse,' Valbourg said. 'Come, let us go somewhere that we can talk—'

'There is nothing to talk about. Don't you understand?' Catherine cried, whirling to face him. 'You have made my predicament a hundred times worse by stepping in where you had no business to!'

'And how many times must I remind you that this *is* now my business because it is clearly *my* involvement in your life that has made him change his mind about giving you your son back.'

Catherine didn't know what to say. Reverend Hailey believed she was having an affair with Valbourg and the fact Valbourg had come to her defence, while admirable, had likely only confirmed his suspicions. 'Lord Valbourg, I appreciate what you tried to do today, but for the welfare of all concerned, please stay out of my life from now on.'

'I will, if that is truly what you wish. But if Hailey believes something of you that isn't true and is punishing you because of it—'

'I must learn to live with it,' Catherine interrupted. 'Your coming here today has only led him to believe there *is* a connection between us, otherwise you wouldn't have bothered.'

'I told him you had the friendship of the Marquess of Alderbury and his family.'

'Which also isn't true,' Catherine said. 'I *met* the members of your family when I was hired to sing for them. That hardly qualifies me as a friend.'

'Nevertheless, I thought the connection to a high-ranking member of the aristocracy would work in your favour,' Valbourg said. 'How many actresses of your acquaintance can make such a claim?'

'Four, and they are all sleeping with their lords.' Catherine sighed and gazed into the distance. What was she to do now? Hailey was bound to be more dead set than ever against her having Thomas. The man he believed to be her lover had come to plead her case. What did that say, if not that Valbourg's interest in her went far beyond that of simple friendship?

'Catherine—'

'No, there is no point in discussing this any further,' she said, cutting him off. 'I shall return to London and then decide what to do next.'

'You will not stay and fight?'

'Not when I haven't a hope of winning.'

'But I'm sure the boy would rather be with his mother—'

'Difficult to say since Thomas doesn't know I *am* his mother.'

The remark stopped Valbourg in his tracks. 'He doesn't *know*?'

'I wasn't allowed to tell him. I have always been introduced as a friend of the family.'

'Then who does Thomas believe his real mother is?'

'I've no idea. That is a discussion I have not had the opportunity of having with my son. And thanks to you, one I probably never will.'

Not surprisingly, Gwen was extremely dismayed to hear of Catherine's failed attempt to speak to Reverend Hailey and to learn that their visit was coming so soon to an end.

'Are you sure there is nothing to be gained by staying and trying again?' Gwen asked after Catherine had related the whole sorry tale. 'Perhaps Reverend Hailey just needs time to come to terms with the situation.'

'I don't think time is going to make any difference. The only thing that might is getting the man who wrote the last report to admit that he exaggerated what he saw.'

'Do you think that's possible?'

'I don't know,' Catherine said. 'But I intend to try.'

'Well, I wish you luck with it, my dear. I know if there is a way of getting Thomas back, you will find it.' Gwen paused for a moment before saying, 'Are you going to see Valbourg when you return to London?'

'No. I made it quite clear I didn't want to see him again.'

'But why? None of this is his fault,' Gwen pointed out gently. 'He went to see Reverend Hailey with your best interests at heart.'

'I know, and it's really not him I am angry with,' Catherine admitted with a sigh. 'I don't think anything was going to change Reverend Hailey's mind, but it is best Valbourg and I don't spend any more time together. He is the type of man one has…a hard time forgetting, if you know what I mean.'

She looked up and met Gwen's gaze. A moment later, she saw understanding and regret dawn in the woman's eyes. 'Ah. So that's how it is. I'm surprised. You told me you had no wish to involve yourself with a man again.'

Catherine blushed. 'I didn't…until I met him.'

'Because he is a marquess's son?'

'No. Because he is Valbourg.' She bit her lip, tugging gently at the soft skin with her teeth. 'I didn't think it was possible to feel this way about a man, Gwen. To feel as though I am only half-alive if he is not near. But I see now that it is… because being with a man like that would not restrict my world. It would enrich it. Fill it with everything it lacks now. It is as though…he has opened my eyes to a world I never knew existed. A world I am richer for having seen. But at the same time, I am poorer because now I know what I shall never have. Not with him. And if not with him, not with anyone else.'

'My dear girl, you mustn't put such restrictions on yourself. There will be other gentlemen. If one has managed to find his way to your heart, others will, too.'

Catherine shook her head, aware there was nothing to be gained by arguing. She had known for some time that she was falling in love with Valbourg, but it was an involvement that had no future for her. He, too, had a child to look after; a boy not much older than Thomas. And Valbourg loved him as deeply as she loved Thomas. But he had promised his sister he would look after Sebastian and he had promised his family he would lead an exemplary life. He couldn't afford to have anyone call his character into question. Not for any reason.

Valbourg was dressing for breakfast when Catherine's letter arrived the following morning.

Lord Valbourg,
I write this as I am leaving for London because I do not wish our last words to each other to be those spoken in anger. I was wrong to lash out at you yesterday. You

*were only trying to help, and good inten-
tions should never be thought ill of.*

*You simply did not know the nature of
the man with whom you were dealing. I did
and could have told you that nothing would
be gained by your efforts, even though you
went with the best of intentions.*

*I wish you well in the future and hope you
will still come and see me now and then at
the Gryphon. Your admiration and respect
mean everything to me.*

Sincerely,

Catherine Jones

Valbourg read the letter three times before
folding it up and slipping it into a drawer. Damn.
He, too, regretted the manner in which they had
parted. He had lain awake half the night, trying
to figure out how to set matters right. He knew
now it had been a mistake to try to make Hailey
see sense. Catherine was right. He should have
minded his own business. But he had been so
sure that talking to Hailey was the right thing to
do. If he could have made the clergyman see that
nothing was going on between them, Valbourg
felt sure Hailey would have released the boy into
her care. Instead, all he had done was make the
situation worse. Hailey had sent the boy away,
further reducing Catherine's chances of regaining custody of him, and now she was angry with

him even though her letter tried to convince him otherwise.

It was a deeply troubling situation and one for which there was no easy answer. Valbourg wasn't used to people challenging his word or calling his integrity into question. To be called a liar by a village parson seemed the absolute height of absurdity—but Catherine was the one who was being punished.

The matter stayed on Valbourg's mind for the rest of the morning. Even when he went out riding with his host, thoughts of Catherine's predicament continued to plague him. She would be well on her way back to London now and he could imagine how unhappy she was. To be driving away with only her servant for company when she had expected to have her son with her as well must be heartbreaking.

He tried putting himself in her place, tried to imagine how he would feel if Sebastian were to be taken away from him. It would be a horrendous wrench. One he would fight with every bone in his body…and that was exactly what Catherine was going through now. For the past five years her only goal had been to regain custody of her son. Everything she had done—or hadn't done—had been with a view to achieving that goal. She had worked hard at becoming the best performer she could be and had saved enough money to be able to afford a house in a decent part of town. She had gone to church and prayed forgiveness for the sin of bearing a child out of wedlock. She had denied herself the pleasures of the flesh because she knew what it would cost her if she partook of them.

Yet she had still lost. She had sacrificed everything...and for what? To be called a whore and be denied the one thing that mattered more to her than anything else in the world—

'You're very deep in thought this morning, Valbourg,' Brocklehume commented at his side. 'I don't believe you've heard a word I've said.'

Valbourg sighed. 'Sorry, Robert. I have been a bit preoccupied.' He reached out and pulled a burr from the gelding's mane. 'Tell me, what do you know of Reverend Hailey?'

'Hailey?'

'The vicar over in Grafton.'

'Oh, him. Not a great deal,' Brocklehume said. 'He calls here occasionally, but I try to avoid him. Tiresome man. Always quoting God's word or pontificating about morality and sin. But then, I suppose that's what clergymen do.'

'What do his parishioners think of him?'

'I've no idea. I don't trouble myself to listen. Julia could probably advise you better. She often gets involved with the goings-on at the church, though I know she doesn't care much for Hailey's wife. Pretty enough, which is likely why he married her, but sharp-tongued and used to getting her own way. There's many who say she rules the roost and, knowing what I do of Hailey's temperament, I'm not surprised.'

Interesting, Valbourg reflected. Hailey had seemed confident enough during their confrontation in the church, yet Brocklehume's description was of a hen-pecked husband. Perhaps Hailey showed more backbone when on his own than when in the company of his wife.

'I understand Hailey's son died some years ago,' Valbourg said.

'Yes. Shame that,' Brocklehume said. 'Will Hailey was a decent boy. Studious, not much of a sportsman, but for some reason he went out riding and took a terrible fall. Died before they could carry him off the field.'

'A shock for his family.'

'Indeed. Many believe it was grief over Will's death that killed Hailey's first wife. Hailey was shaken up, too. He just turned his grief in a different direction.'

'A younger wife?'

'Exactly.'

'Was Will Hailey seeing anyone at the time of his death?'

Brocklehume glanced up. 'Why all these questions, Valbourg? I wouldn't have thought the life of a country cleric would be of interest to you.'

'I had occasion to run into the fellow the other

morning and didn't much like what I saw,' Valbourg said, seeing no reason to dissemble. 'But I assumed you would have spent more time with him, given that the living at Grafton is yours to award.'

Brocklehume grunted. 'Couldn't be bothered finding anyone else. Hailey's father held the living before him and was well liked. This chap wasn't bad until he remarried. However, getting back to Will, there was talk of his being fond of Catherine Jones, but nothing ever came of it. Just as well since his father would never have approved. Miss Jones was just the local schoolmaster's daughter. Hailey wanted better for his son.'

'I wonder what would have become of her if they *had* married,' Valbourg mused.

'She wouldn't have become an actress. I'll tell you that much,' Brocklehume said. 'Hailey's a bit of the old fire and brimstone when it comes to that. But I'm sure Miss Jones has no regrets. She's done far better in London than she would ever have done here.'

The conversation took a different turn after that, but having found out what he wanted, Valbourg let it go. He had no desire to appear too interested in Catherine. Brocklehume was no fool and Valbourg had no intention of giving his host any reason to talk. Still, the discussion had given him valuable insight into Catherine's predicament and, in particular, the present Mrs Hailey's partiality for Thomas. Valbourg was inclined to think the couple hadn't intended to give the boy back at all, in which case his arrival on the scene had not been the cause of the problem, but rather the excuse Hailey had been looking for all along.

Chapter Seven

The idea of finding Stubbs and getting him to admit what he'd done proved a lot harder than Catherine anticipated. The man seemed to have disappeared. He no longer haunted the lane near her home or turned up at her door at all hours of the day or night. Clearly, now that Reverend Hailey had made the decision to keep Thomas, he no longer cared how Catherine lived her life or with whom she spent her time.

Fortunately, Lily—through her blossoming friendship with Mr Hawkins—was able to find out that Stubbs liked to frequent a certain public house near the docks and, after four unsuccessful attempts, Catherine finally tracked him down. He was hunched over a table close to the door, having an animated conversation with another man who looked even more disreputable.

'Well, well, if it ain't the lovely Catherine Jones

come to see old Stubbs,' he said, winking at her. 'Miss me, did you, love?'

Catherine noticed a few of the patrons staring at her in astonishment, but she merely smiled and put her hand on Stubbs's shoulder. 'No, but I would like a word in private, if you don't mind.'

'Ah, well, I don't know about that, love,' Stubbs said. 'Me and my good friend Bert were just enjoying a chinwag over a pint. Bert's in the same line of work, if you know what I mean.'

'I do.' Catherine opened her reticule and took out a coin. 'Perhaps this will help persuade you to delay your conversation for a while?'

Bert's eyes widened as he took the coin and stuffed it in his pocket. 'For that, I'd never talk to me own mother again.' He finished his drink, got up and left.

Catherine, surveying her surroundings, nodded towards a vacant table in a relatively quiet corner of the pub. 'I think that's better suited for our purposes. Would you care to join me, Mr Stubbs?'

'*Mr* Stubbs? You've never called me that before.'

'There's a first time for everything.'

'Aye, I suppose there is.' Slowly, Stubbs got to his feet and made his way back to the corner table. 'So what brings you all the way down here? I didn't think I'd be seeing you again.'

'Why not? Has Hailey given you your marching orders?'

'Pretty much. Got a letter saying my services were no longer required. And between you and me, I'm just as glad. Never did care for him, but I liked *her* even less.'

'Her?' Catherine repeated, sitting down. 'You mean Reverend Hailey's wife?'

'Aye. She was the one who hired me. Told me she needed to know what you were doing and paid me well for the trouble. So what happened?' he asked. 'Did you get the boy?'

'You know very well I didn't,' Catherine said tersely. 'Not after the comments in your last report.'

'What do you mean? I had nothing but praise for you.'

'Please don't lie to me, Mr Stubbs.'

'I'm not lying. I said you *deserved* to get your boy back.'

'That's not what Reverend Hailey told me,' Catherine said. 'He said what he read in that report changed his mind about giving Thomas back to me.'

'Then it couldn't have been *my* report he was reading,' Stubbs said. 'I said I'd watched you for the best part of five years and never once did I see you do anything of a questionable nature. In fact, I was downright complimentary about you.'

'Then how did he know Lord Val—' Catherine stopped '—that a gentleman had given me a ride home in his carriage?'

'Beats me, love. Maybe Moody sent something in. I heard he was back in town. In fact, I saw him a couple of times the week before last. He was hanging around your house. I told him to take himself off. Got a mean streak, has Moody,' Stubbs said. 'And he's had it in for you ever since that night you kneed him in the groin. Not that he didn't deserve it, mind.'

Catherine flushed. 'He *told* you about that?'

'Told everybody in the pub, but for what it's worth, very few took his side. Nasty piece of work,' Stubbs said, reaching for his beer. 'I hope you did him a permanent injury.'

'It wasn't my intention to cripple him, Mr Stubbs. Merely to incapacitate him long enough for me to get away.'

'Aye, and you did that and all. Maybe he'll think twice before attacking a little piece like you again.'

Catherine sat back, astonished to learn that Stubbs had put in a good word for her and that it was more likely Moody who had sent Eliza Hailey the damning report. *And*, in fact, that it was Eliza who had employed men to spy on her. But with the realisation came an idea.

'Mr Stubbs, now that you're no longer in Mrs Hailey's employ, would you consider working for me?'

'You?' Stubbs's eyebrows shot up. 'What

would someone like you be needing someone like me for?'

'To find out where Thomas is.' She proceeded to give Stubbs an abridged version of her conversation with Reverend Hailey.

'Well, I'll be damned,' Stubbs said at the end. 'So Moody messed you up right good and now the boy's been sent away because of it.'

'It would seem that way. I don't know if Eliza did it because she was afraid I might demand Thomas be handed over to me or because she was afraid her husband would. All I know is that Thomas has been sent away and they won't tell me where.'

'Well, it shouldn't be too difficult to find out,' Stubbs said. 'Just means I've got to get back inside the house and bribe a maid or two.'

'Would a maid be likely to know?'

'If not, the housekeeper would, but she's a hard-nosed piece if ever I've met one.'

'I'm willing to pay for the information,' Catherine said. 'Whatever it takes.'

'Tell you what. I'll see what I can find out and you can pay me later.'

'That's a rather trusting attitude, Mr Stubbs.'

'I've watched you for the last five years, Miss Jones. I think I know what kind of woman you are.'

'Fair enough, but to prove I'm serious, take these,' Catherine said, reaching into her reticule and pulling out some coins. 'You may need to bribe a few people along the way.'

Stubbs grinned, his gold tooth shining as he took the coins and slipped them into his leather pouch. 'Always a pleasure doing business with you, Miss Jones.'

It turned out Thomas had been sent to Glendale, a boarding school located about forty miles north-west of London. Stubbs discovered the name of the school, not by bribing Mrs Comstock but by flattering her; treatment Catherine doubted the woman had ever received. But it paid off and, after rewarding Stubbs for his efforts, Catherine set off for the country. She had no idea what she was going to say to the headmaster when she arrived at the school because she had no idea what he had been told by Reverend Hailey. She couldn't claim to be Thomas's mother because, if asked, Thomas would say she was not. But there had to be some other excuse she could use and Catherine sincerely hoped she was able to come up with it by the time they arrived.

After all, she was an actress. Pretending to be someone else was what she did.

Glendale College was a depressing red-brick building located on the outskirts of town. A wrought-iron fence surrounded a small play area for the younger boys and in a dusty field behind the school a few of the older lads tossed a ball back and forth.

Catherine had hoped to remain anonymous, but unfortunately, it seemed her name was well known even in these parts.

'I actually went to the Gryphon the last time I was in London and saw you playing the part of Selene, goddess of the moon,' Mr Norton told her as he escorted her into his office and closed the door. 'I must say I enjoyed it immensely. You have an exceptional voice, Miss Jones. Quite exceptional.'

'Thank you,' Catherine said, feeling that, if nothing else, she and the headmaster were off to a promising start. 'I'm glad you found the performance entertaining.'

'Indeed. So, tell me, what brings an actress of your repute to our humble school?'

'You are too modest, Mr Norton. The reputation of Glendale College is certainly not humble,' Catherine said, knowing nothing about the school's reputation, but feeling it could do no harm to flatter the man. 'As it happens, however, I have come to see you about one of your students.'

'Oh? Which one?'

'Thomas Jo…Hailey. Thomas Hailey,' she said, stumbling a little over the surname.

'Ah, yes, Thomas,' the headmaster said, settling back into his chair. 'Quiet lad. Possessed of a good mind, though he does have an unfortunate tendency to daydream. But we have ways of dealing with that. A boy must be taught to pay attention.'

'But he is such a little boy, Mr Norton,' Catherine said, her protective instincts rising. 'Surely a small degree of inattention can be permitted.'

'Not at Glendale. We don't mollycoddle our boys, Miss Jones. We mete out discipline when and where it is needed. Now, perhaps you would care to tell me what business you have with Thomas?'

Catherine stirred uneasily in her chair. The moment of truth was at hand and she still had no idea what she was going to say. She'd considered telling Mr Norton the truth, relying on his knowledge of the situation and his compassion for a mother and her child to do the right thing, but given what he'd just said, she wondered if compassion was a sentiment he understood.

'Mr Norton, I do have a good reason for being here,' Catherine began. 'One I feel you will understand when I have set forth the facts and made clear the situation—'

'Excuse me, Miss Jones,' Mr Norton said when a knock interrupted the proceedings. 'Yes, Mr Smith?'

The door opened and a tall man wearing spectacles and looking rather nervous poked his head in. 'Pardon me, Mr Norton, but there is a gentleman to see you.'

'Can you not see that I am engaged?'

'Indeed, sir, but the gentleman said it was urgent, and I believe, given who it is, you may wish to see him.' He walked into the room and placed a small white card on the headmaster's desk.

Mr Norton looked down at it and flushed. 'Yes, I think it best I do see him. Would you excuse me, Miss Jones? I have a most dignified caller.'

'Of course.' Catherine stood up, relieved at having been given a bit more time to rehearse what she wanted to say. 'I shall wait in the hall.'

'That won't be necessary,' a polished and all-too-familiar voice said. 'I expect we are here to the same purpose, Miss Jones.'

Catherine whirled, her eyes widening at the sight of Valbourg standing in the doorway. 'What are you doing here?'

'The same as you, I suspect.' Valbourg smiled, a study in aristocratic amiability. 'I've come to collect Master Thomas Hailey and to take him back to London with me.'

Valbourg knew his arrival in the headmaster's office had caught Catherine unawares, but hoping she hadn't been so foolish as to reveal who she was and the reason for her visit, he confidently approached the desk and addressed his next question to the headmaster. 'Have you received a letter from Mrs Hailey, Mr Norton?'

'Mrs Hailey?' The headmaster frowned. 'Not that I am aware of, no. Am I to expect one?'

'You are. Mrs Hailey has been called to London to see her mother, who I understand is in very poor health,' Valbourg said. 'She asked me to collect Thomas on my way back to town and to deliver him to her there. It may well be the boy's last chance to see his grandmother alive.'

He watched Catherine's expression grow even more confused, and before she had time to blurt anything out, he said, 'Would you be so good as to have Thomas's belongings packed and brought down?'

The headmaster looked decidedly flustered at the unexpected turn of events. 'I am sorry to hear the news, my lord, but this is somewhat irregular. The boys are given into my care, you understand, and it is usually only parents or close family members who are permitted to remove them.'

'I understand. And you are to be commended for your attention to duty. But the situation in which we find ourselves does not allow for other family members to be here in time. Now, if you don't mind, I would be most grateful if you would attend to the matter as quickly as possible. My horses tend to grow restless when forced to stand in one place for too long.'

'Of course,' Mr Norton said, sounding no less flustered despite the compliment from a gentleman of consequence. 'If you will give me a moment, I shall…make the necessary arrangements.'

He left the room, shouting instructions to his secretary and leaving Valbourg alone with Catherine, who, despite her confusion, looked utterly beautiful. 'Good afternoon, Miss Jones. Fancy meeting you here.'

Catherine was not amused. 'What exactly do you think you're doing?'

'Is it not obvious?'

'Not to me. I came to take Thomas away.'

'So did I.'

'But this is none of your business!'

'Fortunately for you, I have decided to make it my business,' Valbourg said. 'Because without me, you haven't a hope of getting Thomas out of here.'

'Don't be so sure. How did you know where I was?'

'Your housekeeper informed me of your whereabouts. Lovely lady. Very protective of your welfare.'

'But clearly not of my privacy.'

'Don't be too hard on her. I knew what to say in order to gain her co-operation.'

'I hate to think what that might have been,' Catherine said. Then she frowned. 'I wasn't aware Eliza's mother lived in London.'

'I have no idea where she lives, nor do I care,' Valbourg said, keeping his eyes on the door. 'It is enough that Mr Norton believes she is ill and that Thomas has been called to see her.'

'You mean it's not true?'

'Not a word. If you can think of a better way of getting him out of here, now would be the time to mention it.'

'I was going to tell Mr Norton the truth,' Catherine said. 'Appeal to his good nature.'

'Trust me, it would have achieved nothing. When the boy is brought down, he will not look to you as his mother and you would have been accused of trying to kidnap him.'

'But there has to be a time to start telling the truth!'

'I agree, but this is most definitely *not* that time,' Valbourg said. 'Our only hope of getting Thomas out of here without raising the alarm is to give Norton a valid reason for our being here. Did you say *anything* to him before I arrived?'

'No. I was about to when you knocked on the door.'

'Excellent. Then I suggest you lend your support to my story and pretend it is the reason you are here as well.'

Mr Norton returned momentarily with the assurances that Master Thomas's trunk was being packed and that the young lad himself was being readied for travel.

'How fortunate you were on your way to London, Lord Valbourg,' Mr Norton said. 'Otherwise the timing might not have been so fortuitous.'

'Indeed, but as it happens, there would not have been a delay. Miss Jones also came to fetch the boy,' Valbourg said smoothly. 'It seems neither of us was made aware that the other had been asked to bring Thomas to London.'

'I suspect Mrs Hailey has become a little forgetful, given the seriousness of her mother's illness,' Catherine said, affecting a suitable degree of concern. 'She likely forgot she had asked both of us to escort Thomas to London.'

'Understandable,' Mr Norton agreed. 'My own mother suffered terribly with memory loss in her later years and it was always worse during times of stress. Couldn't remember her own name let alone mine.' He looked up, smiling. 'Can I offer either of you refreshments while we wait?'

'Thank you, no,' Valbourg said. 'We must be on our way as soon as Thomas is ready.'

'Of course. And may I say what an honour it is to make your acquaintance, Lord Valbourg. It is surely an indication of the respect with which Glendale is viewed that one of our students has such illustrious connections.'

Deciding it was wiser not to attempt any kind of rejoinder, Valbourg merely smiled. Moments later, the door opened again and Thomas Hailey was brought into the room.

He was smaller than Valbourg expected, standing a good head shorter than Sebastian and likely twenty pounds lighter. His hair was pale gold and his eyes were the clear, bright blue of a summer sky. But it wasn't his size or even the black eye he sported that caused Valbourg to bite back an oath. It was the boy's striking resemblance to Catherine.

'Miss Jones, why don't you wait for me in the carriage?' he said, abruptly pulling Catherine from her chair and ushering her towards the door. 'I wish to speak to Mr Norton about matters of business.'

'But—'

'Don't worry, I shall be along directly.' Valbourg all but closed the door in her face and then turned to offer his most charming smile to the headmaster. 'Now, Mr Norton, are there any financial matters that need taking care of? I don't know precisely when Thomas will be returning to Glendale, but if any fees are due, I am more than happy to cover them on Reverend Hailey's behalf.'

'That won't be necessary, my lord. Thomas's fees were paid in advance. But I do hope we will have him back with us again soon,' Mr Norton said, smiling down at the boy. 'A Glendale education stands a boy in good stead his entire life.'

'So I've heard,' Valbourg said, lying through his teeth. 'Well, we had best be on our way.' He glanced at Thomas, who was looking understandably bewildered by the proceedings. 'We have a long ride ahead of us.'

'Say hello to Lord Valbourg, Thomas,' Mr Norton said. 'He has come to take you to London to see your grandmother.'

The boy regarded Valbourg, his expression very serious. 'Good afternoon, Lord Valbourg.'

'Hello, Thomas.' Valbourg bent down so that he was eye level with the boy. 'I'm sorry to have to take you out of school, but it is important we get you to London as quickly as possible.'

'I didn't know I had a grandmother in London.'

'Well, you do now, and she is very anxious to see you.' Valbourg stood up and extended his hand to the headmaster. 'Thank you for your help, Mr Norton. Miss Jones and I are most grateful.'

'My pleasure, Lord Valbourg. I shall await Mrs Hailey's letter, but in the meantime I shall pen a note of condolence to her,' Mr Norton said. 'Wishing her mother a speedy recovery.'

'I'm sure she would be most appreciative,' Valbourg said, beginning to wonder if he hadn't missed his calling. He doubted even the great Edmund Kean could have played a more convincing part.

In the courtyard below, Catherine waited anxiously for Valbourg and her son to appear. What in the world was keeping them? And what business could Valbourg have had with the headmaster that had necessitated her being thrust out of the room so precipitously?

'I'm sure it is nothing to concern yourself with, Catherine,' Mrs Rankin said. 'His lordship knows what he is doing.'

'Does he?' Catherine said, not at all convinced he did. Thankfully, the front door opened a few minutes later and Valbourg walked out, holding Thomas's hand. He had to slow his steps in order to accommodate the boy's shorter strides, but all that mattered to Catherine was the fact her son was walking towards her. 'Hello, Thomas,' she said. 'How lovely to see you again.'

He looked surprised to see her, but thankfully, he remembered who she was. 'Hello, Miss Jones. What are you doing here?'

'I've come to take you to London. To see your grandmother,' Catherine added, with a hasty glance at Valbourg.

'That's what Lord Valbourg said, too, but I didn't know I had a grandmother in London,' Thomas said. 'Aunt Eliza never mentioned her.'

'Actually, she is more a close friend of the family's,' Valbourg said, a nod to the servant indicating that he should put Thomas's trunk in Catherine's carriage. 'But you are actually going to be riding back to London with me.'

'*With* you?' Catherine repeated. 'Why not with me?'

'Because there won't be room in your carriage

with Mrs Rankin and Thomas's trunk in it.' Valbourg lifted Thomas into his own carriage, and then turned to smile at Catherine. 'Are you coming?'

Catherine stared at him in amazement. Unbelievable! After all these years, it was Valbourg who would be riding back to London with Thomas, and not her.

'Of course I'm coming.' She returned briefly to her own carriage to tell Mrs Rankin what was happening and then quickly made her way back to Valbourg's.

As soon as she was settled, the carriage set off. Catherine kept flicking nervous glances over her shoulder, half-expecting to see the headmaster come running through the front door, waving his arms in the air and demanding that they return at once.

'It's all right. He won't come after us,' Valbourg said quietly. 'He has no reason to doubt the story I told him. However, I suspect there will be a slight problem when his letter of condolence arrives at Reverend Hailey's house.'

Catherine's eyes widened. 'He is writing a letter of condolence?'

'He thought it the polite thing to do.'

'Then the Haileys will know—'

'That we are on our way to London with Thomas, yes,' Valbourg said, tilting his head in the boy's direction. 'But I suggest we talk about it later.'

Agreeing that it was best they say nothing in front of Thomas, Catherine turned her attention to her son, who was sitting on the seat looking out of the window. He had grown since the last time she had seen him and was clearly in need of new clothes. His shirt had a stain on it, his pants were too tight and one of his shoes was badly scuffed. He was also sporting a bluish-yellow bruise on his right cheek.

'How did you come by that bruise, Thomas?' she asked, tilting his head so she might see it better.

'I fell.'

Catherine looked over at Valbourg, then back at her son. 'In the classroom?'

'No. In the yard,' the boy said, adding as an afterthought, 'I tripped.'

Thinking it was more likely he had been pushed, Catherine said, 'I shall put some ointment on it when we get to London. Are you hungry?'

'Oh, yes, miss.'

Across from her, Valbourg chuckled. 'It has been my experience that little boys are very seldom not hungry.'

'Fortunately, I came with that thought in mind.' Catherine pulled a bright red apple from her bag and handed it to her son. 'And there is another one if you need it.'

'Thank you, Miss Jones!' Thomas bit into the apple, the expression of bliss on his face prompting Catherine to wonder what he would say when he tasted Cook's jam sponge topped with thick cream and dotted with ripe juicy strawberries.

'Will I be going back to Glendale?' Thomas asked between mouthfuls.

'I don't know,' Catherine said, feeling it was probably the safest answer. 'Did you like it there?'

'Not very much. The older boys weren't nice to me and the headmaster was very strict. I was twice sent to bed without supper for not paying attention. I'm glad Lord Valbourg came to fetch me.' He looked up at Catherine and smiled. 'And that you came, too, Miss Jones. I was afraid I wasn't going to see you again.'

'Why not?'

'Aunt Eliza said you wouldn't be coming any more. She said you were too busy being famous.'

Swallowing a swift surge of anger, Catherine said, 'I could never be too busy for you, Thomas. Your aunt was wrong to suggest otherwise.'

'I'm glad.' The boy leaned his head against her arm. 'I like it when you visit.'

Catherine closed her eyes and felt her heart swell to bursting. There was so much she wanted to say to him. So much she needed to ask. But this wasn't the time. Thomas had already been through so much. Telling him that she was his mother now, without having established a relationship beforehand, would only confuse him. He needed time to adjust to the fact he wasn't going back to Glendale, or to the only home he knew.

'Does Megan know I am going to London?' Thomas asked suddenly. 'Will she be coming, too?'

'She may,' Catherine said, exchanging an uncertain glance with Valbourg. 'I don't know what the plans are for her.'

'Megan has always wanted to see London,' Thomas said. 'She likes to look at Aunt Eliza's magazines, the ones with the drawings of pretty ladies. She says they all wear beautiful gowns and ride around in carriages, and have ices and fine tea.'

'What about you, Thomas?' Valbourg said. 'Are you looking forward to seeing London?'

'I should like to have ices and visit a sweet shop, but Reverend Hailey says wickedness lives in the streets and that God-fearing people don't go there.'

'Reverend Hailey exaggerates,' Catherine said, careful not to let her annoyance with the clergyman ring through. 'Lord Valbourg and I live in London and so do a lot of other very nice people.'

'Indeed, I suspect wicked people live in Grafton, too,' Valbourg said, with a wry glance at Catherine.

'Megan said that not everyone who lives in London is wicked,' Thomas agreed. 'She said

Reverend Hailey only told us that so we wouldn't want to go there. But I don't mind. It might be fun. And it isn't as though I don't know anyone because you are here with me,' he said, smiling up at Catherine.

It was as though he had reached out and wrapped his fingers around her heart, Catherine thought, smiling back at him. Surely if he already liked and trusted her, telling him the truth about their relationship wouldn't come as such a terrible shock.

When at length her son grew weary, Catherine slipped her arm around his shoulders and drew him close. 'Go to sleep, Thomas,' she whispered, smoothing the hair back from his forehead. 'When you wake up, we will be in London.'

He nodded and drifted off to sleep within a matter of minutes.

'So, this is why you never took a lover,' Valbourg murmured.

Catherine nodded, her arms still wrapped around her son. 'Hopefully, my reasoning isn't as difficult to understand now.'

'Not at all. But I wish you had told me the truth earlier.'

'Surely you can understand why I did not.'

'Because you gave birth to a child without the benefit of a husband?'

'That, and because I had no expectation of ever seeing you again.'

'And yet here we are,' Valbourg said, gazing down at Thomas. 'He's a fine boy. The resemblance between the two of you is striking.'

'Are we really that much alike?'

'Why do you think I was in such a hurry to remove you from the headmaster's office after Thomas was brought in?'

'I did wonder at that, but I assumed you had your reasons. You always do.' He looked at her and Catherine laughed. 'Oh, dear. Was that terribly rude of me?'

'Terribly. But I have found you to be an unusually candid woman, unlike most of the ladies with whom I am acquainted.'

'Yes, I doubt Lady Susan Wimsley would have made such a remark,' Catherine said. 'She has probably been raised to say and do all the right things. Her making a good marriage depends on it.'

'And yours does not?'

Remembering her conversation with Gwen, Catherine shook her head. 'I've already told you I don't intend to marry. Not only am I an actress, I have a five-year-old son. Not many men would choose to take on a burden like that.'

'Not all men would consider it a burden,' Valbourg said. 'Indeed, I can think of several who would be happy to offer you their name. However, if marriage isn't on the cards, have you ever thought of passing yourself off as a widow?'

'I did when I first arrived in London,' Catherine admitted, 'but I didn't like the dishonesty of it.'

'So you chose instead to pretend you were a virtuous single woman without any encumbrances.'

The implication stung. 'I did what I thought best. At the time, I had no way of knowing if I would ever see Thomas again,' Catherine said. 'Reverend Hailey and I did not part on good terms and I had no way of knowing what the eventual outcome would be. I simply thought it would be easier to pretend I didn't have a child than to tell people I did and explain why he wasn't with me.' She looked at Valbourg, feeling it was time to change the subject. 'Tell me about Sebastian.'

'Sebastian?' He looked surprised. 'What do you know about him?'

'Only what my friend Gwendolyn told me. She said the last time she saw you, your family was in mourning for your sister and that you became guardian of her son as a result of a promise you had given her. Is that true?'

After a moment's silence, he nodded. 'Sarah asked me if I would take care of Sebastian if anything should happen to her and her husband.'

'You didn't think that strange?'

'That she would ask me to take care of Sebastian or that something might happen to her?'

'Either.'

'I admit I did find it a little unusual that I should be the one nominated to look after Sebastian when I had no wife of my own,' Valbourg admitted. 'But I paid it no mind. Sarah and John were both young and healthy. No one could have foreseen what happened to them.'

'But when the worst *did* happen and the responsibility for looking after Sebastian was raised, did no one in your family object to you stepping forward?'

'Good Lord, yes, they *all* objected,' Valbourg said. 'And to be fair, I couldn't blame them. My life to that point had been an endless round of drinking and carousing. I won…and lost…vast sums of money on the turn of a hand and came home at all hours and slept half the day away. All that had to change when Sebastian arrived on my doorstep.'

'Was it difficult?'

'Abominably so. I hadn't realised how selfish I'd become,' Valbourg admitted. 'My life was about doing what I liked. However, I'd given Sarah my word and nothing anyone said or did was going to change that. So, I sent my mistress away with a large ruby pendant, stopped going to hells and became a respectable family man.'

'Your staff must have been surprised.'

'In truth, they were relieved. They all feared for my health and saw Sebastian's arrival as a turn for the better, which it was. Now I can't imagine my life without him.'

'So you don't miss what you had to give up?'

'No, because I gained far more than I lost.' Valbourg glanced at Thomas and said, 'I'm sure I don't have to explain that to you.'

No, he didn't. Having Thomas sleeping at her side was a joy unlike any Catherine had ever experienced. Before now, she'd had only the memory of those first few weeks to sustain her— memories of holding her newborn son in her arms and of rocking him to sleep. Nothing came close to what she felt for Thomas and to have him torn from her when he was only a month old had been the worst experience of Catherine's life. She had existed like a ghost for months afterwards, dragging herself through the days, numbed by the magnitude of her loss. Gwen had tried to rouse her from her malaise, but nothing could lessen the pain of having lost her son; grief compounded by the knowledge she might never see him again. If ever there was a hell on earth that had surely been it.

'No, you don't have to explain,' Catherine whispered, pressing her lips to the top of her son's head. 'I've lived for this day. Dreamt about it, never knowing if it would come to pass. But now that it has I intend to do everything I can…anything I must…to keep Thomas with me. I *won't* lose him again!'

'Then I suggest you start by giving some serious thought to where he's going to live,' Valbourg said. 'Because he can't stay with you.'

'Why not?'

'You must know Hailey will come after him.'

'He might, but this time, the circumstances are different. Thomas is my son—'

'But Thomas doesn't know that,' Valbourg interrupted. 'And if anyone asks, he will be the first to say so. We must be grateful he knows and likes you as much as he does, but it is naïve to think he will say you are someone other than who he believes you to be. You've heard him call Mrs Hailey his aunt. He will expect and may well *want* to go back to her.'

'Then I have no choice but to tell him the truth,' Catherine said, her arm unconsciously tightening around her son. 'I have to make him aware that *I* am his mother.'

'The fact he resembles you so strongly will certainly make it easier to believe, but would you force him to stay with you if he said he wanted to go back to the Haileys?'

It was a question Catherine didn't want to answer…because it was a reality she didn't want to face. 'I don't know. I would never wish to cause him pain, but neither do I wish to give him up before he's had a chance to get to know me and to understand who I really am. That means I'll have to spend as much time with him as I can in the hopes of his eventually coming to love me. Then when I tell him the truth, it won't come as such a shock.'

'Well, I can certainly see why he would prefer to be with you than with Eliza Hailey. I know I would.'

Valbourg's voice dropped on those last four words, and Catherine looked up to see him watching her. But this time, his expression wasn't veiled. She saw exactly what he was thinking—and it caused her heart to turn over. 'Valbourg—'

'No, don't say it,' he said softly. 'I know as well as you do that it's impossible. But that doesn't mean I don't want you, Catherine. I have…for a very long time.'

The words hung in the air between them, a sweet promise of something that could never be. For the first time in her life, Catherine wasn't tempted to come up with a clever rejoinder to something a gentleman said, because for the first time in her life, she didn't want to discourage him. 'I didn't know.'

'Not even after I kissed you?'

'I thought you kissed me to prove a point and not a very flattering one at that.'

'Partially true. I kissed you because I needed to know what lay behind that cool exterior,' Valbourg said. 'But I also kissed you because I wanted to. Just like I've wanted to kiss you every time I've seen you since.'

Catherine closed her eyes and breathed a long, deep sigh. What was she to say? Valbourg wasn't being coy or flirtatious. He was stating openly that he wanted to kiss her. Perhaps even to do more than that. Where did that leave her? 'I honestly don't know what to say.'

'Do you find the thought of my caring about you frightening?'

'No. I find it incredibly flattering.'

He smiled. 'It wasn't my intention to flatter you.'

'Perhaps *flattered* isn't the right word.'

'What is?'

Catherine was quiet for a long moment. 'Happy. Yet at the same time, unutterably sad.'

The slight widening of his eyes told her he understood and, in her heart, Catherine knew they both did. The attraction between them had been growing for weeks. Ever since the night she had gone to Alderbury House and seen Valbourg walking towards her. It had grown with each successive encounter and, for Catherine, it had crystallised today when he had shown up in the headmaster's office spouting a ridiculous story that, finally, had allowed her to regain possession of her son.

But an attraction was all it could ever be. An endless succession of stolen moments conducted in secret because their positions in society were too dissimilar to allow anything else. They could not alter the circumstances of their lives. They could only live with them.

Chapter Eight

They arrived on the outskirts of London after having stopped at an inn for something to eat. Thomas had been delighted with the thick slices of bread and butter with wedges of cheese, thin slices of ham and a selection of jams that made his eyes bulge. Clearly, he had never been treated to the kind of foods Valbourg took for granted.

Catherine ate lightly, her stomach in knots over Valbourg's revelations during the carriage ride. Her recently gained awareness of his feelings for her left little room for thoughts of anything else and she was painfully conscious of the glances he kept sending her way. Once, when their hands brushed, she jumped, as though touched by a hot blade. Yet the sensation had not been one of pain. The frisson of awareness that shot up her arm had been one of intense pleasure, making her wonder what it would be like to be held in his arms.

'Will I be staying with my grandmother?' Thomas had asked between mouthfuls.

Catherine had started to reply, but Valbourg was faster. 'I thought you might like to stay with me tonight, Thomas. My nephew, Sebastian, is anxious to meet you. He is a little older than you, but I suspect you share many of the same interests.'

Catherine had stared at Valbourg, startled by his offer. She hadn't expected him to want to have anything to do with her and Thomas once they arrived in London, let alone to offer his house as a place for Thomas to spend the night. He must have a reason for doing so, but for the life of her she couldn't imagine what it was.

Finally, they arrived in Berkeley Square. Thomas kept his face pressed to the carriage window, trying to take in all the sights and the sounds of the busy square. 'Is this where you live, Lord Valbourg?'

'It is.'

'It's a very fine house.'

'Thank you. And there is Sebastian, standing in the doorway, waiting to greet you.'

Catherine held on to Thomas's hand as they walked up to the front door and the boy standing there. She could feel her son's anxiety as they approached Sebastian, who was both taller and heavier than Thomas, but the boy's smile was open and welcoming as he held out his hand and introduced himself. 'Hello. I'm Sebastian. Would you like to come and see my new puppy?'

'You have a puppy?' Thomas said, eyes wide. 'What kind?'

'I don't know what he is. Except that he is brown and white and has a long feathery tail.'

'He sounds splendid. Does he bite?' Thomas asked.

'Not really. At least, he doesn't mean to,' Sebastian said. 'But he does have very sharp teeth. Come on, I'll show him to you.'

Thomas glanced up at Catherine and she saw at once how desperately he wanted to go with Sebastian. She smiled and let go of his hand. 'Run along and see the puppy. Don't worry, I'll be here.'

It was all Thomas needed to hear. With a wide grin, he ran up the stairs after Sebastian, the two already on the way to being friends.

'I told Sebastian he wasn't to have the puppy in his room,' Valbourg murmured. 'Obviously, he hasn't paid any attention.'

'I can't say I blame him,' Catherine said. 'Who can resist a puppy?'

Suddenly, she felt weary, as much from the tension of the day as from the fact it was getting on for seven o'clock and she had been awake very early. 'Well, I should be on my way—'

'Stay and have dinner with me,' Valbourg said. 'I've already asked Finholm to set two places in the dining room. It won't take long, and you can leave once you're finished.'

'I'm not sure—'

'I am. You've earned a good meal after everything you've been through today.'

An hour later, Catherine sat across from Valbourg in the quiet intimacy of the dining room, after the first course, a savoury creamed-vegetable soup, accompanied by a glass of fine French wine. Thomas, Sebastian and Rory the spaniel were having their meal upstairs.

'I hate to admit it, but perhaps it is a good idea that Thomas stays here tonight,' she said. 'Everything is so new to him, but I can see that he likes Sebastian and feels at home with him.'

'What about the other nights?' Valbourg asked, refilling her glass.

Catherine sighed. 'I know what you're saying, Valbourg, but I don't know what to do. I hate the thought of not being able to see Thomas whenever I want.'

'Who said you can't? You can come here as often as you like, now that you have a legitimate excuse for doing so.'

His voice dropped in a manner that sent shivers through her. 'I don't have a good excuse and you know it,' she said. 'Thomas cannot stay here indefinitely. You are not related to us and I cannot impose upon you in such a manner. I will have to give some thought to what you said in the carriage.'

'You're going to have to make up your mind soon,' Valbourg said, relaxing back in his chair. 'It won't take long for the Haileys to make their way to London, or to send someone in their stead.'

'And when they arrive, Moody will lead them straight to me,' Catherine murmured.

'Exactly, which is why Thomas needs to stay here with me. Hailey's men won't hesitate to snatch Thomas from you, but I suspect they would think twice before taking him from a nobleman's home. In fact, the safest place for Thomas might well be Alderbury House.'

'Absolutely not!' Catherine objected. 'I can just imagine what your father would say.'

'Alderbury is a great fan of yours.'

'There is a vast difference between enjoying my singing and having my son live in his house. I doubt any man would welcome such an intrusion.'

'I don't know,' Valbourg said. 'I would be delighted to have both you *and* Thomas living in my house, if it were possible.'

Catherine bit her lip. 'You would?'

'Do you really find that so hard to believe? I have told you how I feel about you.'

'Perhaps not.' She raised troubled eyes to his. 'I care about you, Valbourg. You must know that. But you must also know that if we were to allow ourselves to move in that direction, there would be serious repercussions for you.'

'Not for you as well?'

'I have Thomas with me now. The onus will be on Hailey to try to get him back. But you still have Sebastian to consider. You know what involving me in your life will do.'

'I dare say if my eldest sister were to find out, she would have Sebastian out of here so fast it would make our heads spin,' Valbourg agreed. 'But you know if the circumstances were different, I would already have asked.' He reached across the table and took her hand in his. 'I thought you were breathtaking as an actress. You are even more beautiful as a mother.'

Catherine gazed down at their locked hands, wondering how something so incredible could have happened to her. She had been the object of lust, of envy, even of jealousy, but she had never been the object of genuine respect and affection. Valbourg was the first man to make her feel that way. He was going to make some lucky woman a very good husband one day.

'Sebastian is delightful,' Catherine said, unprepared for the swift stab of pain the thought brought with it. 'And he loves you. You are as much his father as if you were born to it.'

'He is everything I might hope for in a son,' Valbourg admitted. 'I'd never given the idea of being a father any consideration until he came along. I thought, as most men do, that I would do my part in fathering him and then leave the responsibility for raising him to someone else. Now I find I *want* to be involved.'

'The mark of a good father.'

'I'm not sure about that. How does one know if one is doing a good job?'

'You don't,' Catherine said. 'You simply instil the beliefs in him that matter to you and do your best to raise him the way you would liked to have been raised yourself.'

'Sage wisdom if ever I've heard it.' He raised her hand to his lips and kissed it. 'When did you become so wise, Miss Jones?'

'When I turned ten and Papa gave me a book that contained everything I needed to know.'

Valbourg smiled. 'What was the name of this remarkable book?'

'I don't remember. It fell into the lake and sank before I had a chance to read it, but I assured Papa whenever he asked that it was the most useful book I had ever owned.'

Valbourg laughed and, turning her hand over, ran his finger along her palm. 'You have beautiful hands. I noticed them during your performance at Mary's reception. Small, with long, slender fingers and lovely wrists.' He curled her fingers into her palm and then wrapped his fingers around it. 'You need someone to take care of you, Catherine.

Now more than ever if you hope to raise Thomas on your own.'

'I will be fine,' she said, still a little breathless from his touch. 'I have money enough to provide him with everything he needs and I shall hire a governess to look after him when I am working.'

'So you intend to continue performing?'

'What other choices do I have?'

'You could marry.'

Catherine winced, unable to imagine living with any other man now that she had acknowledged her feelings for Valbourg. 'As I said before, not many men would be happy to take me on knowing I already had two greater loves in my life.'

'Two?'

'Thomas.' Her eyes flew up to his. 'And…the stage.'

His slow smile left Catherine wondering if she had fooled him. With Valbourg, it was impossible to tell.

'You could perform for your family and friends, you know,' he said, 'rather than in a packed theatre. Would that not be enough?'

'I don't know. It wouldn't be the same as singing before thousands of people. Nothing could ever be like that.'

'But how will you know until you've tried? Perhaps you will find other things even more appealing.'

'I cannot imagine what.'

'Can you not?' Valbourg pushed back his chair and slowly got up. Still holding on to her hand, he drew her to her feet. 'You might find being with a man even more exciting.' He turned her around and drew her back against him. 'But it would have to be the right man.'

Catherine's heart began to race. Dear Lord, he felt good…but what they were doing was so wrong. Valbourg could never be a part of her life, yet she was drawn to him, intoxicated by his presence. She felt the strength of his chest against her back, the firmness of his thighs against her torso. He put his hands on her upper arms and bent his head to nuzzle the soft skin of her throat.

Catherine closed her eyes and rested her head against him.

'Ah, my sweet.' His hands left her arms to wrap around her torso and draw her even closer. 'What am I going to do with you?'

She raised her hands and grasped his arms. A longing beckoned; a powerful urge to be close to him in a way she had experienced only once before. But she knew it would be different this time. Because she realised now that what she'd felt for Will paled in comparison to her feelings for this man. 'Valbourg—'

'Richard,' he said huskily. 'If you would call me anything, let it be that.'

Richard. Another step towards intimacy, Catherine thought sadly. A place they dared not go.

'We cannot do this, Richard,' she said in a whisper. 'It will only make matters that much harder.'

'Do you want me to stop?'

'No.' And God help her, she didn't. She wanted his hands on her body and his mouth on her skin. All the long years spent denying herself those pleasures only made her want him more. 'But you must.'

'I would have us share one kiss first.'

'We *have* shared a kiss.'

'No, I kissed *you*,' he said, turning her around to face him. '*We* did not kiss. And I need to know that you burn for me as deeply as I burn for you.'

Catherine knew it was madness to allow this to go any further, but she was unable to resist. She was in Valbourg's arms and he wanted her. That was enough. She raised her hand and drew his head down to hers, but this time when their lips met, it wasn't surprise Catherine felt, but pleasure of the most intense and erotic kind. Her experience of kissing had been with a boy. Valbourg was a man and she was left in no doubt about that as his lips teased and coaxed hers apart. He knew exactly what he was doing, his breath soft against her mouth, his hands cradling her head before his arms drew her close. She was falling headlong into danger, but for once she didn't care. *Richard* was with her. Whatever tomorrow held, all that mattered right now was this moment.

At length, Catherine drew back, the heat of his mouth warming her through. She glanced up at him, a little shy in the aftermath of the kiss, and saw that he was smiling. 'Is something wrong?'

'No. I just never imagined it could be like that.'

She sighed and let her head fall forward on to his chest. 'Nor did I, but I'm not sure we should tempt Fate again by allowing ourselves a repeat performance.'

'If that was a performance, I would demand a repeat of it every night of my life,' Valbourg murmured. 'In fact, I would demand a hundred performances a day. But I do understand.' He bent his head and kissed her once more before stepping back and releasing her. 'The fire between us burns white hot, but it will consume us if we let it. And given what we both stand to lose, it is best we not do this again.'

They were the words he needed to say. Catherine knew that. But hearing him say them brought her no joy because now she *knew* what she would be missing...and it would be even harder going forward.

A discreet knock at the door brought them back to the moment and Catherine reluctantly returned to the table. Valbourg waited for her to sit down before saying, 'Come in.'

Finholm appeared in the doorway. 'Are you ready for the next course, my lord?'

'We are.' Valbourg likewise sat down and winked at Catherine. 'Though I have a feeling it will not be nearly as enjoyable as the last.'

They finished dinner in a leisurely fashion, savouring their time alone together and enjoying the chance to talk freely. Valbourg, who selfishly wanted the evening to go on and on, was in no hurry to see Catherine leave. After finishing a delightful lemon soufflé, he suggested they take their brandy into the drawing room. To his relief, despite the unladylike pastime, Catherine agreed.

'Ah, but you see, I am an actress,' she told him. 'I don't have to behave with the same decorum as the fine ladies with whom you spend your time.'

'And yet, you always have. Not that I object to the way you're behaving now,' Valbourg added, watching Catherine take a sip of her brandy, enjoying the provocative sight of her mouth touching the glass and the perfection of her lips. 'I like being able to enjoy a glass of brandy with you and talk about subjects most young women know nothing about. Or if they do, pretend they do not. It is refreshing.'

'I was raised with a view to meeting the expectations of good society, but once I embarked on a career on the stage, those expectations changed,' Catherine told him. 'Suddenly, I wasn't expected to be demure and retiring or to have good morals…or any morals, for that matter. I was expected to play the part of the actress, and as strange as that sounds, sometimes I did.'

'But not, I suspect, when there was any chance one of Hailey's spies might be watching you.'

'No. The problem was, I never knew *when* they were watching me,' Catherine said. 'So the safest thing for me to do was to assume I was being watched all the time and behave accordingly. That way, I had nothing to be ashamed of and nothing to fear.'

'Until I came along,' Valbourg said ruefully.

She looked at him and sighed. 'I really don't think your behaviour had anything to do with it, Richard. If Eliza wanted to keep Thomas, she would have found a way of doing so. Your involvement simply provided a convenient excuse.'

'So you don't think my kissing you in the street had a negative effect on Hailey's opinion?'

'Oh, I am *quite* sure it had a negative effect,' Catherine said with a soft laugh. 'But if his mind was made up to keep Thomas, it wouldn't have been the deciding factor.'

'So the abstinence and good manners you practised all those years was for naught. You could have taken a lover and it wouldn't have made any difference.'

'It would have made a difference to me,' Catherine said. 'I knew in my heart that what I'd done with Will was wrong. My mother was a governess and my father a schoolmaster. I learned at a young age the difference between right and wrong. That's why I say the mistake I made with Will was entirely my own fault.'

'What did your parents say when they found out?'

'Only my father was alive at the time and he was horrified,' Catherine admitted. 'He didn't shout at me, but I knew how disappointed he was—and that hurt me far more than if he had shouted. I loved him dearly and I knew I had let him down.'

'I suspect we all let our parents down at some point in our lives,' Valbourg said. 'Did they have a happy marriage?'

'Yes, though in hindsight I think there was more respect to it than passion. They both did what they had to rather than what they might have wanted to.'

'In that case, it's not surprising your father reacted the way he did to your situation. He wouldn't have been able to understand how intensely passion can flare between two people.'

'No, and it did,' Catherine said, blushing at having such a frank conversation with a man. 'What I did with Will went against everything I had been taught. Everything I had been brought up to believe. But I was swept up in my feelings, perhaps for the first time in my life. And in that one moment, everything changed.'

Valbourg finished his brandy and got up to pour another. 'How will you feel about all of London knowing you have a child?'

'I suspect the question is going to be how will *they* feel about me. It will certainly change the way people look at me.'

'And the gentlemen who constantly beat a path to your door?'

'I suspect they won't feel the same and, to be honest, I'm glad. Perhaps I won't be such a challenge to them.'

Thinking of the bet standing on the book at White's, Valbourg wasn't so sure. 'You may be wrong, Catherine. Knowing you've had a child simply means you're not a virgin. To some men, that will make you even more attractive.'

'But less to those who do not want the encumbrance of a child.'

They sat together in silence for a time, Valbourg content to sip his brandy as he mulled over everything Catherine had said, while she sat staring into the fire. In the candlelight, her hair shone more golden than silver, while her skin glowed a warm peachy rose. Valbourg knew first-hand how soft it was and wanted nothing more than to take her in his arms and make her forget everything except how it felt to be a woman in the arms of a man who cared about her. But they both knew the folly of allowing themselves to go down that road.

'Well, I suppose I should be going home,' Catherine said, reluctantly getting to her feet. 'It has been a very long and eventful day, and Mrs Rankin will start to worry if I am not home soon.'

'I'll take you,' Valbourg said.

'That isn't necessary.'

'I know, but I want to.' He crossed the room to where she stood and, slipping his hand behind her neck, drew her towards him. 'I may not be able to have you here all the time, Catherine, but I intend to take advantage of the times I do,' he murmured against her lips. 'And being alone in a carriage with you at night is a pleasure I am not willing to forgo.'

Unfortunately, as it turned out, the pleasure was to be denied them both. Finholm came up to Valbourg as they were preparing to leave with the news that Sebastian had thrown up his supper.

'I don't think the fever's back,' the butler said, 'but he says his stomach is upset. Shall I send for the doctor?'

Valbourg glanced at Catherine and knew their time was at an end. 'Yes, you best had. I'm sure it's nothing to worry about, but I would rather have Dr Tennison make that call.'

'I suspect it may have been something he ate yesterday,' Finholm said. 'Cook took him to the shops and I dare say he was given a few treats along the way.'

'In that case, he won't be right until he's had it up,' Valbourg said. He turned to Catherine and sighed. 'Do you mind going home on your own?'

'Of course not. But will having Thomas here be too much trouble? I can take him home if you like.'

'No, there's no need to wake him. If the doctor believes Sebastian has anything contagious, I'll send Thomas home straight away. Otherwise, I shall see you in the morning.'

'All right. Goodnight, Lord Valbourg. And thank you...for everything.'

He couldn't kiss her with his butler standing right there, but Valbourg allowed his gaze to linger on her lips and knew from the colour that bloomed in her cheeks that she understood.

He closed the door and turned to see Finholm watching him. 'I trust, Finholm, that the events of the evening will not be made known to any of my family.'

'Events, my lord?' The butler looked confused. 'What events?'

Valbourg smiled, thinking, not for the first time, that a man in possession of a discreet butler was an extremely fortunate one indeed.

Catherine barely waited until ten o'clock the next morning before setting out to see Thomas.

She had finally fallen asleep with thoughts of her son—and Valbourg—swirling around in her head and, upon waking, realised she was desperate to see both.

Thankfully, Finholm greeted her at the door with a smile. 'Good morning, Miss Jones.'

'Good morning, Finholm. How is Sebastian feeling this morning?'

'Much better, thank you, miss.' The butler closed the door and turned to lead the way into the drawing room. 'I believe he was up during the night, but I think it safe to say that whatever ailed him has now passed out of his system and a timely recovery is expected.'

'I am glad to hear it,' Catherine replied, none the less feeling a little guilty. If Sebastian's recovery was due to his throwing up whatever he had ingested, it likely meant he wasn't suffering from anything contagious. With Thomas living in the same house, that was definitely of concern to her.

Finholm left her in the drawing room and Catherine waited, wondering how Thomas had slept and how he was feeling this morning. Would he still be excited about being in London, or might he already be missing Megan and the Haileys and be longing to return home? Everything was so new to him here. Being in London, sleeping in a stranger's house, even spending time with her, were all experiences that could be overwhelming to a small boy who had been leading a sheltered existence in the country.

Which meant, Catherine realised, that there could be no revelations of any kind today. She had no intention of alarming her son by telling him she was his mother. The timing had to be perfect for that. Too soon and he might take fright and want to return to the Haileys. Too late and it would only become harder for her.

She decided to keep an open mind and see what developed. Then the door opened and Valbourg came in. 'Good morning, Miss Jones.'

The sight of him caused a constriction in Catherine's throat. Heavens, was this how it felt to be in love? Was this breathless anticipation all part of it? 'Good morning, my lord.'

Then the door closed and she was in his arms, his body pressed tightly against hers, his mouth warm and possessive on hers. It was the sweetest greeting Catherine had ever received. 'Are you in the habit of greeting all of your morning callers this way, my lord?' she enquired huskily.

'Only those who look as beautiful as you,' Valbourg murmured. 'The others receive a more traditional handshake.'

Catherine laughed, suddenly feeling wonderfully young and carefree. 'You will turn my head with your flattery, sir.'

His arms tightened around her. 'I would do

anything to see you smile.' He kissed her again and then reluctantly released her. 'So, what have you planned for Thomas today?'

'I thought to take him to the park.' Equally reluctant, Catherine moved out of his arms. 'I suspect he would enjoy feeding the ducks.'

'Then by all means, we must go to the park.'

'"We"? Surely you do not intend to be seen with us, Richard?' Catherine said, fearing for his reputation. 'I cannot think it would be a good idea.'

'It will no doubt raise a few eyebrows, but if we set off now we can be in the park well ahead of the fashionable crowd and, personally, I cannot think of a more pleasant way to spend the morning. It might also make the outing more comfortable for Thomas. Based on what you've told me, you have not been able to spend a great deal of time in his company and there may be some initial awkwardness.'

'You could be right,' Catherine said, grateful to him for having thought of it. 'Will Sebastian be able to come?'

'I think it best he stay in bed a little longer. The worst is over, but bouncing around in a carriage may be detrimental.'

It sounded logical and, with a selfish pang of pleasure, Catherine realised it also meant she would have Thomas and Valbourg to herself for a few hours.

* * *

Her son appeared shortly thereafter, dressed for the day in clothes that looked worn and too small for him. Catherine's temper flared. Was this the best the Haileys could do?

'Good morning, Thomas. Did you sleep well?'

'Yes, though I woke up very early,' he told her. 'I heard people talking in the street, and when I looked out, I saw a lady selling flowers from a basket and a man selling fish from a satchel. And a young boy with a monkey on his shoulder!'

Catherine smiled, remembering her early days in London. 'There are many wonderful things to see and do in London. Lord Valbourg and I thought you might like to go to the park this morning and see the ducks.'

'Ducks!' His eyes widened in delight. 'Will I be able to feed them?'

'Of course. I have already asked Cook for a bag of dry bread to take with us.'

'And I shall see about getting you some of Sebastian's clothes,' Valbourg said, obviously having noticed and possibly sharing Catherine's concerns about the boy's attire. 'I guarantee they will fit better than what you have on.'

They set off in Valbourg's carriage a little later. Thomas was quiet to begin with, but it wasn't long before he was chattering away; asking questions about something he saw or someone who passed.

'Are you always this inquisitive?' Valbourg asked as he turned the horses into the park.

'Yes. Aunt Eliza says I ask far too many questions, but Reverend Hailey says it's all right because I have so much to learn,' Thomas replied with a straight face. 'But even he gets cross with me sometimes and then I stop asking. You don't mind me asking questions, do you, Miss Jones?'

'Not at all. How else are you to learn?'

'I tried telling Aunt Eliza that, but it didn't make any difference.'

'Are you happy living where you do, Thomas?' Valbourg asked.

Catherine shot him a warning look, but Thomas seemed not to mind. 'Yes. Sometimes I wish I could go out and play more, but Reverend Hailey says I must read my Bible and help around the house.'

'He puts you to work?' Catherine said, aghast.

'They don't give me the very hard work to do. But I feed the chickens and collect the eggs and carry Bibles for Reverend Hailey when he goes visiting.'

'When do you play?'

'I don't, very much, but Megan reads to me every night and helps me with my lessons.'

'So you like Megan,' Valbourg said.

'Oh, yes! She told me I must think of her as my sister, even though Aunt Eliza tells me she is not.'

This was followed by a recitation of Megan's good qualities, during which Catherine's spirits fell lower and lower. It seemed that while removing Thomas from the Haileys' influence was one problem, taking him away from Megan was going to be quite another.

'Lord Val, why didn't Sebastian come with us this morning?' Thomas asked.

Catherine's eyebrows rose as she glanced at Valbourg. '"Lord Val"?'

'It's what my nephew calls me,' Valbourg explained. 'Sebastian wasn't feeling very well, Thomas, so I told him to stay in bed. I suspect he will be up and around by this evening.'

'I hope so. I like Sebastian,' Thomas said. 'He doesn't make fun of me the way the other boys do.'

'Why do the other boys make fun of you?'

'Because I'm small.'

'You're not small. You're perfect,' Catherine said. 'I wouldn't change anything about you.'

Thomas's eyes shone. 'I like you, too, Miss Jones. You're beautiful.'

Valbourg chuckled. 'Out of the mouths of babes. But he's right.' He turned to meet her eyes. 'You *are* beautiful.'

They drove around the park with Thomas asking questions about every bird, every high-stepping horse and every elegant carriage he saw. Catherine simply enjoyed being with him and having the opportunity to get to know her son after an absence of so many years. She wasn't sure how Valbourg felt, but judging from his numerous smiles and endlessly patient replies, he didn't find the boy too much of a nuisance. She wondered how many other single gentlemen of his position would be so tolerant.

At last, they drove out of the park, but to Catherine's surprise, their destination was not Valbourg's town house, but Theo and Tandy Templeton's.

'Why are we stopping here?' Catherine asked as he drew the horses to a halt.

'I would have thought it obvious.' Valbourg climbed out and then lifted Thomas down. 'You'll want to introduce Thomas to Theo and Tandy.'

'But they don't know about him,' she whispered.

'Exactly, but they will soon and it will be a lot better if they hear the truth from you. Don't worry,' Valbourg said, leaning in close as she stepped down. 'It won't be as difficult as you think.'

'This is a very big house,' Thomas said, slipping his hand into Catherine's as they waited for the front door to open. 'Does the King live here?'

In spite of her nervousness, Catherine laughed. 'No, the King has an even bigger house. But two very dear friends of mine live here and I want you to meet them.'

'They're actors, like your...like Miss Jones,' Valbourg said, winking as Catherine glared at him. 'And they always have big bowls of sweets. If you're a good boy and ask very nicely, they might give you one.'

'Then I shall be very good,' Thomas whispered as the door swung open and the Templetons' butler stood on the threshold. 'Because I like sweets above all!'

It didn't take Theo or Tandy long to figure out the nature of the relationship between Thomas and Catherine. They knew it as soon as they set eyes on him. Catherine not being able to take her eyes from him was also somewhat revealing.

'So, this is your first visit to London, Thomas,' Theo said, bending down so that he was eye level with the boy. 'What do you think of it?'

'I think it's very nice, sir. I saw a lot of carriages in the park and some very nice horses, too. Lord Val said he would let me ride one of his.'

'Did he indeed? Well, that is a rare treat,' Theo said, straightening. 'Now, I do believe Mrs Carson is baking apple tarts this afternoon. Why don't you run down to the kitchen and see if she will give you one hot out of the oven?'

Thomas's eyes grew round as saucers. 'She wouldn't tell me to take myself off?'

'She most certainly would not. And don't forget to ask her for a nice big dollop of cream to go with it.'

'I've never had cream,' Thomas whispered, as though saying it out loud might lessen the chances of it happening. 'Only Reverend Hailey was allowed cream.'

'Well, in this house, everyone eats apple tart with cream,' Theo said.

'Come along, Thomas,' Tandy said, holding out her hand to the boy. 'I shall take you down to the kitchen and see what we can find. I'm rather partial to Cook's apple tarts myself.'

Thomas went without hesitation, engaging Tandy in a lively conversation about frogs.

'What a delightful boy,' Theo said. 'Perhaps you would like to tell me about him, Catherine? And don't bother making up any stories. If that's not your son, I'll be a monkey's uncle!'

Given no opportunity to lie—and really having no wish to—Catherine said, 'Thomas is my son, Mr Templeton. I'm sorry I didn't tell you the truth before, but I didn't want anyone knowing about him. I thought it would just complicate matters.'

'Perhaps, though I venture to say that bringing him to London now you've made a name for yourself is going to complicate matters even more,' Theo said. 'But never mind that. How did it all come to pass?'

Catherine risked a quick glance in Valbourg's

direction, but other than giving her a nod of encouragement, he remained silent. It was her story to tell and they both knew it. So she did, not leaving out any of the details.

At the end, Theo sat back in amazement. 'Well, that's quite a story. But I find it hard to believe that no one in Grafton ever noticed or commented on the fact that Thomas is your son. The resemblance between you is undeniable.'

'Reverend Hailey made sure no one ever saw us together,' Catherine explained. 'Whenever I went to see Thomas I had to stay in the house or the garden with him. I wasn't allowed to go into the village, and since I left Grafton before anyone knew I was carrying Will's child, no one thought to connect him with me.'

'And no one questioned your visits?'

'Again, not many people saw me coming or going. I went to the manse after dark and usually left Grafton early in the morning. I was only allowed to stay part of one day.'

'Shocking!' Theo snapped, getting to his feet. 'To think a clergyman would behave in such a shoddy fashion. He should be thrown out of the church. What about your father? Have you reconciled with him?'

Regretfully, Catherine shook her head. 'I have sent him letters, but he hasn't answered any of them. I know he is still alive because Gwendolyn…Miss Marsh…occasionally visits him, but he hasn't expressed any desire to see me.'

'Then that is his loss,' Theo said kindly. 'Your father deserted you when you needed him most and he will come to regret that one day. However, we must deal with the situation as it now stands. Do you intend to keep Thomas with you and eventually tell him you're his mother, or will he be returning to the country?'

'I would very much like to keep him and to tell him, when the time's right, that he is my son. But I suspect Reverend Hailey will try to get him back, either by coming here himself or by sending someone else to do it.'

'"Someone else"?'

'The good vicar has been paying men to spy on Catherine since her arrival in London,' Valbourg said, crossing the room to stand beside her. 'They were hired to keep watch on everything she did and to send reports back to Hailey.'

'Abominable!' Theo burst out. 'Dear God, if I ever get my hands on him—!'

'I'm sure God will demand an explanation at the appropriate time,' Catherine murmured, 'but Reverend Hailey is not my only problem. Apparently his wife has formed a very strong attachment to Thomas and is unwilling to let him go.'

'Has she no children of her own?'

'No. Though married seven years, she has not yet given him a child.'

'Ah, so it goes deeper than mere anger,' Theo murmured. 'In all likelihood she is barren and sees Thomas as her only chance of having a son. I take it they don't know where he is at the moment?'

'No, but they will find out soon enough,' Valbourg said, and went on to give Theo a brief summation of the activities of the past few days. Tandy, who came back in time to catch the end of the story, was horrified.

'They sent that poor little boy away to school simply to prevent you from seeing him? That's outrageous!'

'Indeed, and all the more reason why Catherine needs to establish herself as his mother and put an end to this charade once and for all,' Valbourg said.

'Do you think they will try to take him away?' Tandy asked.

'Yes, which is why we must be on our guard at all times,' Valbourg said. 'It is the reason I have suggested Thomas stay with me for the time being. Or better yet, with my father.'

'The marquess knows about this?' Theo asked in astonishment.

'No, but he soon will and I need him to hear the truth about what's going on from me before the rumours start landing on his doorstep.'

'And what rumours might those be?' Tandy enquired.

'Rumours that I have been keeping company with Catherine and a young boy who is clearly her son. People may wonder at the nature of the relationship.'

'I guarantee they'll wonder at it,' Theo said. 'Some may even ask if he is *your* child, Valbourg, and suspect you and Catherine of having a long-standing affair.'

'One that goes back five years?'

'It is not beyond the realm of possibility. Many men have had long-standing relationships with their mistresses. The Duke of Bolton lived with Lavinia Fenton for twenty-three years before his real wife died and he was able to make Lavinia his duchess.'

Catherine blanched. She hadn't given any thought to the possibility that people might think Valbourg was Thomas's father, but Theo was right. It wasn't outside the realm of possibility and she could tell from the expression on Richard's face that he realised it, too.

'I can't help what society thinks,' he said. 'I can only tell them what Catherine wants them to know.'

'Then I put the question to you, Catherine,' Tandy said. 'What are you going to tell people when they ask you about Thomas? Because they will ask and you need to be ready with an answer. Otherwise they will make up their own and that could have disastrous repercussions for both of you.'

There was no need for further explanations. If word of Valbourg's association with an actress, and the possibility that he had fathered her child, should reach the ears of his family, his guardianship of Sebastian would most definitely be in jeopardy.

'I intend to make it very clear that Lord Valbourg is not my lover,' Catherine said, hard-pressed to believe she was saying such a thing in mixed company. 'He has been kindness itself, but I will *not* see him lose Sebastian as a result of his friendship with me.'

'And what of your own future, my dear?' Tandy said. 'How will you feel about everyone knowing you have a child? Your reputation will suffer.'

'I know, but the reason I came to London five years ago was to establish a career for myself and to make enough money to support my son,' Catherine said. 'Thanks to you and Theo, that is precisely what I have done. Now I have my son back and all I want is to be able to live with him and know we won't be separated again. I'll do whatever it takes to make that happen. No one is going to take Thomas away from me again,' Catherine whispered fiercely. 'No one!'

Chapter Nine

The rumours began to fly even sooner than Valbourg expected. Though he and Catherine had driven around the park well before the fashionable hour, it had been long enough for several people to see them together, and with a child that could only have belonged to Miss Jones.

His brother, Hugh, was the first to acquaint him with the details.

'Oh, yes, it's definitely making the rounds,' Hugh said as he and Valbourg mingled with the crowds at Lady Upton's musicale later that evening. 'And it's creating quite a stir. Not only is the lovely Miss Jones *not* the virginal angel we have all been led to believe, she is the mother of a cherubic little boy. And you were the one seen squiring her around the first time she chose to show him off.'

'I took her and the boy for a drive in the park,'

Valbourg said. 'I have done the same with several other young ladies, minus the child of course.'

'Ah, but Miss Jones is not like the other young ladies, is she?' Hugh said. 'She is an actress. And given the sudden appearance of a child, an actress with considerably lower morals than any of us thought.'

'I'll thank you to keep a civil tongue in your head,' Valbourg warned, not in the mood to entertain slights about Catherine. 'You don't know the circumstances.'

'I don't need to. She is an unmarried woman with a child, and if you know what's good for you, you'll stay away from her,' Hugh advised. 'You don't want the wrong kind of story reaching Father's ears and, trust me, he will find out. Better you tell him the truth before he hears it from someone else.'

It seemed Hugh was not the only one who felt that way. Upon arriving at his father's for dinner a few evenings later, Valbourg was confronted by his sister Dorothy, who had also heard the rumours and was not at all pleased. 'Is it true, Valbourg?' she fired at him. 'Are you keeping company with that actress?'

'I am not keeping company with anyone,' Valbourg said with as much patience as he could. 'I took Miss Jones for a drive in the park.'

'What about the boy? They say he is her son.'

'He is and, other than the fact that his father is dead, I know nothing about him.'

'Poor little fellow,' Mary murmured. 'Where has he been living?'

'With his grandparents.'

'Never mind that. What of this dead father?' Dorothy said, refusing to let it go. 'Was he really her husband or is the child a bastard?'

'Dorothy!' Mary gasped.

'Such language is hardly appropriate for the dinner table, Dorothy,' her father chastised.

'I apologise, Papa, but really, we are all adults here and it is better the truth be known. I think he must be illegitimate,' Dorothy said, answering her own question. 'Otherwise why would Miss Jones not have kept him with her all these years? There's never been so much as a whisper about a child. Is she so ashamed of him that she felt compelled to bury him in the country?'

'If that were the case, why bring him to London now?' Mary asked. 'No one knew she had a child and no one needed to.'

'I'm sure she had her reasons,' Valbourg said. 'And since speculation is all you have to go on, I suggest you leave the matter alone.'

'But it is interesting, wouldn't you agree, Valbourg?' Hugh threw in. 'The virgin angel not a virgin at all and quite obviously, not an angel.'

'That's enough, Hugh,' Alderbury snapped.

'I'll not have talk like that when your sisters are present.'

'You needn't avoid it for my sake, Papa,' Dorothy said. 'I think the whole thing is disgraceful! And *you* should know better than to be seen with her, Valbourg. What will people think?'

'Frankly, I don't care.'

'You should. If your name becomes associated with hers, the ensuing scandal would be disastrous. I hate to think Sebastian might hear about it.'

'Sebastian won't hear about it unless someone in my family decides to tell him,' Valbourg said in a tight voice. 'I trust that will not happen.'

Dorothy's nostrils flared. 'I hope you are not referring to me?'

'Don't look at me,' Hugh said, holding up his hands. 'I have absolutely no intention of getting involved in this.'

'No one will say anything because there is nothing to say,' Lord Alderbury barked. 'I will not permit scandal to tarnish the good name of this family, Richard. If you are doing anything inappropriate with this woman—'

'I've already said I am not.'

'Good, then I suggest you not be seen in her company again. As for the rest of you, I want to hear no more about it. Do I make myself clear?'

'As a bell,' Hugh replied.

'Yes, Papa,' Mary said dutifully.

Dorothy looked mumpish, but grudgingly nodded. 'As long as Valbourg does as he's told—'

'Dorothy!'

'Oh, very well. But do not think we are the only ones talking about this, Papa,' Dorothy said. 'Valbourg has set a good example thus far, but it only takes a moment's foolishness to change that. And we must keep Sebastian's welfare in mind.'

'No one is more concerned with Sebastian's welfare than I am,' Valbourg said. 'But I will not be told by you or anyone else who I may or may not keep company with.' He abruptly stood up. 'I will see you in the morning, Father. There are matters I wish to discuss with you in private. Good evening.'

It was an abrupt departure, but Valbourg had taken all he could for one night. Dorothy's snobbery and accusations were getting under his skin. The fact that what she said was partially true did little to assuage his anger. He wanted to be with Catherine. He had been away from her for only a few hours, but he already missed her fiercely. He wanted to hold her in his arms and assure her that everything was going to be all right...even if he had no idea if it was.

More than that he dared not do. To do so would put his guardianship of Sebastian at risk and he was very aware that as the days passed, his need to be with Catherine would only grow stronger. At some point, the price for the pleasure of her company was going to become too high and he would be forced to make a choice.

For his own sake, he sincerely hoped that day was a long, long way off.

It was on their fourth day together in London that Catherine decided to tell Thomas the truth about his parentage. It wasn't so much she felt he was ready to hear the truth as it was that the story was quickly making its own way around town. She knew that if she didn't broach the subject with him soon, someone else might. With that in mind she waited until the two of them were standing by the pond, throwing bread to the ducks, before bringing the topic up. Thomas loved feeding the ducks, and Lily, who had taken to joining them for their afternoon strolls, made sure he always had a full bag of dried bread to throw to them. As Catherine watched him, she marvelled that this precious golden-haired child really was hers and that, after five long years, he was finally back in her life.

'Thomas,' she called when at last his bag was empty. 'Come here and sit by me for a minute,' she said, settling on to a vacant bench. 'There's something we need to talk about.'

It was obvious that obedience had been drilled into the boy. He turned at once and made his way back to her side. 'Yes, Miss Jones?'

'Are you enjoying being here in London with me?'

'Very much, miss. I didn't think I would, but I like coming to the park and spending time with Lord Val and Sebastian. I will have so much to tell Megan when I get home.' He looked up at her. 'When am I going home?'

Catherine caught her bottom lip between her teeth. 'That's what I want to talk to you about. You know I've been coming to see you for the past five years. And I hope you know that I like you very much.'

'I like you, too. You never tell me to be quiet or say that I talk too much. And you always answer my questions. I think sometimes Reverend Hailey wishes I would not ask so many.'

Catherine smiled, charmed by the boy's innocence. 'I'm sure that's not the case. But I am glad you like me because that's what I want to talk to you about.' She stopped and glanced towards the pond, praying she was doing the right thing. 'Has anyone ever talked to you about…your parents?'

Thomas shook his head. 'No. I did ask Reverend Hailey about it once, but he got very angry and told me I wasn't to talk about such things.'

'But you would like to know.'

'Yes. When I see other children with their parents, I would like to know who mine were—' He broke off and looked down at his new shoes. 'Some of them point at me and call me names. I didn't know what they meant, so I asked Reverend Hailey. He told me never to say that word again. He said my real parents were dead.'

The pain went deep, causing Catherine to flinch. 'Reverend Hailey didn't tell you the truth, Thomas. Not all of it.'

'But he's a clergyman. He says people must always tell the truth or God won't love them.'

'Sometimes people don't tell the truth because they think it will spare someone else's feelings. Sometimes, the truth hurts.'

'Did Reverend Hailey lie?'

Catherine stared out across the water, envying the ducks their peaceful existence. 'I know he thought he was doing the right thing, but now that you're here with me, it's time you knew the truth. You see, the reason I have been coming to see you all these years isn't just because I am a good friend of the family. The truth is—'

'Lord Val!' Thomas burst out. 'Look, Miss Jones, Lord Val is here.'

Before Catherine could finish, Thomas slipped off the bench and ran towards the man who had already become something of a hero to him. Not sure whether to be relieved or disappointed that the moment of truth had been postponed, Catherine sighed and stood up. 'Lord Valbourg, what a pleasant surprise.'

'I was on my way to my father's house and thought I would stop by to see if Thomas was feeding the ducks,' Valbourg said, swinging down from his magnificent black horse. 'I vow they are growing so fat they won't be able to float.'

'Should I stop feeding them?' Thomas asked, his brows drawing together in concern. 'I wouldn't want them to sink.'

'I shouldn't worry about it,' Valbourg said, clearly a little guilty the boy had taken his words to heart. 'They do spend most of their day swimming, after all.'

'Thomas, why don't you run along to Lily now?' Catherine said. 'I shall be there directly.'

'Yes, all right. Goodbye, Lord Val.'

'I'll see you again soon, Thomas,' Valbourg promised. He waited until the boy was far enough away before saying, 'Forgive my intrusion, but I had to see you this morning.'

'Is something wrong?'

'I've had a letter from Reverend Hailey.'

Catherine felt her stomach clench. 'He wrote to you?'

'It appears the headmaster at Glendale sent his letter to Eliza and that she was not pleased to receive it. Her husband has informed me that he is shocked by my behaviour, that I had no right to involve myself in the matter and that he expects the boy to be returned to him at once or he will take legal action.'

A sickening dread crept over Catherine, making her feel a little light-headed.

'Are you all right?' Valbourg asked, concerned by her sudden pallor. 'Would you like to sit down?'

'No, I'm fine.' She took a few deep breaths and tried to tell herself it was going to be all right. 'I was about to tell Thomas I was his mother.'

'Ah. Bad timing on my part.'

'That's all right. I'm not sure I was ready for it,' she admitted. 'But I will have to tell him soon because I am *not* sending him back.'

'I'm sure Hailey knows that, too, which is why I want you and Thomas to come with me this morning and talk to my father.'

'Your father! Oh, no, Richard, I can't!'

'You must. There may come a time when you need his help.'

'But surely there are other options.'

'None as secure as having Thomas living with the Marquess of Alderbury.'

'But…have you even broached the subject with him?'

'He knows you have a child and that you and I have been seen together.'

'And?'

'And he cautioned me against doing anything that might create a scandal.'

Catherine felt her hopes deflate. 'So he advised you to stay away from me.'

Valbourg reached for her hand and gently squeezed it. 'I want you to meet him, Catherine. It is important we all know one another and it might well make the difference in Thomas's safety.'

That, more than anything, convinced Catherine of the wisdom of talking to Valbourg's father. It didn't lessen her feelings of anxiety, but she had to believe Valbourg knew what he was doing and that he had the best interests of everyone at heart.

She simply couldn't afford to believe anything else.

They were shown into the marquess's private study; a large room filled with books, solid masculine furnishings and elaborate paintings of horses and hunting scenes. His father was not there, but Valbourg used the time to acquaint Thomas with a large globe that stood on a pedestal in one corner of the room, and to do what he could to set Catherine's mind at rest.

In truth, he had no idea what his father was going to say about this highly unusual meeting. All he knew was that it was necessary. He fully expected Hailey to try to take Thomas back and he had resolved to give the boy as much protection as he could. The fact that spending time with Thomas meant he was also able to spend time with Catherine was an added bonus.

'Has your father read all these books, Lord Val?' Thomas enquired, gazing wide-eyed at the selection of leather-bound volumes.

'A good many of them. Most have been collected by past generations and a few are quite rare. But my father loves to read, and from the time I was your age, I was encouraged to do the same.'

'Reverend Hailey says I should only read the Bible,' Thomas said. 'Though I think he sometimes reads books about history.'

'One can learn a great deal from history,' Catherine said, looking almost as impressed by the shelves of books as her son. 'I have always been interested in the ancient Roman society. They were a highly advanced civilisation.'

'Apart from their questionable morals,' Valbourg said in a low voice. He saw a delightful blush rise in Catherine's cheeks and marvelled that a woman who had given birth to a child and spent so much of her life on the stage could still be embarrassed by the mention of such things. There was so much about her he still had to discover—

'Valbourg? What's this all about?'

His father's gruff voice had Thomas scurrying back to Catherine, who suddenly looked like a doe caught in the hunter's sights. Valbourg stood his ground. 'Good morning, Father. I told you last night I wished to see you about a private matter, and since it concerns Miss Jones and her son, I thought I would bring them both here to meet you.'

'Did you indeed!' Alderbury's mouth hardened

as he moved to stand behind his desk. 'You assume a great deal.'

'Perhaps, but I hope when I explain the situation, you will understand why.' He smiled at Catherine, indicating that she should come forward. 'I'm sure you remember Miss Jones?'

Alderbury stiffly inclined his head. 'I do.'

Catherine performed a graceful curtsy. 'Lord Alderbury.'

'And this is Thomas,' Valbourg continued, unconcerned by his father's lack of enthusiasm. 'He is five and has a prodigious thirst for knowledge.'

To Valbourg's surprise, Thomas walked up to his father and smiled. 'Good morning, sir.'

Alderbury's eyebrows rose. 'What's that on your fingers, boy?'

Thomas gazed down at his hands. 'Breadcrumbs. I was feeding the ducks.'

'Mind you don't touch anything, then.'

'I won't, sir. Though there might be some on the book I was just looking at.'

'Eh? What book is that?'

'That one. About horses.'

'Indeed? Like horses, do you?'

'I think they're splendid. Lord Val said he is going to let me ride one of his, but he hasn't said when.'

'We will have to check with your...with Miss Jones first,' Valbourg said, catching himself. 'I wouldn't want to get in the way of her schedule.'

'I'm sure whatever date works for you will be fine, my lord,' Catherine said, unusually meek.

Valbourg heard his father grunt and watched him cross the room to tug the bell pull. Moments later, a servant appeared. 'Take Miss Jones and Master Thomas to the kitchen and have Cook give them some refreshments,' Alderbury said. 'Perhaps some chocolate for the boy.'

'Chocolate?' Thomas gazed at the marquess with an expression close to worship. 'I've never had chocolate before.'

'Then it's high time you did,' Alderbury said. He nodded at the servant, who quickly came forward and escorted the little boy out. Catherine, after a worried glance in Valbourg's direction, followed, leaving father and son alone.

'What on earth do you think you're doing, Richard?' his father demanded. 'It is bad enough you have been seen keeping company with an actress and her bastard child. Did you have to make matters worse by bringing them here?'

Valbourg wasn't surprised by his father's outburst, nor that he had called Thomas a bastard. Alderbury might be many things, but a fool wasn't one of them. 'I brought them here because they may be in need of your help. Catherine believes—'

'*Catherine?*' his father snapped. 'When did you and the lady become so intimately acquainted?'

'We are not, but neither is our friendship one

that demands a rigid degree of formality,' Valbourg replied calmly. 'Now, if you will allow me to go on…?'

Alderbury grunted again. 'Very well, but be quick about it.'

'The boy and his mother were separated at birth. Thomas has been living with his paternal grandfather and his new wife in the country while Catherine has been here in London making a career for herself. She did so in order to make a life for her and her son, and now that they are together again, Catherine is hopeful of keeping Thomas with her. However, I have reason to believe the boy's grandfather may try to take him away from her.'

'Why? If she *is* the boy's mother—'

'She is, but the boy isn't aware of it.' With that, Valbourg gave his father a brief summation of the situation and his concerns regarding Thomas's safety.

'You're not seriously suggesting the boy stay here with me?' Alderbury said at the conclusion of the tale.

'Only until he has been made aware of the fact that Catherine is his mother and that, if necessary, the proper officials have been alerted.'

'You take a great deal upon yourself, Richard,' Alderbury said. 'You assured me there was nothing going on between you and Miss Jones.'

'There is not, other than a sincere admiration

for what she has been able to accomplish and a genuine respect for the lady herself. Yes, she made a mistake, but she has done everything since that time to prove herself worthy of being Thomas's mother. She has refused countless offers from men wishing to set her up as their mistress and has saved enough money to provide a decent lifestyle for herself and her son.'

'And what of your affection for her?' Alderbury enquired. 'And don't try to tell me you have none. I'm not blind. I saw the way you looked at her.'

Valbourg inclined his head, but took his time answering. 'Whatever I feel for Catherine has no bearing on this conversation. I am well aware of the differences between us and of what I stand to lose were I to involve her in my life. In *any* capacity.'

Again, his father grunted. 'Thank you for being honest with me. I would not be pleased to know you were contemplating any kind of association with Miss Jones, Richard. She is a beautiful woman and I agree she is both talented and refined, but you are my son and must bear the responsibilities of being my heir. She could never be a suitable wife for you nor an acceptable mother to your children. However, I can sympathise with her plight. A child should be with his mother. The Haileys have no right to try to take the boy back or to keep him against his will. So, until the situation is resolved, I will allow him to stay here, provided I am not expected to entertain him or his mother when she calls.'

It was more than Valbourg had expected. 'You will allow Catherine to visit him?'

'Damn it, Richard, I'm not heartless. Miss Jones has obviously gone to a great deal of trouble to get her son back; I cannot imagine she would be pleased at not being able to see him now. Yes, she may visit, but I have a condition of my own to make.'

'Name it.'

'You are to announce your engagement by Christmas.'

'My *engagement*? To whom?'

'Whomever you choose within our social circle. It is time you were married. Past time, in fact. I find I agree with Dorothy in this matter,' Alderbury said. 'You are over thirty and raising a young boy as though he were your own. You need a wife and Sebastian needs a mother.'

'We are doing fine as we are.'

'In your eyes, perhaps, but not in mine. The condition stands. Miss Jones's son may stay here and she may come to visit him as often as she likes. But *you* must make a concerted effort to find a wife by Christmas. I know of several who would be only too happy to receive your proposal.'

But none of them was Catherine, Valbourg reflected. And in that moment, with his father's ultimatum hanging over his head, the knowledge that he was in love with Catherine hit him with blinding and irrefutable force. The feeling had crept up on him, happening almost without his knowledge until now he could think of nothing else.

He was in love with her. He felt it every moment they were together. He woke up thinking about her. Went to sleep with her name on his lips. He lived for the hours they could be together and merely existed during the times they were apart. His desire to have Thomas staying at his house or his father's was merely a way of assuring her constant proximity. Of course he had the boy's welfare at heart, but it was Catherine's company he truly craved. He would have done *anything* to secure that.

But now, in order to guarantee her son's safety, he had to make a promise to forget her. To find another woman with whom to spend his life, even though he knew there would never be another for whom he felt this kind of deep and abiding love. He was caught between two evils: doing what was right for his family, or flying in the face of their disapproval and doing what was right for him.

Valbourg closed his eyes and felt resignation seep into his soul. 'Very well, I shall present my choice to you before Christmas. In return, you will keep Thomas safe until we can be certain that Catherine is in a position to do so.'

'Agreed.' Alderbury held out his hand. 'You're doing the right thing, Val. There really wasn't any other choice.'

After a moment's hesitation, Valbourg took his father's hand, shook it once and let it go. 'There is always a choice, Father. I would simply have preferred you not to be the one to force me into making this one.'

Thomas settled into Alderbury House surprisingly well and soon became a favourite with the entire household. Cook took to making treats for him; sweet pastries and puddings unlike any the boy had ever tasted, and the maids took turn playing games with him in between cleaning the rooms.

Sebastian, of course, was his constant companion and even Lord Alderbury seemed to enjoy having him in the house. On one occasion, Catherine arrived to find her son sitting at the piano in the music room while Alderbury sat in a chair close by. It was not the marquess's presence that caused Catherine to stare at the scene in amazement, but her son's unexpected and undeniable talent. It was a simple étude, yet Thomas played it without a single mistake.

She waited until the piece came to an end before walking into the room. 'Well done, Thomas.

I had no idea you could play the piano so well. Has someone been teaching you?'

The little boy shook his head. 'No. Sometimes I played Aunt Eliza's pianoforte, but only when Reverend Hailey wasn't around.'

'The boy's gifted,' Alderbury said bluntly. 'There's no other explanation for it. He must take after you—'

'Shall we go and see if there are any Eccles cakes, Thomas?' Catherine said quickly. It was the first time Alderbury had offered her more than a grunt, but intimating that Thomas had inherited *any* kind of trait or talent from her was bound to be confusing for the boy. 'I remember Betsy saying Cook was going to bake some this morning.'

'Oh, yes, please. I love Eccles cakes!' Thomas said, scrambling down from the bench. 'Not as much as I love chocolate, but almost.'

'Why don't you run along to the kitchen, Thomas?' Alderbury said. 'You know the way. Your…that is, Miss Jones will be along in a moment.'

'All right,' Thomas said and ran out of the room. 'But don't be long, Miss Jones!'

'I won't,' Catherine said, then turned back to find Valbourg's father watching her. 'You wish to speak to me, my lord?'

'I do.' He put his hands behind his back and rocked back and forth on his heels. 'When are you going to tell him the truth about your relationship?'

Surprised a man like Alderbury would care, Catherine crossed her arms over her chest. 'Soon. I've been waiting for the right moment.'

'There isn't going to *be* a right moment. Do it now, before someone says something accidentally, the way I almost did,' Alderbury said. 'It will come as a shock, but it's better he hear it from you. He must be wondering why you're not taking him back to the country.'

In fact, Thomas had asked her that question again last night after she had read him a story and kissed him goodnight. It caught her off guard because it had been a few days since he had mentioned the Haileys or going home. She knew he missed Megan because it was she rather than Reverend Hailey or Eliza whom he talked about, but Catherine also knew it was wishful thinking to expect him to forget they existed. As much as the bond between them was growing stronger, Thomas still clung to what he knew best.

'You're right. Thomas does need to know,' Catherine said. 'I've just been afraid of how he might react.'

'Miss Jones, I don't know a great deal about you, but one thing I have been able to glean from my son's recounting is that you are a brave and resourceful young woman,' Alderbury said. 'You can do this and you *must* do it. For your sake and

the boy's. Now off you go and get some chocolate,' he said grudgingly. 'It would do you good
to put some weight on.'

Catherine left the room with a smile on her
lips. It was the closest Valbourg's father had ever
come to saying he liked her.

Catherine had planned on taking Thomas to
the park to feed the ducks, but when the clouds
rolled in and a steady rain began to fall, she decided to take him back to Green Street and there,
in the quiet surroundings of her home, to tell him
the truth about his birth. She knew he felt at ease
in her company now. He laughed more than he
had in the past and was constantly looking to her
for guidance. Catherine hoped the news they were
related would make him as happy as it did her.

Mrs Rankin was delighted to see him, of
course. She vowed he had grown an inch since he
had last been in the house, which made Thomas
giggle and ask to be measured. She dutifully
stood him against the wall and performed the
task, and though the forecasted inch didn't mate-
rialise, she did assure him that he was definitely
an eighth of an inch taller than he had been two
days earlier.

The three of them had passed a delightful afternoon. Mrs Rankin had played games with him
while Catherine made a list of everything that

needed to be done. Then, as soon as dinner was out of the way, she took him into the drawing room and sat him down beside her on the dark-green chesterfield. 'Thomas, there's something I need to tell you,' she began. 'Something I've wanted to tell you for a long time.'

Thomas looked up at her and smiled. 'Is it something good?'

'I think so, but you must tell me how you feel about it, too. It has to do with your real mother and father.'

His eyes went wide. 'Do you know who they are?'

'Yes. Sadly, your father died before you were born, but you do have a mother and I am very, very happy to tell you that, contrary to what Reverend Hailey has led you to believe, she is alive and well.' Catherine stopped and took a deep breath, praying she was doing the right thing. 'What would you say if I told you...I was your mother?'

She thought for a moment her heart might explode. Thomas looked at her, his mouth forming a silent 'O', his blue eyes opening wide. '*You're* my mother?'

'Yes.'

'Truly?'

'Truly.'

'But...why didn't you tell me?'

'Because your aunt thought it would be less

confusing for you to think of me as a friend,' Catherine said, knowing the lie had nothing to do with Thomas and everything to do with Eliza. 'And she thought you might wish to stay with me rather than them and they didn't want that to happen.'

'But you're my mother,' Thomas said, his forehead furrowing. 'I *would* rather have been with you.'

There was nothing he could have said that would have made Catherine happier. 'And I wanted you with me so very much, my darling boy. It was very hard seeing you only twice a year, but that was all I was allowed.'

'Why do I live with Reverend Hailey and Aunt Eliza?' Thomas asked. 'Didn't you want me?'

'Of course I wanted you, but when you were born, Reverend Hailey thought I wasn't able to look after you, so he said he would take care of you until I could. But we're together now and I don't want us ever to be apart again. But you must tell me if that's what you want, too.'

'I do, very much,' Thomas said. 'But won't Reverend Hailey and Aunt Eliza be angry?'

'I suspect so. They love you and won't be happy at the thought of you coming to live with me,' Catherine said, not wishing to turn the boy against them. 'But I am your mother and they knew that all along.'

'What about Megan? Will I ever see her again?'

'Of course you will, though perhaps not right away. We'll need to let Reverend Hailey and your aunt come to terms with what's happened and that may take a little while. But I'll make sure you don't lose touch with Megan. She can come here and stay with us,' Catherine said. 'Do you think she would like that?'

'More than anything!' Thomas said, brightening.

'Then she shall. She could go to the park and feed the ducks with you.'

'I think she would rather go to the shops.'

'Then we shall visit the shops and then go to the park,' Catherine said, suddenly feeling as though anything were possible. 'Whatever makes you happy, dearest.'

Thomas sat quietly for a moment, chewing on his bottom lip. Then, looking up at her, he said, 'You said my father died. Do you know who he was and what happened to him?'

The question was inevitable and Catherine felt it only fair that she be as honest with Thomas as possible. 'Your father was Megan's brother, Will. He died before you were born. He went out riding one day and took a bad fall from his horse.'

Thomas's brow furrowed. 'My father was Megan's brother?'

'Yes, which means Reverend Hailey is actually your grandfather.'

Thomas looked startled. 'But why doesn't

Rev…that is, Grandfather ever talk about him? Doesn't he miss him?'

'I'm sure he does, but I think it hurts him too much to talk about it,' Catherine said gently. 'The important thing is that *you* know I'm your mother and that I love you very much. And it would make me very happy if you said you would like to stay here in London with me.'

'I would like that, Miss…Mama,' Thomas said, shyly. 'But will you write to Megan and tell her why I'm not coming back?'

Catherine nodded, suddenly feeling tears well up in her eyes. 'I will do anything you want, my darling boy. Anything to make you happy.' She drew him into her arms and hugged him. 'I have waited five long years to make you mine again, and now that I have, no one is ever going to take you away from me again.'

Chapter Ten

A̲fter a long and eventful day, Catherine took Thomas back to Alderbury House, feeling happier than she had in years. The dreaded secret had been revealed and not only was Thomas accepting of her new role in his life, but he had also expressed himself delighted. She couldn't wait to tell Alderbury she had met his challenge!

Unfortunately, the marquess had gone out to an evening engagement, so Catherine took supper with Thomas in the nursery before taking him up to his bed and tucking him in. She started reading him a story and, though he proclaimed he wasn't at all sleepy, it didn't take long for him to fall asleep.

Catherine didn't mind. It had been an emotional day and she was looking forward to getting home and crawling into her own bed. But as the carriage made its way back to Green Street, it was not Thomas she found herself thinking about, but Valbourg, and how much closer they had become since their return to London. Though they had not been intimate and likely never would be, there was an ease between them now that hadn't been there before.

Perhaps her life really was changing for the better, Catherine mused. If she could keep Thomas with her and maintain her career on the stage, she would have everything she wanted.

Except Valbourg. He could never be a part of her life. No doubt he would eventually marry and start a family of his own with someone of whom his father approved. A mistress was not part of that scenario because Valbourg had to abide by society's—and his sister's—rules about what did and did not constitute a respectable family man's behaviour.

Still, Catherine resolved to content herself with whatever time she was able to spend with him and to ask for no more than that. She would devote herself to raising Thomas and to furthering her career. Those were the two most important considerations in her life.

The hackney drew to a halt in front of her house. Catherine stepped down and paid the driver, then pulled out her key. She was almost at her door when another carriage came around the corner and drew to a halt in front of the house next to hers. A moment later, the door opened and a middle-aged man got out, wearing a tweed jacket over light-coloured breeches tucked into polished brown boots. In his hand was a piece of parchment and on his face, an expression of frustration.

'Excuse me, I wonder if you could help me,' he said, walking towards her. 'I am new to London and looking for a gentleman who supposedly resides on this street.' He glanced at the parchment again. 'A Mr Howard. Do you know him?'

Catherine shook her head. 'I'm sorry. I do not. Have you no house number?'

'I'm not sure. A friend gave me the directions before I left Brighton, but I'm having trouble reading them.' He smiled ruefully and stepped a little closer. 'I must have left my spectacles at home.' He held the parchment out to her. 'Can you see a house number written down anywhere?'

Catherine took a quick look and saw a lot of very small writing. 'I don't know.' She bent to have a closer look. 'Yes, there it is. Mr Howard at...I think it says number twenty-five, but the writing is very— *Wait!* What are you doing?'

The man, who seemed to have lost all interest in the paper, had grabbed her by the arm and was pushing her towards the carriage.

'Stop!' Catherine shouted. 'What do you think you're doing?'

'Taking you for a ride,' the man said, all trace of amiability gone.

'How dare you! Get away from me!'

'Oh, no, my virgin angel, I have no intention of going away. In fact, I plan on getting very close indeed.' With that, he gripped her around the waist and all but lifted her off her feet as he tried to shove her into the carriage.

Thankfully, Catherine remembered her training. She let herself go completely limp, and when he loosened his arms to get a better grip, she twisted around and lifted her knee straight into his groin.

The unexpected move had the desired effect. He dropped her at once and doubled over in pain. "You little bitch! I'll make you pay for that.'

'Not tonight you won't!' Catherine hissed, running for the door.

Thankfully, Mrs Rankin must have heard her shouts and was holding it open. 'Dear Lord, are you all right?'

'I'm fine.' Catherine shut the door and locked it behind her.

'What happened? I heard you shout—'

'We'll talk about it in the morning,' Catherine said, unsure if she was trembling as a result of anger or fear. 'Right now I need a brandy.'

'I'll bring one right up.' Mrs Rankin pushed her gently towards the stairs. 'You go up and get ready for bed. Are you sure you're not hurt?'

Catherine closed her eyes and took a long, deep breath. 'I'm fine.' But she wouldn't have been had she not been able to incapacitate her attacker. The man had clearly intended to push her into the carriage and then take her God knew where for only God knew what purpose. Although, judging from what he'd said, she had a pretty good idea what he'd had in mind.

Had this something to do with the wager Valbourg had warned her about? Her attacker had obviously planned an elaborate ruse to catch her off guard and had waited for the right moment to spring. But having done so and been foiled, he would no doubt be angry; doubly so because she had dealt him an injury. He wouldn't forget that any time soon and Catherine knew she would have to be on the lookout for him.

The stakes had just doubled. Like it or not, the safety and well-being of both her *and* her son were now at risk.

In the weeks that followed, Catherine existed in a constant state of anxiety. She had no idea if the man who'd accosted her would try again, but she was constantly on the lookout for late-night carriages or dark strangers lurking on her street. She also kept a close watch on Thomas, still fearful that Reverend Hailey or one of his men would appear at her door and try to take him away. She refused to believe Valbourg's assurances that the clergyman must have simply accepted what had happened and moved on.

'He was so adamant I wasn't going to have

Thomas,' Catherine said as she and Valbourg sat on the grass together under the shade of a large oak tree one sunny afternoon. 'I can't understand how he would let this go without any kind of retaliation.'

They had driven out to the country with a picnic hamper tucked in the back of the carriage. Catherine had suggested bringing the boys, but Valbourg asked that it be just the two of them because he needed to talk to her about a matter of considerable importance. He assured her his father would look after Thomas and Sebastian while they were gone.

Selfishly, perhaps, Catherine had agreed, welcoming the opportunity to spend a few hours alone with Valbourg. For whatever reason, he hadn't been able to spend much time with her of late and she missed him terribly. She had even dispensed with the formality of bringing Mrs Rankin along to act as chaperon. What was the point? As an unwed actress with a child, she had very little modesty left to protect.

'Perhaps Hailey has come to his senses and realised that Thomas belongs with you,' Valbourg said, biting into a crisp green apple. 'After all, you are his mother.'

'That didn't matter to him in the past. I'm sure you remember what he said about my morals and character.'

'People often say things in the heat of the moment, only to regret them later. Hailey probably didn't like you standing up to him and I expect he liked my doing so even less. But in the end, he must have realised there was nothing he could do.'

'I hope you're right,' Catherine said. 'It would be a relief to have one less thing to worry about.' The fact she was still a target for that unknown man was a different issue altogether, but one she had kept to herself. Valbourg clearly wasn't in a position to do anything about it. 'So, what did you want to talk to me about?'

Valbourg looked at her and then tossed the apple away. 'There's something I have to tell you, Catherine. Something I've been putting off, but that I can't any longer. It's not fair to either of us.'

He was deeply troubled. Catherine could see it in his expression. 'What's wrong?'

He reached for her hand and held it tightly. 'You know I care about you and that I care *for* you. I would do anything I could to avoid hurting you.'

'I know that. You have been nothing but kind and honest with me since the night we met.'

He raised her hand to his lips and kissed it, his smile holding more than a trace of sadness.

'I have been…asked to do something I would avoid if I could, but that in all honesty I cannot.' He gazed down at their intertwined fingers, then up into her eyes. 'My father is insisting that

I marry. I am to announce my engagement by Christmas.'

'*Christmas!*'

'I'm sorry. This isn't what either of us want, but I really have no choice.'

It was the last thing Catherine had expected to hear—and the last thing she wanted to. 'I suppose I shouldn't be surprised. You are Alderbury's heir, after all. You had to marry some time.'

'True, but until recently, I hadn't given the matter any thought. I was happy with my life and content to see it continue along the same lines. But my father isn't happy and is insisting I marry.'

'I see.' Catherine stared down at the ground. She would have withdrawn her hand, but Valbourg held on to it. 'Do you have…anyone in mind?'

'No. The only woman I care about is the only woman I cannot have.'

She looked up and saw in his eyes all that he felt for her…and it broke her heart. 'Oh, Richard, what are we going to do?'

'I don't know. We always knew this was impossible.'

'I know.' Catherine stared at their hands, wondering how she would ever bear being separated from him. 'There are too many obstacles.'

'I told myself that as well, but it hasn't made any difference. I've wanted you for so long,' Valbourg said. 'Ever since the first time I saw you in the theatre. There was something so wonderfully alive about you. You captivated me then and I've only grown more fascinated by you since. But it has to come to an end and I thought it only right that I tell you now. Because it will, naturally, affect the amount of time we are able to spend together. And once I am married—'

'You will have no time to spend with me at all,' Catherine said, trying to be brave, but also aware that not even her best acting skills were equal to the task. 'I wish I could say I don't care or that I won't miss you, but I will. Terribly. Every day of my life.'

He drew her into his arms and settled her in the bend of his knees, cradling her against his chest. How long she sat there, Catherine didn't know. She simply put her arms around his neck and clung to him, staying as close as possible. How was she to live without him? She wanted to be everything to him: friend, lover, wife…but in reality she could play none of those roles. He was destined to marry a woman with a title as lofty as his or at the very least an upbringing as noble. There was simply no place in his life for an actress.

'I'm sorry, Catherine,' he murmured, his lips pressed against her hair. 'If there was any other way, I would take it, but it isn't just my future that's at stake. I have to consider Sebastian and I hate to think what would happen to him if he were taken away from me. I love him as my own; the way you love Thomas. I don't know what I would do without him.'

'Hush,' Catherine said, reaching up and putting a finger to his lips. 'No one is going to take Sebastian away because you are going to do what you must. You are going to find a nice young lady and ask her to marry you. Then you are going to settle down and start a family of your own so that Sebastian will have brothers and sisters to grow up with.' Her voice caught. 'You cannot do anything else, Richard. You know that.'

He did. She could see it in his eyes. But knowing she was doing and saying the right things made her no happier. She loved him too much for that.

At length, the picnic came to an end. Valbourg was quiet as he packed away the remnants of their meal and folded up the blanket. Though the sun still shone, Catherine felt a chill that had nothing to do with the weather. Everything had changed. He helped her into the carriage and put the horses to a walk, but to her surprise, they did not take the road by which they had come, but instead went deeper into the forest, at length arriving at a charming cottage.

'Where are we?' Catherine asked as Valbourg jumped down and held out his hands to her. 'Whose cottage is this?'

'It belongs to a friend of mine who is in India at the moment and who asked me to check on it every now and then. He comes here to paint when he's not travelling around the world.' Valbourg pulled a key from his pocket and unlocked the front door.

Catherine could tell at once that it was the home of an artist. A large easel stood in the centre of the living room and paints and brushes were scattered around the room. A number of half-finished canvases leaned against the walls, lending a general air of creative haphazardness to the cottage.

She turned around to find Valbourg watching her. 'It's delightful, but…why have you brought me here?'

'To give you a choice.' He walked towards her and took both of her hands in his. 'My life is going to change in the next few months, Catherine. I won't be able to see you often, if at all. So while I still have the chance, I want us to be together. But only if that's what you want, too.'

It took a moment for Catherine to understand what he was suggesting. When she did, she gazed down at their hands and realised the weight of the decision staring her in the face. He wanted to make love to her…and she wanted it, too. Wanted it with an intensity that made her bones ache and her body heavy. Even now, the blood was pounding in her veins at the thought of lying naked in his arms.

'I do want it,' she admitted huskily. 'More than I have any right to. But are you sure it is the right thing to do?'

'No, but neither do I wish to spend the rest of my life wondering what it would have been like to make love to you,' he said. 'I will care for the woman I marry, but she will never be you, Catherine. No one will ever be you.'

It was all he needed to say. The question had been asked…and answered.

Catherine nodded and smiled as they walked into the bedroom together. She was not in the least afraid and yet she knew full well that what was about to happen would change both of their lives for ever.

In the aftermath of love, they travelled home, closer as a result of what they had shared and united by the power of their feelings for one another. But there was sadness there, too, because now more than ever, they knew what might have been and what they were giving up.

What had happened today would never be repeated.

Valbourg reached for her hand and pressed a fervent kiss to the soft skin of her palm. Catherine, whose entire body was still tingling from their lovemaking, felt her heart turn over. How would she get through the long, lonely years knowing he was married to someone else? That he would hold another woman in the darkness and that in her body, he would plant his seed. How was she to live with the knowledge that more than anything, she wanted to be that woman? The one he loved and who would be the mother of his child...

'What are you thinking?' he murmured against her temple.

'Nothing that serves either of us well.' Catherine closed her eyes and shook her head. 'Thank you, Richard. I will never forget this afternoon.'

'Nor, I'm afraid, will I.'

There were no further declarations. No bemoaning what fate held in store for them. They both knew what was and what wasn't allowed. Valbourg could fly in the face of convention, but his reputation would suffer for it. He would be shunned by those who mattered; be denied access to the houses of good society and be cut off from those who cared about him. He might even be disinherited. It had been known to happen.

And she would be castigated for being the cause of his disgrace. They would call her a scheming, manipulative woman who thought only of her own needs. A woman who would bring him down to her level because she loved him and wanted to be with him.

Catherine refused to do that. She loved him

too much. And knowing how deeply the disgrace would affect him gave her the courage to do what needed to be done.

After they parted company today, she would not see him again.

They arrived at his father's house and made their way inside. As soon as they did, Catherine knew something was terribly wrong. Worried faces met them at every turn and they were taken at once to Lord Alderbury's study, where they found him pacing back and forth.

'What's wrong?' Valbourg asked immediately.

Alderbury turned and Catherine saw something in his face that terrified her. 'What's happened?' she asked, taking a step towards him. 'Where's Thomas?'

He looked at her and his face was white and rigid. 'He's gone,' he said in a tortured voice. 'A stranger took him. And I have absolutely no idea where.'

It was her worst nightmare come true. Catherine felt Valbourg's hands close around her arms just before her legs gave way.

'Where did this happen?' he demanded as he guided her to a chair and helped her sit down.

'In the park,' Alderbury said. 'Tippings took the boys to see the ducks. They were feeding them when they heard a commotion nearby. Tippings said he turned to see what the noise was, and when he looked back, Thomas was gone.'

'Dear God!' Catherine whispered.

'Did anyone see who took him?' Valbourg demanded.

'A woman was standing nearby. She said a man came out of the bushes and grabbed Thomas, then started running towards a carriage. Sebastian ran after them, but the man was too fast. Both the woman and Sebastian gave Tippings as good a description as they could, but the carriage disappeared before he could get back in his own and follow it. Tippings brought Sebastian home immediately to tell me what had happened.'

'And what have you done since?' Catherine demanded, getting to her feet. 'Has a search been launched?'

'Of course, but so far nothing has turned up.'

'What did the man look like?' she whispered, feeling a chill settle into her bones.

'Tall and heavy-set, with dark hair and a beard.'

Valbourg shared a glance with Catherine. 'It wasn't Hailey.'

'I didn't expect it would be,' Catherine said. 'He'd have someone else do his dirty work, but it doesn't sound like Moody or Stubbs either. He must have hired someone new. Someone I wouldn't recognise. No doubt the man's already on his way back to Grafton with Thomas.'

'Miss Jones, I truly am sorry,' Alderbury said. 'You left him in my care—'

'You can make your apologies when I have my son back,' Catherine said coldly. 'I know you don't approve of me or of him, but out of respect for your son, I'll leave it at that.' She gazed at Valbourg for a moment, then turned and walked out of the room.

A moment later, Valbourg heard the front door close…and knew what he had to do. 'I'm going with her.'

Alderbury flinched. 'Do you really think that's necessary?'

'I do. Her son has just been kidnapped and she's going to need my help.'

'I'm sorry, Richard. Truly I am. I sympathise with Miss Jones's predicament and feel terrible that it happened while the boy was in my care,' his father said. 'But there's nothing we can do. The authorities have been alerted and I have every confidence they will find the boy. I strongly advise against your getting involved.'

'Sorry, Father, but I already am involved. I have been from the start,' Valbourg said, heading for the stairs. 'I'll see you when I get back. And then we will talk again. You can be sure of it.'

Catherine was getting into a hackney when Valbourg arrived.

'You're coming with me,' he said. 'In my carriage.' He paid the driver and transferred her small valise into his carriage. She was deathly pale apart from two bright spots of colour that stood out in her cheeks.

'You can't get involved in this, Richard.'

'I already am. You'll need me there for moral support, if nothing else.'

'What will I do if I can't get him back?' she said in a choked voice. 'Hailey may refuse—'

'Hailey *will* refuse, and when he does, we will threaten, intimidate and verbally browbeat if we have to. Anything short of violence if it means we will get Thomas back.'

'I wish I could be as confident. Any man who would do something like that in broad daylight—'

'I suspect he was counting on the element of surprise,' Valbourg said. 'Whoever's been watching Thomas knows of his fondness for the ducks. He was probably just biding his time until the right moment came along.'

'Unfortunately, it did so when your father was responsible for his safety,' Catherine said, the bitterness evident in her voice. 'I thought the idea of moving Thomas there was so that he would be safe.'

'And he was…until Tippings turned his back. At least we have a description of the man who took Thomas.'

'It doesn't matter. We know who's behind this,' Catherine said. 'Thomas will already be on his way back to the Haileys and getting him away will be even more difficult than it was the first time.'

'You forget, Thomas knows you're his mother now and will likely kick up a fuss when he realises he's been taken from you.'

Catherine closed her eyes, biting her lip. 'I can't lose him, Richard. I *can't*. It would tear me apart.'

'I know and we are going to get him back.' Valbourg placed his hands over hers. 'Trust me, Catherine. We won't let Hailey get away with this a second time. When we leave Grafton, Thomas will be coming with us. I give you my word on that.'

They reached Cheltenham in good time and went straight to Gwendolyn's house. There, Catherine acquainted her friend with the details of the situation.

'Lord Valbourg, it is good to see you again,' Gwen said, in a polite yet friendly manner, 'though I am truly sorry for the circumstances.'

'As am I,' Valbourg said. 'But we anticipate a good outcome. For now, Catherine needs to rest.'

'I have no intention of resting. We must go immediately to the Haileys,' Catherine said. 'I won't give him any more time with Thomas than I have to.'

'I understand your concern, my dear, but in this

instance I think Lord Valbourg is right,' Gwen said gently. 'You have been travelling at a frantic pace, with thoughts of Thomas uppermost in your mind. You will do better to rest for the evening and start out fresh in the morning. I suspect you will be able to approach the situation more calmly and your conversation with Reverend Hailey will reflect that.'

'But what if he uses the time to send Thomas away again?' Catherine said. 'How will I find him? Stubbs won't be able to help me now.'

'I don't think Hailey will send Thomas away,' Valbourg said. 'Thomas knows you're his mother and he'll tell anyone he can. He might even put up a fight. My guess is Hailey will keep him close to home, where he can keep an eye on him.'

It was impossible to tell whether Valbourg's hunch was right, but, knowing she needed sleep, Catherine agreed to set out first thing in the morning.

She fell into a heavy but restless sleep, finally getting up and dressing long before a servant arrived with her cup of morning chocolate.

They set off not long after, but when they arrived at the manse, there was no sign of Thomas.

'The master told me to tell you he's got nothing to say to you,' Mrs Comstock said coldly. 'Now take yourself off and don't be calling here again.'

'I beg your pardon,' Valbourg said, stepping

forward. 'If you value your job, you will tell Reverend Hailey that Lord Valbourg wishes to see him and that it will be the better for him if he makes himself available at once.'

Catherine was quite sure the stern-faced housekeeper had never been spoken to in such a manner and one look at Valbourg's face must have convinced her it would be wise to pass his message along. But she did not invite them in, instead closing the door in their faces.

'Charming,' Valbourg murmured. 'A fire-breathing dragon sent to guard the door.'

'I'm sure she succeeds with everyone else,' Catherine said, finally managing a smile. 'I would turn tail and run if you spoke to me like that, too.'

The hardness in his face vanished. 'I never would speak to you like that.'

The door opened momentarily and the housekeeper reappeared. 'Mrs Hailey has agreed to see you. The vicar is engaged with diocesan business.'

'Yes, I'm sure he is,' Valbourg said, letting Catherine precede him into the house.

The housekeeper led them to a different room this time, one in Mrs Hailey's realm, judging from the feminine décor, and left without another word.

Eliza entered shortly thereafter. She looked as lovely as ever, but Catherine saw the gleam of anger in her eyes. 'How dare you come here!'

she said, not wasting any time with pleasantries. 'Have you not done that poor boy enough harm?'

'*I* have done him harm?' Catherine repeated incredulously. 'You're the one who's keeping a child who doesn't belong to you. You're the one who arranged for him to be kidnapped in London and brought back here.'

'Of course, after you took him from Glendale under false pretences,' Eliza shot back. 'I expect the authorities will take a dim view of that—'

'There is no need to bring threats into this,' Valbourg said coldly. 'Miss Jones is the boy's mother. She has a right to take him.'

'She gave up that right when she left Thomas here as a baby.'

'I did not leave him!' Catherine said. 'Your husband *took* him from me. You were there. You know exactly what happened.'

'As I said, when you left him here and ran away to London to become an actress, we had no choice but to take poor Thomas in and raise him as our own.'

Catherine stared at the woman in disbelief. 'Is *that* the story you intend to put about? That I *abandoned* my son?'

'It is your word against ours, Miss Jones, and I guarantee, we will win. Who would take the word of an actress over that of a clergyman?'

'Someone who is well acquainted with both,' Valbourg said. 'Miss Jones is head and shoulders above you when it comes to integrity and compassion, Mrs Hailey. But we are ignoring the central person in this drama. Why don't you ask Thomas with whom he wishes to live?'

'Don't be ridiculous. He is five years old,' Eliza said angrily. 'He cannot know what is best for him.'

'Since he will be the one living with the outcome of the decision, I think he is eminently qualified to speak on his own behalf.'

'Nonsense! I refuse to allow him to take part in this. And I resent you telling me what to do, Lord Valbourg, because this really is none of your business. I understand that you and Miss Jones have a relationship, but that does not entitle you to come into my house and—'

'Madam,' Valbourg cut in icily, 'you will tell your husband that Miss Jones and I will return tomorrow morning at ten o'clock to pick up her son. Unless you wish to find yourself standing in a court of law, I suggest you have Thomas ready. Do I make myself clear?'

Out of the corner of her eye, Catherine saw a movement near the door, then heard the creak of a floorboard. She turned to get a better look, but no one was there. Clearly, whoever had been eavesdropping on their conversation had decided not to linger. It seemed the staff went in fear of Elizabeth Hailey, too.

She turned back in time to hear Valbourg say, 'Good day, Mrs Hailey. Come along, Miss Jones.'

They left without waiting for the housekeeper to show them the way. Catherine was silent until she reached the carriage. Then, 'Why did you let her get away with that? She came right out and accused *us* of being in the wrong.'

'And I'm not sure a court of law wouldn't agree with her,' Valbourg said. 'Emotion doesn't come into it when you're dealing with barristers, Catherine. They base their legal pleadings on fact and the fact is we did remove Thomas from Glendale under false pretences. The court might well say the Haileys were within their rights to take him back by whatever means possible.'

'But he is my son! I know you're probably tired of hearing that, but it is the truth!' Catherine said, on the brink of tears. 'He belongs with me—and I believe that's what he would say if he were asked.'

'I agree, but it doesn't solve our problem right now. I suggest we go back to Gwen's house and sleep on it.'

They were halfway home when Catherine suddenly sat up straight. 'Richard, would you mind taking me somewhere else before we go back to Gwen's?'

'Not at all. Where would you like to go?'

'To a place I haven't been in six years,' she

said quietly. 'To see a man I miss very much and parted with badly.'

Valbourg ran his fingers along the reins. 'Are you sure you want to do this today?'

'I must. I may not have the courage to do it again.'

Her father hadn't changed a great deal. He looked older and greyer than Catherine remembered, but other than that, he was the same. He was sitting in his garden, reading a book, and looked up at the sound of the carriage. When it slowed and came to a halt in front of his house, he put down his book and stood up.

Catherine watched her father approach the gate and felt the past six years slip away. It was as though she was a little girl again, rushing home to tell her father where she had been and what a good time she'd had. He would pick her up and tell her she must have eaten an entire pie because she was much heavier than when she had left. Then he would put her down and they would walk into the house together and all would be well with her world. But she wasn't that little girl any more, and as she stepped down from the carriage, Catherine was very aware of how much had changed. 'Hello, Papa,' she said.

'Catherine?' His expression changed from uncertain to incredulous. 'Is it really you?'

She offered him a tentative smile as she pushed

open the gate. 'I came back to see Reverend Hailey. But I wanted to come and see you as well.'

They stood staring at each other, six feet—and six years—separating them.

'Well, I'll leave the two of you alone,' Valbourg said, glancing from one to the other. 'I'll come back in an hour, shall I?'

Catherine nodded, wondering if an hour would pass in the blink of an eye—or feel like an eternity. Valbourg squeezed her hand before leaving, and then she was alone again with her father.

'I know we parted badly, Papa,' she said, deciding to take the lead. 'And I know how you felt about me when I left. But that was a long time ago and I have missed you so very much. I wanted to come back and see if there was any chance of reconciliation between us. It would mean the world to me to know I was forgiven.'

Catherine wasn't sure how he would react. She was prepared for disdain, even for anger. She was not prepared for tears. 'Oh, my dearest girl.' He came forward and grasped both of her hands. 'How I have longed to write to you, only to stop every time, overcome with shame for the way I treated you. You cannot know how grateful I am that you have finally come home.'

Chapter Eleven

In the quiet of the garden, father and daughter sat and talked over the events of the past six years. Tears flowed, laughter echoed, and for the first time in a long while, Catherine felt a sense of peace in a part of her heart that had been broken for so long.

'I feel dreadful for the way I treated you, Katie,' her father said, slipping back into his childhood name for her. 'I was so concerned about what people would say and about the shame I thought you brought on our house—'

'I *did* bring shame on us, Papa,' Catherine interrupted gently. 'I made a terrible mistake and I am so very sorry. It was never my intention to hurt you.'

'I know. I think I knew it at the time, but I was too stubborn to admit it.'

'You were also dealing with Mama's death,' Catherine said. 'What I did… What happened between Will and myself couldn't have happened at a worse time.'

'No, but your mother was gone. You were still here and you needed me, and I wasn't there,' her father said. 'However, with time comes wisdom and I have learned a great deal over the past six years. I am so grateful for having the chance to sit and talk with you again, Katie, and to hear about your life in London. I read the reports in the papers. You've done well for yourself and I am so very proud.'

His words brought tears to Catherine's eyes. How many nights had she lain awake dreaming that one day her father might say something like this? 'You don't know how much it means to me to hear you say that, Papa.'

'Do you think I will be able to see little Thomas?' he asked, his voice tentative again. 'I should very much like to meet my grandson.'

'You haven't met him?' Catherine said. 'I thought the Haileys would have taken him to church.'

'They did, but he was never allowed away from Eliza,' her father said. 'And given that they were trying to pass him off as Eliza's nephew, there was no reason for them to introduce him to me.'

'But did no one comment on the resemblance between Thomas and myself? Lord Valbourg says we look very much alike.'

'I doubt anyone thought to connect the two of

you. You've been gone so long, and though a few people said they thought they had seen you, they couldn't be sure.'

'The Haileys insisted I arrive and leave at night,' Catherine told him. 'So as to lessen the chance of anyone seeing me.'

'Ah, that would explain it, I suppose. Still, if anyone suspected you of being Thomas's mother, no one said anything to me. But then, why would they? Most people knew we parted badly, though I explained it was because of your desire to perform on stage rather than as a result of...well, the other. It seemed easier.'

Yes, it likely would, Catherine thought sadly. Anything, even a career on the stage, would be better than having to admit your only daughter had borne a child out of wedlock.

'What about Lord Valbourg?' her father asked. 'I was surprised to see you in the company of such an illustrious gentleman. Is there an understanding between you? It would be a very good match for you if you have earned his affections, Katie.'

Catherine smiled and shook her head. 'Life in London has taught me nothing if not reality, Papa. Lord Valbourg has been kind to me, but that is all. He will be announcing his engagement before Christmas, though I would ask you to keep that to yourself, since he hasn't asked the lady yet.'

Her father looked at her for a long time, then

nodded. 'Thank you for clearing that up. I did not wish to say anything out of place, but I did think there was something between you. I saw the way he looked at you before he left. But perhaps it was just hope in these old eyes. Still, I would be honoured if you and his lordship would consider having dinner with me this evening. I suspect you will be returning to London soon?'

'I am not sure when we will be heading back,' Cathcrine said, 'but I would be delighted to have dinner with you and I shall ask Lord Valbourg when he returns if he is free to join us. I know he has friends in the area. He may have made arrangements to join them for the evening.'

Catherine knew Valbourg hadn't made any plans, but if he preferred not to spend the evening with them, he would at least have a plausible excuse.

As it turned out, however, Valbourg was delighted to join them.

'Splendid!' her father said as the three of them stood by the gate. 'I shall have Mrs Rowntree prepare a special dinner in honour of the occasion. She constantly complains that it is terribly boring having to cook for a widower. Now we shall see what culinary masterpiece she is able to put forward!'

They parted with great affection and Catherine climbed back into Valbourg's carriage in a much better frame of mind than she had left it. 'Perhaps my luck is changing,' she said as the horses set off. 'I had no idea my meeting with Papa would go so well, but I am happy and relieved that it has.'

'It was good to see the two of you getting along,' Valbourg said. 'I wasn't sure what I would find when I returned. Had you been sitting on the grass by the gate with your head in your hands, I wouldn't have been surprised.'

Catherine laughed. 'When you left, I had no idea what I would be doing. But Papa was as pleased by the opportunity to put the past behind us as I was.' Her smile faded as she remembered one part of the conversation. 'He asked if it would be possible to see Thomas. The Haileys haven't brought him here to meet his grandfather.'

'In their eyes, there would be no reason to. If Eliza was trying to pass Thomas off as her nephew, he would have no connection to your father.'

'That's what Papa said, but the Haileys know the truth and it was cruel of them to deny Papa the right to see his own grandson.'

'They may have thought he had no interest in the boy. You said the two of you parted on bad terms and the rest of the village must have been aware of it,' Valbourg pointed out. 'Nothing remains secret in a place like this. I wouldn't be surprised if quite a few people suspected you of being Thomas's mother, but were afraid to say anything. You might even hear from some of them before we leave.'

Catherine didn't put any stock in Valbourg's statement. People were too caught up in their own lives to worry about anyone else's. If they spoke to her at all, it was to congratulate her on her success on the London stage.

At least those who were kind enough to speak to her. Some simply ignored her, making it very clear what they thought of her career in the theatre.

'Never mind the rest of them, I know for a fact Mrs Humphries thinks you're marvellous,' her father said over dinner that evening. 'I suspect she was peeking through her curtains for a glimpse of you when you arrived. Especially with Lord Valbourg at your side.'

'Oh, dear, I've likely started another round of gossip in the village,' Catherine said with a sigh. 'You will have much to contend with after I leave, Papa.'

'And contend with it I shall,' he said, grinning. 'I shall put in their place those who dare to criticise you and agree with those who tell me you are marvellous.'

'And how will you deal with those who ask about Thomas?' Valbourg enquired. 'Or do you think it unlikely the subject will arise?'

Mr Jones looked thoughtful for a moment. 'I honestly don't know. As I told Katie, there are some who suspect her of being Thomas's mother. No one has said anything directly, of course, but it is impossible to deny the events that took place around that time.'

'I intend to fight to get Thomas back, Papa,' Catherine said quietly. 'Reverend Hailey told me he would return Thomas to me when he was five if I did everything he asked of me, and I have. That was what kept me going. I had to prove myself worthy and financially capable of providing for Thomas. Thanks to my work, I have been able to do that.'

'Then why did Reverend Hailey change his mind?' her father asked. 'Surely a clergyman would be the last person to go back on his word?'

Catherine felt Valbourg's eyes on her, then told her father the details of the story, only omitting the kiss she and Valbourg had shared in the carriage. Thankfully, his reaction was the same as Valbourg's.

'So he condemned you on the reports of others,' he said at the end of the recounting. 'And he had you spied upon! Shocking! I shall tell him what I think the next time I see him.'

'No, Papa, you mustn't say anything!' Catherine said. 'Please do not involve yourself in this. Lord Valbourg has offered to help me. He knows the right people to talk to.'

'I can't make any promises, of course, but I will do everything I can to that end,' Valbourg said. 'I have connections with those who may have some sway in the matter.'

'Well, I am very glad to hear it. My poor Katie has suffered enough,' her father said. 'I long to see her happy again. Yes, Mrs Parkes?'

The housekeeper bobbed a curtsy. 'Excuse me, Mr Jones, but there's a young lady to see you. Or rather, to see Miss Catherine and his lordship.'

'Who is it?'

'Miss Megan Hailey, sir. And she said it was very important that she see Miss Catherine as soon as possible.'

'Yes, of course. Show her in,' Mr Jones said. 'I wonder what on earth has brought Megan here at this time of night?'

'Thomas!' Catherine whispered, her throat tight. 'Something's happened to Thomas.'

'Don't go jumping to conclusions,' Valbourg cautioned as the door opened and Megan walked in, the hood of her cape pulled low over her face. 'Good evening, Miss Megan. What a pleasure to see you again.'

'Lord Valbourg!'

'Is Thomas all right?' Catherine said, too concerned with her son's welfare to waste time with greetings. 'Has something happened?'

'Nothing's happened, miss. Thomas is fine,' Megan assured her, slipping back her hood. 'Good evening, Mr Jones.' She glanced shyly at Valbourg. 'I didn't know whether you would be here or not, my lord.'

'Mr Jones kindly invited me to stay for dinner,' Valbourg said with a smile. 'Do your parents have any idea you're here?'

Megan shook her head. 'They are dining with Mr and Mrs Bullen and won't be home until late, so I thought it would be safe to come.'

'But why *did* you come?' Catherine asked, her voice calmer in the wake of hearing that Thomas was all right.

The young girl bit her lip. 'Is it true, miss? Are you really Thomas's mother? I heard what Step-mama said to you this afternoon and I remember what Papa said to Lord Valbourg in the church, but I didn't know what to think. So I thought I should come and ask you for the truth.'

Catherine's eyes widened in surprise. So, someone *had* been listening at the door this afternoon…and that someone had been Megan. Catherine felt her father's and Valbourg's eyes on her and realised how important the moment was. 'Yes, Megan, I am. And since you heard the conversation, you know why Thomas is not with me.'

Megan sighed. 'I always thought Eliza's story seemed a little odd. She never talked about having a sister or a brother who might have had a child. She just said Thomas was her nephew and that she had to raise him because no one else could. Now I understand why. It was all a lie.'

Catherine got up and crossed the room to put her hands on the girl's shoulders. 'I am so sorry. You shouldn't have had to find out like this, but it is better you know the truth.'

'I know. And I know you love him. I can hear it in your voice when you talk about him.'

'I do love him,' Catherine said. 'With all my heart. And I came back to get him because he belongs with me.'

'I know that,' Megan said in a sad voice. 'I know that's what I would want if he were my son.'

Having made that pronouncement, she turned and walked out of the room.

'Megan?' Catherine said anxiously. Surely the girl hadn't come all this way just to satisfy her curiosity about Thomas's birth? But when the door opened again, Catherine had her answer. 'Thomas!'

'Mama!' He ran to her arms and buried his face in her skirts. 'You came back! I was afraid I wasn't ever going to see you again.'

Catherine scooped him up and held him tightly in her arms. 'You should have known better,' she murmured into his hair. 'No one's going to keep us apart, my darling. Not any more.'

'This is a wonderful thing you've done, Megan,' Valbourg said quietly. 'But I fear your father will be very angry when he finds out.'

'I know, but I shall speak to him in the morning and try to make him understand.' Surprisingly, Megan didn't look afraid. 'He's not a bad man, Lord Valbourg. He's been a wonderful father to me. We were always close, and after Will and then Mama died we became even closer. Then Eliza came along and everything changed. After Papa married her, she took charge of the household and everyone in it. She tolerates me because she knows how much Papa loves me, but I don't think she likes me very much.'

'I'm sure that's not the case,' Catherine said gently.

'Yes, it is,' Megan said. 'But I have learned to make the best of it. For the most part, I try to stay out of her way and not to make her angry.'

'This is going to make her very angry,' Valbourg said.

Megan looked at him with an expression far too mature for a girl of her tender years. 'I know, but what matters is Thomas. I never knew if his real mother was alive or dead,' she admitted, glancing at Catherine again. 'Now that I do and understand how hard you've worked to get Thomas back, I can't ignore that and let Eliza have her way. She was wrong to try to keep Thomas.'

'Still, neither your father nor Eliza will approve of what you've done,' Catherine said. 'They may punish you.'

'If they threaten to do anything, I shall tell

Papa I will leave as well. I don't think he would like that very much.'

'No, he wouldn't,' Valbourg said. 'He does love you, Megan. I saw that in the church the day we met. Nevertheless, you are a very brave girl and we are eternally in your debt. If you ever wish to come to London, you can be assured of having a place to stay.'

The girl's eyes lit up. 'Really?'

'You have my word on it.'

'I can't thank you enough for this, Megan,' Catherine said. 'Is there anything I can do for you?'

'Just send me a letter when you are back in London and let me know everything is all right.'

'We will,' Valbourg said. 'And I think we should probably set off at once. I would rather be well on the road to London before Reverend Hailey returns home and finds out Thomas is gone.'

There was a round of embracing and many tears as Megan and Thomas said their goodbyes.

'You will come to see me in London, won't you, Meggie?' he said, clinging to her.

'Of course I will come! You know how much I want to see London and now I shall have the very best reason for doing so!'

After another round of hugs, Megan slipped away. Thomas seemed inclined to stay close to Catherine, but the first thing she did was introduce him to her father, who had been watching the boy avidly since his arrival in the room. 'This is your other grandfather, Thomas. Grandfather Jones.'

'Hello, Thomas. I'm very pleased to meet you at last,' her father said, tears shimmering in his eyes.

Thomas looked equally serious. 'Hello, Grandfather. I'm sorry it's taken so long.'

'It doesn't matter, because we know each other now. I hope we will be seeing a lot of each other in the future.'

'I promise you will, Papa,' Catherine said. 'But right now, we had best hurry. Like his lordship, I would rather be well on our way to London before the Haileys find out what has gone on this night.'

They stopped briefly at Gwen's house to pick up their belongings and say their farewells.

'Goodbye, dearest,' Gwen whispered as she hugged Catherine close. 'I shall come and see you in London very soon. I think it is about time I had a little adventure of my own.'

'You would be more than welcome and I would love to see you,' Catherine said. 'And please do go and see Papa. He mentioned you at dinner tonight.'

'He did?'

'Yes, and judging from the colour in your cheeks, you might enjoy seeing him as well.'

After one last embrace, Catherine hurried out to the carriage where Valbourg and her son were already waiting. Thomas fell asleep not long into the journey, curled up in Catherine's lap.

* * *

'Do you think Megan will be all right?' she asked after a long silence. 'We owe her so much. This could never have happened without her.'

'It certainly would have been a great deal more difficult,' Valbourg agreed. 'But I expect she will be fine. She has a good head on her shoulders and, though Eliza may make her life miserable for a while, I believe she will be able to convince her father that she has done the right thing. If not, I suspect we will see her in London very soon. In which case, I shall ask Mary to sponsor her next Season.'

'You would do that?'

'Happily. Mary will delight in buying her new clothes and dressing her up like a proper lady. And she will introduce Megan to the kind of gentlemen she would never have met in Grafton.'

Catherine smiled as she gently rested her chin on her son's head. She was glad the worst was over and that she and Thomas were together again. Though the memory of the kidnapping in the park was still fresh in her mind, she felt confident that as long as she kept a watchful eye out in future, she would be able to keep him safe.

But what about when she was performing? She wouldn't be able to take Thomas with her when she went to the theatre for rehearsals in the morning, or for her performances every night. He needed to be schooled and to have a safe environment in which to grow up.

Was it time to think about giving up the theatre and becoming a full-time mother?

'So, when do you start performing again?'

Catherine glanced at Valbourg in amusement. 'Have you developed the ability to read minds as well as everything else, my lord?'

'No, but I suspected it might be in your thoughts. Having Thomas living with you will necessitate certain changes in your life, just as Sebastian's arrival necessitated changes in mine.'

'I know. I just haven't had time to figure out what they are. But I will. And you have weighty matters to ponder as well,' Catherine said, striving to keep the sadness from her voice. 'Christmas is not all that far away.'

Valbourg turned his head away, a muscle twitching in his jaw. 'You know this is not how I would have matters between us, Catherine.'

'I know, but it is the only way they can be.'

He didn't pursue the matter, as they both knew she was right. He couldn't have a life with her. His father would be furious and his sister apoplectic. But it wasn't their life to live, Catherine thought angrily. It was Valbourg's, and she desperately wanted to spend it with him. She wanted to go to bed with him every night and wake up in his arms every morning. She wanted them to be able to enjoy all that life had to offer. Was that really asking so much?

For the first few days after their return to London, Catherine kept a close eye out for the presence of strange men or suspicious carriages lurking in the area. On the few occasions she and Thomas went to the park, she held on tightly to his hand and went right to the edge of the pond with him to feed the ducks. He slept in a new bed in the room next to hers and every night she made sure the window was securely locked.

Thomas didn't seem to mind all the extra attention. He was quiet his first few days back in London and seemed almost as reluctant as Catherine to set foot in busy public places. He had endured more in a month than most children did in a lifetime, but as the weeks passed and nothing of an untoward nature happened, they both began to relax and settle into their new routines.

Of Valbourg, Catherine saw nothing. No doubt he was spending time with Sebastian and his family. She hoped he occasionally found time to think of her and remember with pleasure all that had passed between them, even though she knew nothing was going to change. By necessity, his focus would be on his future. Christmas would be here before they knew it.

She was pleased and relieved, however, to receive a letter from Megan Hailey. It was brief, saying that both her father and Eliza had been very upset over what she had done, but that she had convinced her father not to take any further action with regard to Thomas. She said she was looking forward to seeing Thomas again when she came to London in January, and that she hoped she might be able to stay with Catherine until things were more settled at home.

Catherine had folded up the letter and immediately sat down to write one of her own. Megan hadn't gone into detail about what had happened, but Catherine had read between the lines. She suspected Reverend Hailey had forgiven his daughter for interfering, but that Eliza had not. She was unlikely to have let the girl off lightly, in which case, Megan was welcome to stay for as long as she liked. Catherine rather liked the idea of having both a son and a 'daughter' living with her.

Theo Templeton decided to stage a few more performances of *Promises* before closing for the year. The first couple of times Catherine took Thomas with her, reluctant to let him out of her sight. She knew Mrs Rankin would have defended the boy with her life, but she felt better knowing he was in the building with her. He stayed with Theo or Tandy during the performances, but as soon as they were over, he was back with her.

She saw Valbourg for the first time about a month after their return from the country. She had been invited to a soirée given by Lady Duffington, a woman who, like the Templetons, often invited artists and businessmen to her gatherings, and it was there in the elegant blue-and-gold drawing room that Catherine saw him again. He had a lady by his side; a beautiful young woman dressed in the height of fashion, her dark hair caught up with an elegant arrangement of flowers.

'Lady Phoebe Shore,' Tandy whispered in her ear. 'Daughter of the Earl of Montpare. Her parents arc actively encouraging the match.'

'She's lovely,' Catherine said, turning away. 'I assume Lord Alderbury approves.'

'Why not? The girl's an heiress and her blood is as blue as his. They know the same people, move in the same circles and understand what is expected of them.'

'Do you think he loves her?' Catherine asked, not really wanting to hear the answer.

'I don't know. At one time, I thought his affections lay elsewhere,' Tandy said softly, 'but Valbourg has always been a difficult man to read.'

Catherine caught the expression of concern... and sympathy...in the older woman's eyes and knew Tandy had figured it out. 'I feel sure,' she said, 'that...whoever that other woman was, she knew how lucky she was to have had his good opinion, even if only for a short time.'

Tandy sighed, pressed an unexpected kiss to Catherine's cheek, then moved away, leaving

Catherine to stare into her glass and pretend her heart wasn't breaking all over again.

'So, the delightful Miss Jones is back in society. We missed you.'

Catherine raised her head, surprised to see Valbourg's brother standing beside her. 'I'm sure no one noticed my absence, Lord Hugh.'

'You underestimate your charm, dear lady. I always notice the absence of a beautiful woman, especially one so closely aligned with my family.'

'I can't think what you mean. I have nothing to do with your family.'

'Come, Miss Jones, you sang at my sister's betrothal celebration, your son stayed with both my father and my brother before that unfortunate incident and your name continues to crop up during conversations at breakfast, lunch and dinner,' Lord Hugh said. 'I almost feel as though we should set a place for you at the table.'

Catherine managed a strained smile. 'I'm sure your father is happy to have Thomas out from underfoot.'

'I'm not so sure. He speaks quite often of the boy. Indeed, at times I do believe he misses him,' Lord Hugh said. 'So Val brings Sebastian round more often for visits. Naturally Sebastian is distraught that he cannot see his friend any more. It seems the two of them became thick as thieves during their brief time together.'

'Thomas misses Sebastian, too,' Catherine admitted. 'It would have been nice had their friendship been allowed to continue.'

'Nice, but unrealistic. The grandson of a marquess does not play with the bastard son of an actress. Oh, I'm sorry. Was that cruel?' Lord Hugh asked as a flush rose in Catherine's face. 'Yes, I suppose it was. But we cannot ignore the facts, can we, my dear? There are simply too many obstacles standing in your way, which is why my brother's courtship of Lady Phoebe is being so actively encouraged. You really never stood a chance.'

The implication that she had somehow set out to win Valbourg's affections stung. 'I am well aware of the differences between us, Lord Hugh,' Catherine said quietly. 'Lord Valbourg helped me through a difficult period and I will always be grateful to him for that, but I am not so foolish as to believe there was ever a chance of our association developing into something more.'

'Fie, Miss Jones, you don't expect mc to believe that, do you? You must know he's in love with you. Not that any man *wouldn't* feel that way, of course,' Lord Hugh mused. 'God knows, I'm a little in love with you myself. But my intentions would be strictly dishonourable whereas Valbourg's would be eminently laudable. I'm sure that is why he is feeling so wretched about the entire affair.'

Catherine put her glass on the table, aware that

her hand was trembling. 'You're wrong, Lord Hugh. Valbourg is well aware of his obligations and would never allow himself to fall in love with someone like me. He is courting Lady Phoebe and I wish them both happiness, if that is whom he chooses to marry.'

'Personally, I'm not sure he will. My money is still on Lady Susan Wimsley. She looks a lot more like you,' Lord Hugh said. 'I say, are you all right, Miss Jones? You've suddenly gone quite pale.'

'I'm fine,' Catherine said woodenly. 'But it's time I went home.'

'What a pity. Barely five minutes in my company and you are already running away. Ah, well, hopefully we will be seeing each other in the not-too-distant future,' Lord Hugh said, adding with a wink, 'Now that the truth of your background is known, there doesn't seem to be much point in perpetuating the Angel myth, does there? We all know what you really are.'

His smugness left Catherine in no doubt as to his meaning and, afraid the evening would only get worse, she headed for the front door. She had made a mistake by coming to the soirée this evening. She had no intention of making a second by remaining.

She was waiting for a carriage when Lord Tantemon and Lord Lassiter approached.

'Well, well,' Tantemon said. 'The Angel has

left her little cherub at home and is mingling once more in society.'

'Good evening, my lord,' Catherine said, keeping watch for an approaching hackney.

'Not leaving us already?'

'Perhaps she is not feeling well,' Lassiter said. 'She does look a little pale. I suggest she spend the rest of the evening in bed. I know that would make me feel better. Especially if it's my bed she spends it in.'

Catherine sighed. 'Surely you have better things to do than harass me, my lord.'

'As a matter of fact, I do not. Not so fast, Miss Jones,' he said as she started to walk away. 'You and I have a score to settle. The last time we met, I suffered at the hands of your champion.'

'Lord Valbourg is not my champion.'

'No? He certainly acted the part, and I have been meaning to take him to task over it. I did not appreciate his ungentlemanly handling of my person.'

'Had you behaved in the manner of a gentleman, he would have had no reason to handle you.'

'Ooh, saucy wench. Calling *my* morals into question when all of London knows you have none. A turnabout, wouldn't you say, Tantemon?' Lassiter said with a sneer. 'The Virgin Angel revealed for the whore she is.'

Catherine didn't stop to think. She just reacted—and the sound of her palm striking Lassiter's cheek echoed in the darkness.

'By God, you'll pay for that,' the man snarled. He grabbed her by the arm and raised his hand to strike, but Catherine twisted around and landed a hard kick just below his knee. His leg buckled and he went down, swearing viciously.

Unfortunately, as he went down, Tantemon lunged. 'Come, my pretty, I know better than to get that close.' He grabbed Catherine around the waist from behind, and the next thing she knew, her feet were off the ground and she was being thrust into a carriage.

That was when she screamed.

For Valbourg the evening was interminable. He had spotted Catherine the moment he'd walked into the room, but, grimly aware that other eyes were focused with equal interest on him, he had kept his distance, gritting his teeth when Hugh had begun a conversation with her. He also noted the exact moment she left, prompted, he felt sure, by something his brother must have said. Tact had never been one of Hugh's skills.

Now, however, it was Hugh who walked swiftly towards him, breaking into his conversation with Lady Phoebe to say, 'I say, Val, a word if you don't mind. Excuse us, Lady Phoebe,' he said, taking Valbourg's arm and drawing him away. 'I don't want to alarm you, but there's a bit of a discussion taking place between Miss Jones and a few of her more ardent admirers. You might like to go and intervene. I would have, but I don't have your quick right jab. Or your blistering left hook. And I fear both will be required.'

Valbourg saw the expression of concern on his brother's face and quickly made his way outside. Upon reaching the street, he was astonished to see Lassiter lying on the ground and Tantemon doing his best to force Catherine, kicking for all she was worth, into a carriage.

He reacted without thinking. He grabbed Tantemon by the shoulder, spun him around and aimed his fist into the peer's face, feeling skin and bone flatten under the power of the blow.

Blood spurted and Tantemon staggered backwards, putting his hands to his face. 'What do you think you're doing? You've broken my nose!'

'You're lucky that's the only thing I broke!' Valbourg shoved him out of the way and reached into the carriage. 'Are you all right?' He helped Catherine out. There were tears on her cheeks and scratches on her arms, but her clothes were intact and he was relieved to see her nod.

'Yes. Take me home, Richard. Please.'

The strain in her voice made him want to turn on Tantemon then and there, but because they had already had enough drama for one evening, he simply ordered his carriage and helped Catherine into it. As soon as they were away, she was in his arms, her slender body racked with sobs, the tears flowing freely down her face.

Valbourg didn't say a word. He just held her, knowing this was where she belonged. So much had happened over the past few weeks. So many dreams shattered. No wonder she had finally reached her breaking point.

At last, when the tears and the sobs began to ease, he took out his handkerchief and gave it to her. 'I saw Lassiter lying on the ground. Was that a result of the technique you mentioned the first night we met?'

She laughed, although it came out like a sob. 'Not that p-particular one, no.'

'Really? Judging from his expression, I thought it might have been,' Valbourg replied. 'Just as well, since I likely would have killed him.'

'Oh, Richard,' Catherine said, dabbing at her eyes. 'You really mustn't joke about such things.'

'I'm not joking. That's the second time Lassiter's crossed the line when it comes to you and I'm damned if he'll do it again. Nor will Tantemon. I have a score to settle with both of them.'

He had hoped to set her mind at rest, but all the threat seemed to do was make her sadder. 'It's always going to be like this, isn't it?' she whispered. 'Men believing I'm a whore. Believing they can take advantage of me.'

Valbourg rubbed his thumb gently across her cheek. 'You *must* marry, Catherine. I know you don't want to, but it is the only way of assuring your safety. Is there not someone for whom you feel a small degree of affection?'

'Yes. But he must choose another...and I would not ask him to do otherwise.'

Valbourg sighed and pressed his lips to her hair, wishing they could stay in the carriage for ever. He wanted the rest of the world to disappear and leave them alone, but they both knew that wasn't possible. Nevertheless, they stayed in each other's arms for the duration of the trip, and it wasn't until they drew to a halt in front of her house that Catherine slowly sat up.

'Thank you, Richard. I don't know what I would have done if you hadn't been there tonight.'

'I have no doubt some other gallant gentleman would have come to your rescue. I must remember to thank Hugh when I get home.'

'Hugh?'

'He was the one who came and alerted me to what was going on.'

'Really?'

'I know. I was surprised, too.' He grasped her chin and, pulling her towards him, tenderly kissed her. 'Will I see you again?'

Her eyes shimmered and she looked away. 'I think it best you don't. Goodnight.'

He would have walked her to her door, but she insisted he remain in the carriage. Nevertheless, he watched her every step of the way, refusing to drive on until he saw her front door open and close and knew she was safely inside. She turned only once to look at him…and Valbourg knew it would be a very long time before he forgot the expression of sadness in her eyes.

That night, lying in bed, Catherine made a decision. She knew she could not go on living the way she was. The strain of having to see Valbourg at society functions, her constant fears surrounding Thomas's safety, and now concerns about her own welfare were taking their toll. She was sleeping badly and losing weight. If nothing changed, her performances would begin to suffer and she couldn't afford to let her personal life negatively affect her professional one. If she retired from the stage, she wanted it to be because she *chose* to leave, not because her performances deteriorated to the point where people no longer wanted to see her.

As a result, after breakfast the next morning, she sat down to write letters to her father and Gwen, telling them of her plans to leave England. As she saw her thoughts taking shape on the page, Catherine knew she was doing the right thing. It would not be easy starting over in a foreign country, but she had faced bigger challenges and overcome them. Now, with Thomas by her side, it was time to start again.

That done, she changed and got ready to go

out. The letters had been difficult to write, but compared to the meetings she was about to have, they were as easy as breathing. She would not leave England without saying goodbye to the people who had done so much for her and with whom she had formed such a close and special relationship.

'I will finish the season out, of course,' Catherine told Theo and Tandy as they sat together in the room where they had enjoyed their first conversation. 'But I will not be returning next year.'

'This all seems rather drastic, my dear,' Theo said. 'Are you sure this is what you want to do?'

'I believe it is more a case of what I *must* do,' she told him. 'I can't go on living my life in fear. That won't be good for Thomas or myself.'

'Will you ever come back?' Tandy asked.

'Maybe, when people have forgotten my name and my story. But I suspect it will be a long time before that happens.'

'Dearest child, we will miss you terribly,' Theo said, the regret in his eyes confirming the truth of his sentiments. 'Not only because we are losing our best performer, but because we are losing the friendship of someone who has come to mean a great deal to us and whom we both hold very dear.'

'Thank you,' Catherine said, genuinely touched. 'I hope you know how much your support and encouragement have meant to me. I wouldn't be where I am today without it. You believed in me when I didn't believe in myself.'

'Because you never truly appreciated how rare your talent was,' Tandy said. 'We did. And I know I speak for Theo when I say how thrilled we were to be able to promote that skill and watch it propel you to the forefront of the industry. You will always have a place with us, Catherine, if you want one.'

'Indeed, I sincerely hope we *will* have the opportunity of working together again,' Theo said. 'But you must do what you feel is best for you and Thomas right now.'

Deeply touched, Catherine hugged them both, wondering if she would ever meet such wonderful people again, and then walked out to the waiting carriage. It would seem strange not coming here after her performances; even stranger not to see Theo on a daily basis. He had become a huge part of her life.

But as difficult as her farewells to the Templetons had been, Catherine knew her next goodbye would be much harder.

'You're leaving?' Valbourg said when they were alone in his study. They had not embraced. Valbourg had started to approach her, but she had held up her hand to stop him. 'In God's name, why?'

'Because I must. I no longer feel safe in London,' Catherine said. 'I have given this a great deal of thought, Richard. Indeed, I have lain awake at nights, trying to make up my mind. But now I have and I know it is the right decision. Every day, I wake up wondering if this will be the day Hailey or one of his men try to take Thomas away. And every night I go to bed thanking God nothing happened.'

'But there are things we can do to ensure his safety,' Valbourg said. 'Steps we can take. You don't have to leave London.'

'Unfortunately, it's not only Thomas's safety that is at stake. I fear for mine as well.' She had never told him about the man who had attacked her, nor did she intend to. But he had interceded on her behalf with Lord Tantemon and that was enough. 'Every night, I wonder if this will be the night some man tries to take advantage of me. If tonight, someone will emerge from an alley or come up behind me and force me into his carriage. I can't live with that fear hanging over my head, Richard. And you know there's a very good chance it will happen.'

She didn't tell him that the other reason she wanted to leave London was the fact that every day she stayed, there was a chance she would open the newspaper and see Valbourg's engagement announcement emblazoned across the society pages. 'I can't go on like this. I have to get away.'

'But...where will you go?'

'North, most likely,' Catherine said, regretting the necessity of a lie. 'Gwen knows some people in the Lake District. She's already written to ask if it would be convenient for us to stay with them.'

His face looked as though it had been chiselled out of stone. 'When do you plan to leave?'

'As soon as the arrangements can be made and my belongings packed up. Possibly the end of next week.'

'So soon.' He looked away, his eyes heavy. 'Have you told Theo and Tandy of your plans?'

'Yes. I just came from there.'

'I can't imagine they were pleased. They've grown very fond of you.'

Remembering Tandy's tears, Catherine felt her own throat tighten. 'They understand my reasons. And they will find other actresses to play my roles. I must look on this as...a great adventure,' she said, trying to sound as though she meant it.

Valbourg nodded, though the expression on his face told another story. 'Will you advise your father of your plans?'

'I have posted a letter this morning, telling him what I intend to do. Now that we are reconciled, I want to keep him informed of what I'm doing and where I go. Gwen, too. But I would rather no one else know. I would prefer not to leave a trail for anyone to follow.'

Valbourg sighed and finally crossed the room to where she stood, reaching for her hands and raising them to his lips. 'What am I going to do without you?'

'You will go on,' Catherine said in a choked voice. 'You will marry and have a family and live your life as it was meant to be lived. But for what it's worth, I will always remember you. And I wouldn't change a moment of what we've shared. *No one* can ever take that away from me.'

'Will you at least write to me?' he asked.

Sadness centred in her chest and radiated outwards. 'What would be the point? You will be engaged by Christmas and likely married by the spring. Your wife will not appreciate you receiving letters from another woman. Nor would your family. They don't want me in your life, Richard. They've made that painfully clear.'

'Because they don't understand.'

'They don't have to.' Catherine felt her heart break. 'That's just the way it is.'

Chapter Twelve

⤙⤙⟨⟩⤚⤚

Valbourg stood for a long time after Catherine left, the sweetness of their parting kiss lingering on his lips, his body hard and aching for her. Was this how he was meant to spend the rest of his life? Dreaming of a woman he couldn't have? Remembering the few stolen moments of exquisite passion he had shared? What possible chance for happiness lay in store for him if he was unable to forget Catherine and move on?

It certainly wasn't fair to whomever he married. His wife, whether it be Lady Phoebe or Lady Susan, would know that she came second, just as he would know he was only going through the motions. In his heart he would understand that whatever he did, he would be doing it because it was expected of him, rather than because it was what he wanted. There would be no love in his marriage or satisfaction in his life. Nothing close to the joy he'd experienced since falling in love with Catherine.

Nor had he any idea how he was going to face his father again. It wasn't logical or fair that he blame Alderbury for his separation from Catherine, but Valbourg did, and he doubted those sentiments were going to change. She was leaving because she was afraid to stay in London. Circumstances were forcing her to leave behind everything she knew in order to make a better life for herself and her son. She was being incredibly brave...and he was not.

That awareness brought him up sharply. Catherine was doing what was best for herself...but *he* was doing what was best for his family. If he were to do what was best for him, he would be with Catherine. He would disappoint his father and alienate everyone he knew. He would certainly prove Dorothy right and most likely lose Sebastian. But at the end of the day, when his future stretched long and empty ahead of him, what really mattered? The opinions of others or his own happiness? Could he really turn his back on Catherine and watch her walk away simply because everyone else told him he was doing the right thing by letting her go?

His father was playing billiards when Valbourg called later that evening.

'Richard, what a pleasant surprise. Have you come to play?'

'Actually, I've come to talk,' Valbourg said, watching his father chalk the tip of his cue. 'I have something to tell you.'

'Very well.' Alderbury took his shot and then set his cue on the table. 'Brandy?'

'No, thank you.'

'Mind if I have one?'

'Not at all. I suspect you'll want one before we're through.'

'I'm not sure I like the sound of that,' his father said. 'What's this all about? Have you come to tell me you've proposed to Lady Phoebe?'

'I'm afraid not, though it does concern a lady.'

'Lady Susan Wimsley, then.' His father grinned. 'I thought you were more partial to her, and to tell you the truth, so am I.'

'It's not Lady Susan either.'

'No? Lady Juliet Ransome? Mary said she saw the two of you riding in the park the other day.'

Taking pity on his father because he would never guess the correct name, Valbourg said, 'The lady to whom I refer is Catherine Jones.'

'Miss Jones?' His father's smile abruptly disappeared. 'I thought we'd already said all that needed to be said about her.'

'In *your* mind, perhaps, but after what I learned yesterday, I realise there is a great deal more to say.'

'Oh? And what exactly did you find out?'

'That she has made up her mind to leave London, possibly as soon as next week.'

'Well, that is her business, of course,' his father said, looking visibly relieved. 'Though I suspect her audiences will be disappointed. They'll just have to wait until next Season to see her again.'

'She isn't coming back,' Valbourg said. 'She told me she is afraid Reverend Hailey will try to take Thomas away from her and that she fears for her own safety from the men who continue to pursue her.'

'Then she should let one of them set her up as his mistress,' Alderbury said. 'Gain the protection of his name and have done with it. There must be someone who doesn't care that she has a child.'

Valbourg shook his head. 'She refuses to become any man's mistress. And even if she did, who can say it would prevent other men from trying to seduce her? A gentleman's code of honour is hazy where mistresses are concerned.'

'Yes, I suppose it is, but what have her plans to do with you, Richard? Why are we even having this conversation?'

'Because I would like to ask her to marry me,' Valbourg said quietly. 'And I would like your blessing.'

'My *blessing*?' Alderbury snapped. 'Are you mad? The woman is an actress. With a child.

Have you any idea of the shame you would bring upon the family by doing this?'

'I know what the family will think of my decision, but gentlemen loftier than myself have run off with actresses or married their mistresses,' Valbourg said. 'The Duke of Bolton married Miss Fenton twenty-three years after she became his mistress. If I married an actress, it would no doubt create a scandal for a time, but like everything else, it will pass. But I can assure you, my feelings for Catherine will not.'

'Rubbish! You haven't given this any thought!'

'I have given it nothing *but* thought, and nothing you can do will cause me as much grief as the thought of living the rest of my life without her.'

'I won't hear of it! I forbid you to do this!'

'I thought you liked Catherine.'

'Whether I like her or not has nothing to do with it. She is not worthy of being your wife! Marry Lady Phoebe or Lady Susan,' Alderbury said. 'They at least have had the benefit of an upbringing similar to your own.'

'There is nothing wrong with Catherine's upbringing,' Valbourg said, lowering his voice even as his father's rose. 'Her mother was a governess, her father a tutor. She is educated, refined and capable of moving at any level of society. *You* shun her because she is an actress.'

'Yes, and so should you. Marry the girl? Certainly not. Do you care nothing for your reputation? Your responsibilities to this family? And what about Sebastian? Have you spared a thought for him? Because I promise you, you *will* lose custody of him if you marry that woman,' Alderbury said. 'No grandson of mine will *ever* be raised by a whore!'

As far as Valbourg was concerned, the conversation ended there. His father wasn't going to change his mind, and Valbourg knew that if he continued to see Catherine, there would be no going back. His bridges would be well and truly burned. But for the first time in his life, he didn't care.

'If you *ever* say anything like that to me again, I will walk out that door and never come back,' Valbourg said in a low voice. 'Catherine deserves neither your contempt nor your condemnation. She is an intelligent, talented and incredibly giving woman. Yes, she made a mistake, but she has paid for it a thousand times over. And after having met and spent time with Thomas, I can no longer view it as a mistake. As for Sebastian, I regret more deeply than I can say that I will no longer be his guardian, but under the circumstances, I can see why it would be wrong of me to continue in that role. So, if you proceed with this, I will speak to Mary and Lord Tyne and ask if they would be willing to take him once they are married. Then I shall apply to the Court of Chancery to have his guardianship changed.'

'But there is no need for *any* of this, Richard!' Alderbury said, clearly frustrated. 'Think with your head for a moment. Consider all you would be giving up. Wealth, position, the respect of your peers. Is all that worth throwing away on a whim? Take her as your mistress if you must, but do *not* marry her. You will live to regret it.'

'What I will live to regret,' Valbourg said quietly, 'is that my feelings for her have driven a wedge between you and me and forced this distance between us. I will *never* regret being with her. Cut me off without a penny and erase my name from the family Bible, but I *am* going to be with Catherine one way or the other.'

'Damn it, Richard, I've already lost Sarah. Don't make me lose you as well.'

'That is your choice, Father. I know what I have to do.'

'Fine. Then go and be with your whore,' Alderbury said bitterly. 'And may you both be happy.'

Realising there was nothing more to say, Valbourg left the room. It was too late for apologies or second-guessing. His relationship with his father was over. It might well be the last time he ever walked through that door. All he could do now was pray that the door to Catherine's heart was still open.

He called on her the same evening, knowing Thomas would be in bed and that they wouldn't be disturbed. What he intended to say needed to be said without interruption.

'I didn't expect to see you again,' Catherine said as she led him into the drawing room. 'Has something happened?'

'You could say that.' Valbourg walked across the room to the fireplace and stood looking down into it. 'My father and I had words this evening.'

'"Words"?'

'An argument.'

'About what?'

'What do you think?' He looked up and knew from the expression on her face that she had guessed.

'Oh, Richard. Why do you provoke him? You know how he feels about me.'

'I don't care. He needs to know how *I* feel about you.'

'But you can't *have* any feelings towards me. You have responsibilities. Obligations——'

'None of which have anything to do with the way I feel about you,' Valbourg interrupted. 'Marry me, Catherine. Marry me and we will raise Thomas and Sebastian together.'

'Marry you?' She stared at him, wide-eyed with disbelief. 'Do you hear what you're saying? If you married me, you wouldn't *have* Sebastian. We've talked about this before, Richard. You know there can be nothing between us.'

'Why not? Such alliances are not unheard

of. Dukes and earls have done it. I told my father as much.'

'Dukes can do as they please and wealthy noblemen don't have the Marquess of Alderbury as their fathers,' Catherine pointed out. 'Alderbury would be horrified as would the rest of your family.'

'But if he were not?'

'He will be.'

'But if he were not…'

Catherine sighed. 'This is pointless, Richard. Your father has made it very clear how he feels about me. And you haven't answered my question.'

'Which one?'

'The one about losing Sebastian.'

'I won't lie and tell you I don't care because I do. I love Sebastian like a son. But you *are* my life, Catherine,' he said with quiet intensity. 'I've tried to picture my life without you in it…and I can't. As for marrying someone else, it's a poor husband who marries one woman…when he is so deeply in love with another.'

He loved her. Catherine closed her eyes, not sure whether to laugh or cry. He loved her. Loved her enough to give up Sebastian. Loved her enough to go against his father and ask her to marry him. They were the words she had longed to hear. Words she had imagined in her dreams. But now that he had said them, she realised it didn't matter. She couldn't let him do it. He was the one who would suffer the most for their liaison. The one who would be shamed in the eyes of the world. How could she destroy who he was and all he stood for? How could love justify such selfishness?

'I love you, Richard,' she whispered. 'I've made no secret of that. But I will not marry you. Too many people would be hurt. And you would lose everything.'

'If I were to lose you, then, yes, I would have lost everything.'

Catherine closed her eyes, fighting for the strength to say what she must. 'What about your father? He may not disinherit you, but he can choose to have nothing more to do with you. In his eyes, and in those of your family, you would cease to exist. You would become an outcast; unwelcome at any of their homes. You would never see your nieces and nephews. Have you thought about that?'

A muscle flexed in Valbourg's jaw, evidence of the control he was exerting. 'There must always be sacrifices in matters like these, but what matters most is how we feel about each other.'

'No, it isn't,' she whispered. 'What matters most is doing what is right.' Her brows drew together and she had to force herself to say the words. 'If we were to marry, Thomas would still be a bastard. Your marrying me won't change that.'

'I know. But I am happy to raise him as my son…because he *is* yours.'

'And what about any children we might have together?' she continued. 'Your father would never recognise them. Never see them. Would you wish that upon them? Know they would never be accepted as members of your family because of our actions?'

Valbourg laughed, but it was a bitter, cynical sound. 'What are you trying to do, Catherine? Side with my father and convince me not to marry you? Do you not care that I love you so very much?'

'I care deeply,' Catherine said, the pain of losing him nearly taking her breath away. 'It would be so much easier if I did not. But I know better than you what our life would be like because I have already experienced that life. I know what it is to be looked down upon and ignored. How it feels to be treated as though you have no feelings. How can I inflict that kind of humiliation on you and our children? On myself?'

He put his hands behind his neck and glanced towards the ceiling. 'I cannot control how society views the situation, Catherine. It would be enough that I could have my father come to terms with it. However, I will ask you this. Are there *any* conditions under which you would agree to marry me?'

She walked slowly across the room. 'Yes. If your father said he had no objection to our marriage *and* that he would allow you to retain guardianship of Sebastian, I would marry you in a heartbeat. But without his approval, my answer must remain no. I will not be the cause of your dishonour, my darling. I love you too much to bring that kind of destruction to your life. Or to watch you fall out of love with me when you wake up one day and realise all you've sacrificed to be with me.'

His hands fell to his sides, the expression in his eyes bleak. 'I will never stop loving you, Catherine. Know that as surely as you know the sun will rise tomorrow. But just as I know the sun will rise, I know my father will not change his mind and agree to our marriage.'

'Then this discussion is over.'

'For now. But I don't intend to give up. Not until you tell me you don't love me.'

'I won't ever say that. I can't. But I know this is the right thing to do.' Then, because it *would* be the last time they would be alone together, Catherine walked up to him, took his face between her hands and kissed him, committing to memory the warmth of his mouth, the taste of his skin and the wonder of his love. 'Goodnight, my darling. And goodbye.'

Catherine did not write a letter to Lord Alderbury. She simply showed up on his doorstep, dressed in the most elegant of her gowns and the most fashionable of her bonnets. He might not think well of her as a person, but she refused to let him think she was unfashionable or lacking social grace.

Thankfully, the butler let her in and settled her in the drawing room, seemingly unaware that she was not his master's most welcome guest. Alderbury arrived a few minutes later, the expression on his face far from welcoming. 'What are you doing here?'

'Good afternoon, Lord Alderbury.' Catherine rose to greet him, her smile polite but cool. 'I know you have no wish to see me, but I have a very good reason for calling.'

'I'm sure you think you do,' he snapped. 'However, had I known you would have the temerity to call, I would have left instructions that you be denied entrance.'

'Then how fortunate you did *not* know of my intentions, since I think you will wish to hear what I have to say.'

'I cannot imagine there is anything you could say that would be of interest to me.'

'Not even that I am here because your son asked me to marry him?'

She watched Alderbury's mouth open and then abruptly close again. 'So it's done. Well, I'm sure you're very pleased with yourself at having wrung such a proposal from my son.' He walked to the other side of the room and kept his back to her as he said, 'Did he tell you he asked for my blessing and that I refused to give it?'

Catherine flushed. 'Yes.'

'So you've come here to throw in my face the fact that my son disobeyed me and asked you anyway?'

'Not at all. You were right to withhold your consent.'

'Don't placate me, Miss Jones. I haven't the patience for it.' He spun around and glared at her, his eyes dark and condemning. 'You must know he will lose Sebastian over this.'

Catherine lifted her chin. 'Yes, I know. That's why I'm here. I don't want to see that happen any more than you do.'

'Spare me the platitudes. We both know you don't give a damn about my son or care what happens to his nephew,' Alderbury spat. 'You see Valbourg as a means to an end. A way out of your current predicament and a method of bettering your life through marriage. Well, I won't have it.' He bent to the desk and pulled open a drawer. 'How much do you want?'

Catherine frowned. 'I beg your pardon?'

'Money. That's why you really came, isn't it? To tell me how much it will take for you to go away quietly.'

As the meaning of his words sank in, Catherine blanched. 'You don't understand—'

'Oh, I understand. You came here today boasting that my son asked you to marry him and then tell me you're glad I didn't give him my blessing. Do you really expect me to believe you don't have an ulterior motive?' He pulled out a ledger and flipped it open. 'How much do you want?'

'I don't want your money,' Catherine said, unable to keep the bitterness from her voice. 'If you weren't so caught up in your own pride, you would realise why I'm here and what I've been trying to say. Your son did me the great honour of asking me to be his wife. *I* was the one who turned him down.'

Alderbury looked up. 'You *refused* him?'

'Of course I refused him. Do you think you're the only one who realises how wrong it would be for him to go through with this?' Catherine said angrily. 'The only one who recognises how terrible it would be for him to lose everything he was born to? I love your son as much as he loves me, Lord Alderbury, but I know what people will think if he goes through with this marriage. What *you* will think of him. And I refuse to bring that kind of shame on his head. That's why I turned him down and why I've decided to take Thomas and go abroad.'

'"Abroad"?' It was Alderbury's turn to frown. 'Richard said you were leaving London. I assumed he meant for another part of England.'

'That's what I wanted him to believe. But I intend to go somewhere with Thomas where I can live without the constant fear of discovery. Without the stigma of being thought a whore because I have a son and no husband. That's why I came here today, Lord Alderbury,' Catherine said. 'So that you might know that I *do* love your son enough to turn him down and because you must now do everything you can to convince him to marry someone else. Someone who will be a loving wife to him and a good mother to Sebastian and to the rest of the children they will have. You must help him to move on.' She started towards the door. 'I do care about your son's future, and about your grandson's.'

'Wait. Wait, I said!' he barked when she kept on walking. 'Are you honestly telling me you're not going to try to hold on to him? Even though he's told you he loves you and asked you to be his wife?'

Catherine nodded, not trusting herself to speak. She wanted to cry, but she wouldn't give Alderbury the satisfaction. What little pride she had left meant too much.

Alderbury was silent, too. Finally he bent and wrote something in the ledger. 'Here.' He tore it out and walked across the room to hand it to her. 'Consider it a parting gift.'

Catherine took the slip of paper, saw what he had written and then slowly and deliberately tore it up. 'I have no need of your money, my lord. Nor would I take it if I had. I would never put myself

in a position of obligation to you.' She dropped
the pieces of Alderbury's cheque on the floor and
walked out of the room, feeling better in one respect yet at the same time a hundred times worse.

She didn't want to admit that having told Valbourg she would marry him if his father approved,
she had come to see Alderbury today in the hopes
he might change his mind. That she might have
been able to say something that would have made
a difference. She had seen very quickly that Valbourg was right. His father's mind was made up.
He was not going to change it on the strength of
her visit. And as long as he felt that way, Catherine knew she would never be in a position to
entertain Valbourg's proposal.

It was at Lady Rigby's musicale that Valbourg
found the clarity he was seeking. He was standing
beside Lady Susan and her mother, both of whom
looked very pleased that Lady Susan had been
named the favourite to become his wife, when
he noticed his father talking to Lord and Lady
Matheson, a couple who made no secret of the
fact they detested one another. A few feet away,
Valbourg's sister Mary stood next to her new husband, who was obviously madly in love with her
and wasn't in the least reluctant to show it.

There before him were the two choices a man
could make when it came to marriage, Valbourg

realised. To be madly in love with one's spouse—or barely able to tolerate them.

He knew which he preferred—but it was seeing the two examples side by side that reinforced his decision and gave him the strength to do what he must. He made his excuses to Lady Susan and her mother and then walked across the room to join his father and the Mathesons.

'Ah, Valbourg,' Matheson said, 'I was just saying to your father that the two of you should join us at Twillings next month for the shooting.'

'Thank you, Lord Matheson. We might take you up on that,' Valbourg said pleasantly. 'Father, might I have a word?'

'Hmm? Oh, yes, of course, my boy. Excuse us, Charlotte, Matheson. We'll finish our conversation later.'

With a jovial smile, his father fell into step beside him. Valbourg said nothing, going over in his mind what he wanted to say. To his surprise, however, his father spoke first.

'Thank you for rescuing me back there, my boy. I wanted to get away from Matheson, but wasn't sure how to go about it diplomatically.'

Valbourg glanced at his father in surprise. 'I thought you liked him.'

'I do, but the tension between him and Charlotte is unbearable. You can't get within twenty feet of them and not feel the antipathy. Pity they ever married. I don't believe there was ever any genuine affection there.'

Relieved, Valbourg began to smile. 'Thank you, Father.'

'For what?'

'For making what I am about to say a lot easier.'

'Eh? And what is it you intend to say?'

'That I have decided to go with Catherine, if she'll have me.'

'Go *with* her?' Shock and something akin to fear registered on the older man's face. 'You can't go with her. You're my heir!'

'Yes, but since you cannot approve of what I'm doing and I am going to do it anyway, I thought I might as well say goodbye now and have it over with. You've made it very clear how you feel. The choice is you or her…and I've chosen her.'

'Damn your eyes!' Alderbury said, though the words lacked conviction. He sat down heavily in the nearest chair and rested his elbows on his knees. 'I never thought it would come to this. I thought you of all people would respect my wishes. That you would do the right thing.'

'I almost did. I know what is at stake, Father,' Valbourg said in a low voice. 'I know how much the family's honour means to you, just as I know that one day I will be the Marquess of Alderbury and carry all the responsibilities that go with the title. But seeing Lord and Lady Matheson tonight brought the truth home to me and made me see what's important in a man's life. It made me realise that if I *do* the right thing, I might well end up like them. A worse fate I cannot imagine. I'm sorry to go against your wishes, because I truly have no desire to antagonise you or abandon the estate. But I *will* not be forced to marry against my wishes,' Valbourg said. 'I love Catherine with all my heart and I know she loves me. She is the woman I want to spend the rest of my life with. Knowing that, how can I propose to someone else and expect to enjoy any kind of happiness or satisfaction in the future?' He glanced in the direction of the Mathesons, who were even now standing with their backs to one another. 'You said it yourself, Father. They should never have married. Is that what you wish to hear someone say about *my* marriage in twenty years' time?'

Alderbury said nothing, but his defeated look saddened Valbourg. His father had always been so strong; so incredibly sure of himself. Even in the days following his wife's death, he had not broken down or given way to grief. Sometimes, Valbourg wondered if his father had ever even felt it.

'She came to see me, you know,' Alderbury said abruptly. 'Your precious Miss Jones. She came to the house and told me you had asked her to marry you and that she had turned you down.'

Valbourg's eyes narrowed as he gazed at his father. So, Catherine had bearded the lion in his den. What a remarkable young woman she was. 'I suspect she told you why.'

'She told me she knew it would ruin you. She said she was going away because it was the only way she had of sparing you. Then she tore up my cheque and walked out.'

Valbourg stiffened. 'You offered her money?'

'I thought that's why she'd come. When I told her I wouldn't allow you to marry her, I thought she would ask for money and then take herself off. But she turned me down. Even when I said it was a parting gift, she told me she had no need of it and tore the paper up right in front of me.'

Valbourg smiled. He could picture Catherine doing that, standing in front of his father, tearing up his cheque and dropping the pieces on the floor. She would not be browbeaten by him or anyone else. She would state her opinion, tell his father what she thought and then walk away with her head held high and her principles intact.

Poor Alderbury. He had no idea who he was up against. 'She is good at making her point heard,' Valbourg said as he sat down next to his father.

'Yes, she is. But do you know, I respected her for it. It took courage to come and see me. She told me she was in love with you and that it was because she loved you she had turned you down.'

Valbourg sighed. 'She refuses to be the cause of my alienation from the family. Or of my losing Sebastian. Apart from the latter, I said it didn't matter, but she wouldn't listen. Her mind was made up and nothing I could say was going to change it. Not even a proposal of marriage.' He glanced at his father. 'So what did you do after she ripped up your cheque?'

'I sent her away rather harshly, I'm afraid. Then I lay awake the entire night, thinking about what I'd said to you and to her, and wondered why no one would listen to me. But it wasn't until just now I realised how wrong I've been.'

'"Wrong"?'

'Mmm. Seeing Matheson and his wife brought it home to me, too. Very few people know this, Richard, but many years ago, before he met Charlotte, Matheson was in love with a woman who worked on the estate. I don't remember what position she held. Governess, perhaps, or nursery maid. It doesn't really matter. What does is that he was madly in love with her and by all accounts she felt the same way. But the old earl frowned on their friendship and sent the girl away. Matheson was devastated, of course. He stopped going out, stopped doing all the things he'd done before he fell in love with her and became withdrawn and angry. Four months later, he married Charlotte Parsons, the woman his father had chosen for him. Sadly, they disliked each other on sight. Likely because Charlotte knew Matheson was in love with someone else, and that he didn't… couldn't, I suppose…love her.'

'Did they ever try to make it work?' Valbourg asked.

'I've no idea. Over the years, their mutual dislike turned to hatred and then to indifference. Hence the current state of affairs. Something I wouldn't wish on my worst enemy. I certainly wouldn't wish it on my own son.' Alderbury turned his head and looked at Valbourg. 'I don't want you ending up like Matheson, Richard. I want you to be happy in your marriage and in love with the woman you marry. The way I was with your mother.'

'I wasn't sure you actually *did* love Mama,' Valbourg said. 'After she died, you became so remote. So unemotional. You never broke down. Never cried. And I never heard you talk about her again. It was almost as though you erased her from your memory.'

'I tried to…but not because I didn't care about her. I loved that woman with all my heart,' Alderbury said quietly. 'Her death tore me apart. So I tried to forget her and everything we had together. I thought that by not talking about her, the memory would fade. But it didn't. Nor did my love.'

'I'm sorry,' Valbourg said, aware it was one of the most honest conversations he and his father had ever had. 'I honestly thought you didn't care.'

'I know, because that's what I wanted you to think. I was selfish. I discouraged you from talking about your mother because it was too damn painful for *me* to hear you go on about how wonderful she was and how much you missed her. Because I missed her, too. You never forget the love of your life. And hearing you talk about Miss Jones and knowing you would walk away from me and everything you have rather than lose her just reminds me of how important love is. And of how terrible it is to live without it. So, I take back what I said. Marry her, if you must. You have my blessing.'

Valbourg could hardly believe his ears. 'Are you sure?'

'Quite sure. Is she the woman I would have chosen for you?' Alderbury shook his head. 'Absolutely not. But love doesn't ask who we should fall in love with. It just happens. And so, you must go back to Miss Jones and ask her to marry you again. But this time, tell her your father has no objections. The only thing I *would* ask is that she give up the stage and become a proper wife to you.'

'I don't know if she will be willing to do that,' Valbourg admitted. 'The stage means the world to Catherine. It has given her everything she has— including her son. How can I ask her to give that up?'

'You are giving up a great deal to be with her,' Alderbury pointed out. 'Surely it is not so much to ask that she give up a little to be with you.'

Valbourg stared down at the floor, quite certain

Catherine would not think that giving up the stage was a little sacrifice. 'I will ask her again and see what she says. Then I will tell her you have given us your blessing…because that is the *only* condition under which she would accept my proposal.'

Alderbury raised an eyebrow. 'It is?'

'You are not the only one capable of driving a hard bargain.' Valbourg held out his hand. 'Thank you, Father.'

'Don't thank me yet,' Alderbury said, nevertheless gripping his son's hand. 'Go and find your young lady and get this straightened out. I have no intention of travelling halfway round the world to see my grandchildren!'

Catherine stood by the dresser and checked the contents of the last trunk. With the exception of the clothes she and Thomas would need for the voyage, everything else was packed. A few small cases would travel with them on board, but the rest would go on ahead for delivery to her new home in Italy.

Italy! Catherine pressed a hand to her heart as though to still its furious beating. It sounded so far away. So foreign. But she had made the decision to leave England and it was best not to delay her departure. She hadn't heard from Valbourg for nearly a week and her resolve was weakening. She desperately wanted to see him. It was the longest they had gone without speaking since they had become close, and the loneliness was already tearing her apart. If she didn't leave soon, she would do something foolish, like end up on his doorstep begging him to take her back. He had obviously taken her words to heart and had moved on with his life. Now she had to move on with hers.

It was the reason she had stopped reading the society columns. She was afraid of what she might find.

Of course, fear of seeing his engagement notice didn't prevent Catherine from thinking about him, or ease the tight knot of pain every time she did. She loved him so much the thought of being away from him was like a dull ache that refused to go away. But that was how matters had to be, and really, there were many positive things about moving to Italy. The warm Italian sun and the fresh Tuscan air. The anonymity of the countryside and the remote villa where she and Thomas would be staying; a place where no one would know anything about her life in London or her past in Grafton.

She would become plain Mrs Jones, a widow with a child. She had moved beyond the stigma of lying about her past. Part of her reason for going to Italy was to start a new life. If pretending to be a widow made it easier, so much the better.

'Excuse me, Catherine,' Mrs Rankin said from the doorway, 'but this just arrived for you.'

Catherine turned—and felt the air go out of her lungs. *A pink rose tied with a white-satin bow.* 'Where did that come from?'

'A gentleman came to the door. He said he had heard rumours you wouldn't be performing at the Gryphon any more and that he wanted to see you in person. To give you this last rose.'

Catherine stretched out her hand, aware that it was shaking. 'Where is he now?'

'In the drawing room.'

So, the mystery was at last to be revealed. Strange that he would choose her last night in England to do so. Still, better late than never.

Without a word, Catherine started down the stairs. She practised a dozen opening lines, everything from surprise that he had found her to expressing annoyance that he had kept her guessing so long. In the end, she decided to let him open the conversation.

On the threshold of the drawing room, Catherine stopped and took a deep breath. Then, lifting her chin, she opened the door and walked in.

He was standing by the window with his back to her, but she would have known him anywhere. 'Richard!'

He turned slowly, his beloved face wreathed in smiles. 'Good afternoon, Miss Jones.' He glanced briefly at the rose in her hand. 'I see you received my final tribute.'

'Dearest man, has it truly been you all along?'

'Of course.' He walked towards her, his gaze holding hers. 'I told you no lies when I said I fell in love with you the first time I saw you. You were Flora, goddess of spring. A vision of loveliness in a white gown adorned with pink roses. Then the next time, you were Miss Delacorte; a young lady who wore gowns the same colour as the pink roses she took such pains to grow because she needed them to decorate her mother's grave.' He nodded at the flower in her hand. 'I began to associate you with pink roses, but knowing I could never be a part of your life, I decided to send them to your dressing room, hoping that through them, I might tell you how I felt.'

'But you never enclosed a card or allowed your servant to mention your name,' Catherine said. 'Not so much as a word to let me know who you were.'

'I thought it better that way. Then, if we ever did meet, there would be no need for explanations.'

'Oh, Richard.' Catherine bit her lip. 'I can't believe it was you all along. I wondered about it, of course. Every night when the rose arrived, I tried to imagine who might have sent it. But even after we met, I never dreamt it was you.'

'Then my coming here tonight is a surprise?'

'Totally, and in more ways than one.' A smile

trembled over her lips. 'I thought I was never going to see you again.'

'I know. And you're leaving for Italy tomorrow.'

She gasped. 'How did you know where I was going? Mrs Rankin and Lily were the only people I told and I swore them both to secrecy.'

'Yes, well, I'm afraid Lily isn't quite as trustworthy as you think, at least not when it comes to your happiness,' Valbourg admitted, moving closer. 'Something over which she seems to feel I have some control.'

'Does she now?' Catherine said, desperately trying not to laugh. 'Well, I shall have a word with my dresser the next time I see her. She should have known better than to divulge my plans. And *you* should have known better than to ask her.'

'True, but the stakes were too high to play fair,' Valbourg said. 'Short of travelling to Italy myself, I realised this was my last opportunity to see you and to ask you to marry me, so I wasn't about to waste that chance.'

Hope flared, bright and shimmering, only to be doused by the cold waters of reality. 'Oh, Richard, we've been through this before. You know what I said about needing your father's permission—'

'You have it.'

Catherine took a quick breath. 'I beg your pardon?'

'Father has given us his blessing. I have a letter in my pocket attesting to it.'

'But he doesn't like me—or approve of me. Whatever made him change his mind?'

'You did.' Valbourg took her by the hand and led her to the love seat. 'He told me you had been to see him.'

Catherine flushed. 'Did he tell you the nature of our conversation, or what I said?'

'He told me enough that I understood what he accused you of and how you reacted. You stood up to him and he was impressed.'

'I thought he was going to explode.'

'My father often gives that impression. He tends to act first and think later. It is the reason I do the exact opposite.'

'Which to my way of thinking is infinitely preferable,' Catherine said, chattering nervously, too afraid to put too much stock in what he was saying.

'He did make one stipulation though,' Valbourg went on. 'And I suspect it will have a bearing on your answer.'

'Oh?'

'He said he would agree to our marriage, but that he would very much like to see you stop performing in public.'

'He wants me to give up the stage?'

'Yes.'

Catherine glanced down at her hands. 'What did you tell him?'

'I said I couldn't guarantee your answer because performing is what you were born to do and that if it *was* your wish to continue, I wasn't going to pressure you into stopping. But I said I would ask and I have. The rest is up to you.'

'I hardly know what to say.'

'Then let me say something before you give me your answer. I know you have concerns about our being together, Catherine, and, yes, there will be challenges, but I don't care as long as we're together. I want you to be my wife. If that means living in Italy, I'll have my belongings packed and we will both get on that ship tomorrow. If it means staying in England, we can leave London and settle in the country somewhere. However, I should warn you that if you turn me down, I *will* follow you to Italy, and I will buy a villa down the road or an apartment across the square and I will court you in English and Italian until you say yes.'

'But if you marry me, you *will* lose Sebastian,' Catherine said. 'Your father's blessing surely doesn't extend to that.'

'I think it does,' Valbourg said. 'When I told him I intended to apply to the courts to award custody of Sebastian to Mary and Tyne, he realised how serious I was and made no further mention about my giving Sebastian up. Dorothy will have a fit, of course, but I don't care. I love you and

I intend to do everything I can to be with you. *And* to keep Sebastian. If you're willing to have both of us, that is.'

'I wouldn't dream of splitting you up.'

'Good, because I think Italy will be good for the boys. And Thomas will need a playmate until he can make friends with the local boys.'

Catherine stared up at him. Was this really happening? Had Alderbury truly given his permission? 'May I see your father's letter?'

He looked wounded. 'You don't believe me.'

'It's not that. I want to see what he said.'

With a faint smile, Valbourg drew out the letter and handed it to her. Catherine read it over twice before saying in astonishment, 'He's given us his blessing...and he has apologised to me for his behaviour.'

'As I said, Father often regrets his actions once he's had time to think about them. But he wants me to be happy, Catherine. And if that means being with you, he's willing to allow it.'

Deciding it was time to stop resisting, Catherine dropped the letter and threw herself into his arms. 'Darling Richard, you have made me the happiest woman in England. I love you desperately,' she murmured against his lips. 'I was so afraid I was going to lose you.'

'Well, you're not. You have come to your senses at last and agreed to marry me. And conveniently, our honeymoon is already planned, though it would have been better, I suppose, had we set off as a married couple. No matter, we can either marry when we get to Italy or ask the captain to marry us on the ship. By the way, where exactly in Italy are we going?'

'Florence. Gwen is friendly with a couple who live in the city, but who own a small villa in the surrounding hills. She wrote and told them Thomas and I were looking for a place to stay and they kindly offered us the use of it until we were able to find a place of our own.'

'Splendid. Florence is magnificent and the countryside around it spectacular. I suspect we will have no trouble finding a place that suits us,' Valbourg said. 'We may even be able to find a theatre for you to perform in.'

Catherine shook her head. 'That won't be necessary. As much as I love performing, I love you more. And given that your father has agreed to our marriage, I am more than happy to agree to his request. After all, if I was willing to go to Italy in the first place, I was obviously prepared to surrender the stage. Marrying you doesn't change that. We shall come back to England, and I shall give private performances for you and the boys. That will be enough for me.'

'If there wasn't a little boy asleep in the bedroom next to yours, I would take you upstairs and ask for a private performance right now,' Valbourg said, his voice deepening as his gaze dropped to the creamy expanse of her throat. 'But for the sake of propriety, I'll wait. I have the rest of my life to show you how much I love you.'

'Yes, you do. But I don't think there would be anything wrong with getting a little rehearsal in ahead of time,' she said in a husky voice. 'Do you?'

Valbourg laughed, a warm, throaty sound that sent shivers along Catherine's spine. 'You know what they say, my darling. Practice makes perfect. And I have a feeling it's going to be a very long time before either of us feel we have no room left for improvement.'

* * * * *

& *Special Offers*

Every month we put together collections and longer reads written by your favourite authors.

Here are some of next month's highlights—and don't miss our fabulous discount online!

On sale 20th June

On sale 4th July

On sale 4th July

Save 20%
on all Special Releases

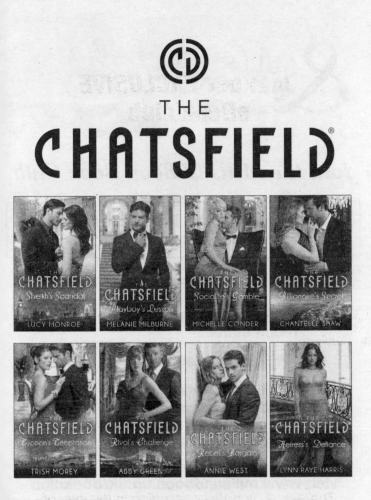

 MILLS & BOON® *Book Club*

Join the Mills & Boon Book Club

Want to read more **Historical** books?
We're offering you **2 more** absolutely **FREE!**

We'll also treat you to these fabulous extras:

  Exclusive offers and much more!

  FREE home delivery

  FREE books and gifts with our special rewards scheme

Get your free books now!

visit www.millsandboon.co.uk/bookclub
or call Customer Relations on 020 8288 2888